E.J. RUSSELL

BAD BOY'S Bard

Fae Out of Water
Book Three

Cover art: Natasha Snow Designs, http://natashasnow.com
Edited by Rachel Haimowitz

ISBN: 978-1-947033-64-1

Second edition
September 2023

Contact information:
ejr@ejrussell.com

E.J. RUSSELL

Fae Out of Water
Book Three

A MYTHMATCHED NOVEL

About
Fae Out of Water

Once upon a time, there were three brothers, nobles of the Seelie Court of Faerie, who set out to seek their fortunes. The eldest—

Scratch that. Rrrrrewind.

Nowadays, when tales are told in micro bursts on tiny LED screens, rather than spun out by the glow of a midnight campfire, even Faerie's elite have to get with the program.

The Kendrick brothers have traded longbow for briefcase, battle steed for Harley, and enchanted harp for electric guitar. But while they're finding their feet in the modern world, instead of gaining their fortunes, they stumble straight into love.

CHAPTER ONE

"Niall. Do you know how long I've been searching for you?"

At the sound of his brother's impossibly deep voice, Niall O'Tierney jumped to his feet, knocking over his stool.

Eamon advanced into Niall's quarters, his broad shoulders barely clearing the door. "I'm sorry. I didn't mean to startle you."

"You didn't." But jumping to attention when he was addressed was a hard habit to break. "What brings you to my little corner? Shouldn't you be getting ready for your wedding?"

"That's why I'm here." Eamon eyed the fire roaring in the hearth. "How you can suffer through this heat is more than I can fathom."

Niall righted the stool. "Heat? My dear brother, compared to what I'm used to, your Keep is positively arctic."

Eamon's forehead wrinkled in concern. "I'm sorry. I should have—"

"It's all right. You needn't treat me like an invalid." *Even if I am one.* "Don't forget, I've survived a night drinking with the duergar. And that involved shots of fermented dragon bile infused with crushed holly berries."

Eamon smiled, shaking his head. "How you could stomach that—"

"Oi. It was a wager, all right? Besides, it netted me a boon. I'll call it in one day."

Eamon's smile widened. "No wonder they're so nervous around you. I'd never thought duergar capable of anxiety."

Niall shrugged. "Just takes the right leverage." Niall had always known how to apply it.

"Yes. Well." Eamon cleared his throat. "There are several issues that we must discuss before the Convergence ceremonies. Some things that might . . ." He grimaced. "Disturb you. I wish you to be prepared."

Niall bowed his head. "You needn't ask, Your Highness. I appreciate the consideration."

"Ah, give over, Niall. You don't need to address me that way. We're brothers."

"Yes, and you're the King by Faerie's acclamation, even though you're putting off official coronation until after the Convergence. We wouldn't want to scandalize the court by an unseemly display of informality."

"You mean we wouldn't want to give anyone else the chance for insolence."

"That too. I'm surprised the whole court didn't forget that Tiarnach had any sons at all, let alone two of them."

"All the more reason for us to present a united front. Tonight is a critical juncture. If we—"

A startled cheep from the doorway made them both turn. Peadar, a brownie who'd been one of Niall's staunchest allies for most of his life, cringed at the threshold, his arms full of velvet and fur. "Your pardon, Majesty, Highness. For the interruption. I bring Prince Niall's clothing for the feast and the ceremony."

Despite the reforms Eamon had already put in place after deposing their father, the lesser fae on the Keep staff who'd toiled under the old King couldn't make the transition to the more lenient regime overnight. They still instinctively expected a blow at every transgression, no matter how small.

Niall could relate. Thanks to his own punishment at Tiarnach's hands, he had the same reaction himself.

He strode across the room and took the bundle of clothing from Peadar's arms. "Please don't call me Highness. I'm not a prince." Not anymore.

Peadar looked down his long nose. "Those as act like a true prince are treated as one. Highness." He bobbed his head at Eamon and scurried out.

Niall returned to the hearth where his brother was waiting. "I'm sorry. What did you want to discuss?"

"Do you recall the Seelie traitor we left in the underworld along with Father when we rescued you?"

"You mean the Daoine Sidhe—the one-handed one, who spewed such invective when you removed his mute curse?"

"The very same." Eamon scowled. "He was Caitrìona's—that is, the Queen's—former Consort until he tried to usurp her throne."

Niall chuckled, his laugh still sounding like an unoiled hinge, since he'd had so little opportunity for amusement in the last two centuries. "Jealousy doesn't become you, Your Majesty."

"I told you not to call me that."

"Is that an order?"

Eamon sighed. "Of course not. But I want to be your friend again, Niall, not your sovereign. I've missed you."

And here I've been acting like a typical self-absorbed Unseelie arsehole. "Forgive me, Eamon. I missed you too, and I've never even asked. What were you doing during my unfortunate incarceration? Finding new and creative ways to make Tiarnach's life miserable?"

"No. I . . . I spent it in exile. I returned the same night you did."

Niall goggled at him. "What? Why have you never told me this?"

"When have I had the opportunity?" Eamon's voice took on an exasperated edge. "You've spoken barely a word to me in the entire two weeks since your release. You dodge me, hiding here in your quarters, or down in the kitchen, huddled by the fire, surrounded by lesser fae who regard me like I might suddenly turn into Father and dash their brains out against the hearth."

"So you're telling me Tiarnach got rid of us both? Was it . . . was it my fault?"

"In a way . . ."

"Shite," Niall muttered. "I brought nothing but misery to everyone I cared about. If I had known—"

"Peace." Eamon held out his hand and Niall clutched it perhaps harder than he should have, but Danu's tits, if he'd known Tiarnach would vent his fury on *Eamon* . . .

"I'm so sorry."

"Don't be." Eamon squeezed Niall's hand in return. "I don't blame you for Father's decision. Although he used my assistance to you as an excuse, I have no doubt he'd have found another reason to curse me in the end. He was convinced one or the other of us was plotting to usurp him."

Niall forced a smile that was doubtless a parody of his old irreverent grin. "A rather prophetic fear, at least in your case."

"More like a self-fulfilling prophecy. If he hadn't been obsessed with punishing you, with killing Gareth Cynwrig—"

Niall's belly clenched, and he dropped Eamon's hand as if it were molten iron. "Don't. Please." Niall had taken the sentence Tiarnach had meted out—every stroke of the lash; every hour, every day, every year of the futile backbreaking labor. Stoking the fire, hauling piles of metal scrap from one cavern to another, working the bellows as Govannon forged weapon after weapon—only to melt them down again into scrap and leave Niall to drag it all off to the scrap room to begin the cycle again the next day. He'd taken it, and gladly, because Tiarnach, certain Niall would break and be brought to heel, had declared none but Niall would kill Gareth. Niall had clung to that, believing that as long as he remained imprisoned, Gareth's life was safe.

"But surely—"

"I'm not ready to talk about him." *I may never be ready.* Because not two days before he'd been liberated, his back still bloody from another unscheduled flogging, he'd learned it had all been for nothing. Tiarnach had confessed gleefully that he'd grown tired of waiting and killed Gareth himself.

Niall could only hope Tiarnach had been more merciful to Gareth than he'd been to his own sons. *How likely is* that, *you bloody great twit?*

"Niall." Eamon laid his arm across Niall's shoulders and Niall flinched, his back no more fully healed from that last beating than his heart had healed from Tiarnach's final blow. Eamon dropped his arm. "I'm sorry. I thought—now that you're back in Faerie, haven't you recovered yet?"

"When the whip is wielded by a god, my brother, not even a fae royal can heal the wounds."

"I never thought Govannon was so very cruel."

"He's not, at least not purposely. But he's neither judge nor jury—only the jailer, and indifferent to anything but atoning for his own guilt. Once Tiarnach condemned me, Govannon's duty was to carry out the sentence. So he did."

Eamon closed his eyes, his face contorting with pain. "Believe me, if I had known what Father had planned, I would have done everything in my power to dissuade him."

"Your belief in the power of words is touching, but nobody has ever convinced Tiarnach to change his mind. To do so would be to admit he was wrong in the first place. Inconceivable."

"I was fully aware of Father's ruthlessness, but I never imagined he'd take leave of his reason so completely."

Niall gripped Eamon's forearm. "It's done. In the past. Leave it and tell me what's got you worried about the future."

"Very well. According to Fionbarr, we need—"

"Who's Fionbarr?"

"He's First Mage now, the primary architect of the Convergence spell. He says that in order for the Convergence to succeed, *all* fae—and no one else—must be present, inside the gates, when the spell takes effect. That means both Father and Rodric Luchullain must be brought into the Keep from the forges."

Niall shivered. Once again under the same roof as the man who was unfortunately his father? *I'll bear it. I must.* "Will I need to be present then, or share the room with him?"

"No. I'll make sure you're advised well in advance, and Fionbarr has orders to take them to the dungeons directly. They're shackled with a druid-made chain, and Fionbarr will be escorting them, along with a full cadre of guards."

"Very well. Is there anything else?"

Eamon ducked his head, looking as shamefaced as six feet eight inches of solid muscle could. "The procession from the Keep to the Stone Circle will leave soon after the feast. Caitrìona's entourage will leave her pavilion in the Seelie realm at the same time."

"A parade." Niall applauded slowly. "How festive."

"I'm afraid you must be part of it, Niall. I'd spare you if I could, but your presence is necessary for the spell. Also . . ." Eamon's gaze dropped to his feet. "I would ask you to stand by me at my handfasting."

Ah, shite. How could he refuse? "Of course. But I warn you—I'll not be able to stomach the feast. You're on your own there."

"I suspected as much." Eamon withdrew a small velvet bag from his belt pouch. "I want you to have this."

Niall took it, hesitant to look inside, but by the weight and size, the bag held an item not much bigger than his thumbnail. "What is it?"

"Fionbarr calls is a binding stone. Caitrìona has the mate to it. We'll offer them to him on the altar as the final part of the Convergence spell."

Niall thrust the bag back. "Then you keep it."

Eamon closed his fist over Niall's. "No. You've been disregarded in Faerie almost since your birth because of

Father's attitude and court politics." Eamon released Niall's hand and smiled wryly. "Your own antics didn't help, of course. Baiting the trows with enchanted dice? You were lucky to escape with your head."

Niall shrugged, then winced at the chafe of his shirt on his back. "I was in no danger. They were too busy trying to cheat each other to wonder why I won every third throw."

"Nevertheless, I want you to be part of this new Faerie. We're so few now, where once we were many. All fae should feel welcome: Unseelie, Seelie, greater, lesser, Scots, Irish, Welsh—and whatever of the Cornish, Manx, and Bretons we can find. You're somewhat of a hero to the lesser fae, you know."

"Me? I never did anything special."

"No? As I recall, the incident with the trows involved a pack who'd attacked a bauchan den. And somehow the courtiers who lost most disastrously at your famous card parties were the ones who were most churlish to the Keep's staff."

Niall shifted uneasily. He hadn't realized he'd been quite so transparent in his targets. "Those arseholes simply thought they were better players than they actually were."

"Niall. Accept it. You were treated as an outsider your whole life, and I know it hurt you. I don't blame you for your rebellion. In fact, I envied your courage at the same time I despaired of your recklessness. I'd never have dared oppose and flaunt our Father's will as you did."

Niall held up his abraded wrists. "Much good it did me in the end."

Eamon grasped his biceps. "I want you to be a part of this ceremony. Integral to it. Like it or not, you're the standard bearer for the disenfranchised."

"So if I can be brought back into the fold, there's hope for anyone?" Niall couldn't help the scorn in his tone.

"Think of it this way—if you refuse, will all who look to you as a champion believe that the new order will be as corrupt, as rigid, as the old? Do this for me, Niall, please. Do this for Peadar and Heilyn and all the other lesser fae who look to you for fair treatment."

Niall took a deep breath. As little as he wanted to plunge back into politics, how could he refuse Eamon this simple request? It was little enough.

Eamon, however, had done the impossible—forged alliances between natural enemies, defeated his own curse, deposed Tiarnach—and won the Seelie Queen as his mate. Yet the first thing he'd done afterward had been to release Niall from captivity.

A public gesture in support of his brother and the Queen. What could it hurt? He could always hide out again afterward.

"Very well. What must I do?"

"Fionbarr will call for the stones at the proper time in the ceremony. You only need to come forward then and hand this one to me. Stand next to me during the handfasting."

"Will Caitrìona have someone at her side as well?"

"She will, but not family. Her champions, Lord Cynwrig and Lord Maldwyn."

Niall flinched and turned away, staring out the narrow embrasure at the forest beyond the Keep. Gareth's brothers. He'd never met them, but he'd heard of them. They couldn't have taken the news of Gareth's death well, yet they'd still chosen to take part in the ceremony. *They'd know about Gareth's life in the years I lost—how he filled his days, what made him smile, his music . . .* If Niall's heart weren't still so raw from the loss, and if he weren't certain they'd hate him for his betrayal, he'd beg them for the tales.

"Have you studied the documents I gave you? The details of the Convergence spell?"

"A bit." Niall glanced guiltily at the rolls of parchment on his table. "There are a lot of them."

"Yes, because it's a very complicated spell. I'd value your opinion."

"Me? But I'm not a mage."

"No, but you're clever, far cleverer than me. That cleverness is something Caitrìona and I desperately need in the combined court. She has her trusted advisors in the Cynwrig brothers. I have only you."

Niall shifted uneasily from foot to foot. "Surely Fionbarr—"

Eamon waved one giant hand. "Fionbarr is interested in the Convergence only as a magical puzzle. He has no real allegiance to me, or to anything other than his own study of magic."

That raised the hair on Niall's neck. "Perhaps that is something you should worry about. A man with power but no loyalties is more dangerous than a known enemy."

"You see?" Eamon said heartily. "Again, you show how much I need you."

"Nonsense. Besides, until I've recovered fully, I'm of no real use to you—no better than a human, like my mother. There are enough at our own court who never considered me a fit prince for that reason alone. If you couple that with my reputation?" Some twist in Niall's half-human heritage had given him the ability to discern the crack in another's character, the flaw that when stressed would cause them to shatter. And once he'd seen it, he couldn't resist applying the necessary pressure. It hadn't made him popular. "Do you think they'll accept me in your . . . what do you call it? Administration, like the Outer World governments call it?"

"They'll have to learn."

Really, Eamon? Are you still so naïve? "But that's the point. They may not be able to. Not without help. I can accept change because I'm half-human. True fae might take more persuasion."

"You're a true fae, and I'll challenge any who say different. Besides, who better than you to persuade? You persuaded the last Seelie bard into your bed."

Niall froze, hands fisting in the folds of his cloak. "How dare you, Eamon? How *dare* you?"

Eamon's perfect brow puckered. "What do you mean? You did, just as you said you would, then defied Father to keep him."

"And that got me chained in the forges for two hundred years. And Tiarnach killed Gareth anyway."

Eamon blinked, then pity flickered across his face. "Oh my dear. I didn't realize— Gareth isn't dead."

Niall staggered back until he stumbled against the stool, his heart knifing sideways in a painful thump. "Not . . . not dead?" He could barely force the words out of a mouth gone dry as bone dust. "Don't toy with me, Eamon. Please."

"I would never joke about such a thing. He's alive. In fact, he'll be here tonight."

Niall's knees gave out and he collapsed, missing the stool completely and falling on his arse, uncertain whether the sounds tearing from his throat were hysterical laughter or racking sobs.

Chapter Two

"Gareth, what the hell?" Spence banged a discordant chord on his keyboard. "That's the third time you've fucked up that bridge. I didn't think you fae bards *could* fuck up."

"Since I'm the only one there is, it's kind of hard to find a basis for comparison." Gareth fingered the chord progression again. It wasn't that difficult. "Sorry, guys. I'm . . . my mind's not on the music at the moment."

"This moment or any moment in the last two weeks." Tiff unslung her bass and set it on its stand.

"What she said." Hamish bounced behind the drum kit, flipping one stick. Gareth scowled at him. Hamish always agreed with Tiff on everything—but it didn't do him a damn bit of good. She still wouldn't go out with him.

Josh laid his violin in its case and moved to the front of the practice room. "Look, everyone. It's been a tough time for Gareth. We all know that, right?" Josh fixed each of them in turn with his wide brown gaze. Trust Josh to make the peace.

Unfortunately, it made Gareth feel like an even bigger arsehole, since he'd let Josh down more than the rest of Hunter's Moon. The two of them hadn't written a new song for the band in months. At some point, the fans would get tired of hearing the same old shite in every concert and start drifting away.

He owed it to Josh—to the whole band—to get it together.

"Too bad you don't have 'it' anymore, ain't it, boyo?"

Gareth's fist clenched around the neck of his guitar. *Gods-bedamned Voices.* Would he ever be rid of them? He'd hidden his bardic talent in the days millennia ago when he and his brothers had still lived in Annwn, before the Unification, before Arawn abandoned the Welsh fae and Annwn disappeared. He'd hidden it for as long as he could, but when Arawn discovered it, he'd decreed Gareth needed training.

Unfortunately, there'd been no living fae bards to teach him, so Arawn found a dead one: Gwydion himself.

To this day, the voices of the dead, who'd first invaded his thoughts when he'd been sequestered with Gwydion during his training, always found the chink in his armor, in his confidence. Usually music kept them at bay; it was the one thing he was good at, after all. But his music was abandoning him now too.

Ever since the Queen had decreed that the Seelie and Unseelie realms would merge, that Gareth would be cheek to jowl with the creatures he'd loathed since the day one of them had taken his first and only lover—his *human* lover—his music, the bedrock of his life, had cracked like a wren's egg.

This evening, it would all happen—the Convergence, the handfasting between the Queen and her Unseelie monster betrothed—and Gareth was ordered to be there, whether he liked it or not.

No wonder he'd fucked up the bridge.

"Thanks, Josh, but they're right. You deserve better, and I'll try to get it together. I promise. After tomorrow—"

"Why will that be any better?" Spence asked. "If you're this whacked out just thinking about the Convergence, how are you gonna act when it's a done deal? Hell, when *you* have to help make it happen."

Damned good question. "I don't have to participate in the spell. I'm just playing at the feast."

"So you can nip out right after?" Hamish asked.

I wish. "No. I have to stay for the ceremony. All fae are required to be present."

Hamish launched a drum stick into the air. "You think you can be there without wanting to stab a few Unseelie in the eye?" He grinned. "As I understand it, some of 'em only have one eye to start with."

"I can handle it." *I hope. As long as I don't see* that *one. The one who kidnapped Niall.*

"Do you want company?" Josh asked. "I mean, we've played in Faerie before. We can do it this time too if it would help."

"Nah. Thanks, mate, but this is a fae-only event. Not even my brother-in-law can go, nor Mal's bloke." Gareth winced when he remembered the vile words he'd flung at Mal and Bryce that night in the Stone Circle. He switched off his amp and sat down heavily on the beat-up orange sofa in the corner of the room. "The worst part will be facing my brothers. I was kind of a dick to them last time I saw them."

"'Kind of'?" Tiff snorted. "From what you said, I'm surprised Mal didn't drop-kick you out of the Circle—right after Alun ran you through."

Gareth sighed. "I'd have deserved both. But sometimes—"

"That's right, boyo. Sometimes you have to let them know how much hate you really *have. For the Unseelie swine. For the Queen who failed you. For your sodding brothers—"*

No! Not my brothers. They'd put up with his moods, year after interminable year, granting him more indulgence than he had any right to deserve. Which filled him with shame. Which gave the Voices a way in again.

Goddess, he missed Niall. When they'd been together, it had been the only time the Voices were truly silent.

"You'll be back in time for our next gigs, though, right?" Josh sat down next to him. "The second Portland show is the replacement for the one we had to cancel last summer. If we bail again—"

"Don't worry. The feast and the ceremony are the only requirements." Then he could get the hells out of Faerie before he had a psychotic break.

Eamon's disclosure left Niall on edge, unable to decide whether he most wanted to see Gareth again or hide in the dungeons until the whole thing was over.

No hiding in the dungeons. Not with Tiarnach and his Seelie accomplice there.

When Gareth saw him again—*if* Niall had the courage to show himself—what would he think of the wreck Niall had become? He couldn't do much about his wounds, but the least he could do was look less . . . feral.

To save the Keep staff the burden of hauling water to his quarters, he skulked down to the bathing rooms used by the lesser fae, then stood staring at the steaming water as he realized he couldn't go in without compromising the dressings on his back. Heilyn, a bauchan who acted as Eamon's valet, found him there. Clucking in concern, they shooed Niall into the water, holding towels for him when he emerged. Then they trimmed Niall's hair and rebandaged his back.

He spent the rest of the day next to the fire in his bedroom, alternating between trying to make sense—unsuccessfully—of the Convergence spell documents and peeking in the looking glass, wondering what Gareth would see when they were face-to-face once more.

He laid out the clothing Peadar had brought him earlier. Royal blue velvet and ermine? Gold bullion embroidery? Not bloody likely. He dug out one of his old, less ostentatious court outfits from his dusty trunk and struggled into it. The doublet was too tight through the chest and arms, putting agonizing pressure on his back. The breeches, though . . . they might work if—

No. This was ridiculous. Danu's tits, was he actually attempting to *primp*? What good would that do? Even if he were suddenly as perfectly beautiful as Eamon on the outside, the inside would still be rotten with his lies and deceptions.

Best to make the outside match.

He donned his old loose clothing again and made himself concentrate on the spell, his back to the window. But as the day aged, he couldn't help but glance over his shoulder to check the sky for the green of midafternoon, when the pre-Convergence feast was to begin.

Gareth. Alive. Here. All Niall had to do was walk down the corridor, cross the throne room, and enter the Great Hall and he'd see him again. He clutched the quill he'd been using to make desultory notes. Was he grateful? Overjoyed? Terrified? Yes and yes and yes.

Why was it that the one thing you thought you wanted above everything else was the last thing you could face?

I can just take a peek at him, I don't have to talk to him yet. Niall wasn't sure he was ready for that. He was not the same man that Gareth had known. He was broken. Scarred. Damaged. But above all, *Unseelie and assassin.*

He'd never revealed those little details. One of the gifts from his human mother—other than his connection with the *ethera* that allowed him to understand and adapt to changes in the Outer World—was the ability to appear fully human without resorting to *glamourie.* He'd been masquerading as human when he'd tracked Gareth to the eisteddfod in Corwen, only half-serious about making good on his wager with Tiarnach to deprive the Seelie Queen of the one thing she had that the Unseelie court could never boast: a true bard.

Tiarnach, being the unimaginative bastard that he was, probably thought he'd ordered Niall to kill Gareth. After meeting Gareth—and falling in love with him—Niall had hatched the brilliant notion of convincing Tiarnach that the way to score off the Queen was not to kill the bard, but to bring him to the Unseelie court as Niall's consort instead.

Tiarnach was not impressed by the brilliance of Niall's plan. Niall had gotten chained in the forge instead, and had never seen Gareth again.

But now, he had that chance. Would Gareth still be angry that Niall had left without a word? If Niall were to explain the reasons for both for the deception and the abandonment, would Gareth forgive him? He'd never thought to have the opportunity, not after Tiarnach's last crazed announcement.

I'll never know if I don't try.

When Gareth crossed into Faerie late that afternoon, nausea roiling in his belly and anger prickling his skin, he wasn't sure he could avoid the psychotic break after all.

"You know what they did after they took him from you? What they always do to humans? They fucked him. As many times as they wanted. Every day. Every hour. And they made him want it. Made him beg for it. The glamourie *can counteract the pathetic love you were so sure was yours."*

"Shut up," Gareth growled.

"I didn't say anything." Alun, Gareth's older brother, stepped out of the shadows under the trees.

"Sorry. I wasn't talking to you."

Alun looked at him uneasily. Gareth didn't blame him. How did you apologize for being a total arsehole to your brothers? *Groveling is in your future.* He'd have to face it, but it wouldn't be easy.

"This way." Alun didn't waste words. He was probably afraid that Gareth would launch into another tirade.

Gritting his teeth, Gareth followed through the trees and across the unseen—but definitely felt—barrier from the Seelie sphere into the Unseelie.

They walked along in silence, Gareth humming under his breath to keep the Voices at bay, forming guitar chords on his left thigh to keep his hands from shaking.

Out of nowhere, a large gate suddenly barred their way. Mal stood outside it, thumbs hooked in his belt. *Both hands.* At least his brothers were whole and curse-free now.

"That's because both of them found truuuuue looooove. *Something you'll never find. You'll be broken forever. Just like us."*

"Gareth. You made it." Mal made a slight motion, as if to hug Gareth in his old enthusiastic way, but hesitated.

Bugger that. Gareth took two giant steps forward and grabbed Mal in a hug, burying his head on his shoulder. "Goddess, Mal, I'm so sorry for what I said to you." He'd accused Mal of more than one unthinkable act—not only a treasonous conspiracy with the Unseelie, but also with forcing a permanent partnership on a non-fae, like some renegade old-school Sidhe. Although Mal's lover wasn't a defenseless human like Niall. He was a gods-bedamned druid.

Oak and bloody thorn, Gareth still couldn't wrap his head around the notion of his brother mated to a druid. Not as bad as if he were to take an Unseelie to bed, but druids and fae had been wary of one another for millennia for good reason.

Mal chuckled, and his arms came around Gareth, patting him on the back. "No worries, mate. We all have our bad days, right? Bryce says I have enough of them for any ten other bastards. But if you're going to give me a cuddle, at least get a haircut first. These bloody curls in my face—"

Gareth pulled back. "Fuck you. I like it this way."

Mal's grin dimmed a bit. "I know."

Niall liked it this way. "Never mind." He turned to Alun and gave him a hug too, even though it was hampered by the sword sheathed along Alun's back. "Thank you for standing by me." He stepped away. "Thank you both."

"There was never a question, Gareth. You ought to know that." Alun's eyes were serious, his tone holding no recrimination. "We're brothers. We've always got each other's backs."

Mal slapped Alun's shoulder. "Then we'd better get our backs inside before we're late to the party. The Queen will forgive a lot, now that she's crazy in love, but she's still a stickler for punctuality."

Mal opened the gate and led them up to the Keep proper, where two guards—one a Daoine Sidhe from the Seelie court, and one a hulking Unseelie trow—flanked the open doors.

Light spilled out onto the path, and inside fae milled about the entrance hall, some in the elaborate finery of high humanoid fae—both Seelie and Unseelie, Gareth suspected. The non-humanoid, in nothing more than mottled skin and fur, were de facto Unseelie, excluded from the Seelie realm by the elder gods' notion of what constituted beauty.

Gareth took a deep breath, drawing strength from the presence of his brothers beside him, of the harp on his shoulder—his brothers and his music, the two things he could always depend on.

"You sure about that, boyo?"

Gareth bit back a retort and marched forward. "Let's do this." To drown out the Voices, he attempted to keep up desultory conversation with his brothers, while avoiding contact with the Unseelie as unobtrusively as possible. The humanoid ones were nearly indiscernible from Seelie courtiers. The only differences were the side glances and sneers they cast at the Kendrick brothers as they made their way through the corridor.

"Great Hall's yonder." Mal pointed to a vast archway off to the left where the tide of chattering fae was already heading. "The feast will be there. They've even got a minstrels' gallery, believe it or not. The old Unseelie King must have snatched his architect from the Plantagenets." He winced. "Sorry, Gareth. Bad joke."

"No worries, Mal." In truth, Gareth was relieved. If he retreated to the gallery for his command performance, he wouldn't have to be among the crowd.

The brothers were borne along with the throng, which began to disperse to the tables that ringed the room. Mal nodded at the far end of the hall, to a dais shoulder height above the floor. "We'll be sitting yonder, along with Eamon and the Queen, and a couple of the Unseelie honchos. Fionbarr, the mage who's casting the spell; Eamon's brother; a bloke who's the Lord High Something-or-other—"

"Lovely." A Seelie page passed by with a tray of silver goblets full of wine. All three of the Kendricks took one. Gareth downed half of his at one go. *I'll need another one of those soon.* "I assume we'll be on the Queen's left?"

Mal snorted. "Not like I perused the fecking seating chart. I expect we'll sit where we please."

Alun nodded at the bauchan standing at the end of the dais, his head just visible above the table. "I think the steward will point us the way."

"Hey, it's Heilyn." Mal raised cup in an air-toast, and the bauchan tugged its green forelock, baring its rows of sharp teeth in what passed for a grin. "Heilyn's all right. A good fellow with a cudgel, not to mention the go-to fae for any supplies, if you catch my meaning."

"Mal, must you?" Alun growled.

"Supplies? You mean—" Gareth gulped, stomach roiling. Mal had actually had sex in the Unseelie realm? "You . . . and an Unseelie?"

"Are you daft, man? With Bryce, after Rodric and his barmy ex-Majesty were dispatched to the hells." Mal frowned. "Place was too good for them if you asked me."

Gareth shrugged, trying to rid his mind of the image of Mal with an Unseelie. "Sorry. But you can't blame me for jumping to conclusions, considering your reputation."

"That's all in the past, mate. Bryce is all I'll ever need."

Imagining Mal with a druid wasn't much better. "With the Queen about to mate with her monster—" *Make nice.* He forced a chuckle. "To be honest, I never knew Her Majesty had such a taste for blue."

"Blue?" Mal asked.

"Her soon-to-be-consort's skin, of course. Blue and scaled. A far cry from Rodric Luchullain, but maybe that's the point."

Mal frowned. "Hold on, mate. You know Eamon was under a curse, right?"

"Curse?"

"Shite, I forgot. When you saw him, he hadn't transformed yet. That's not how he really looks."

"Really? I—I suppose I didn't think about it."

A short fanfare from the bells of invisible trumpets played, and the crowd's noise dropped to a low murmur.

"That's the cue for the grand entrance, so you'll meet him directly. If you like Alun, you'll like Eamon—he's got nearly as big a stick up his arse as our brother when it comes to duty."

Most of the crowd had already taken their seats, but all now stood in a scrape of chairs as the Queen entered the Hall on the arm of a tall, dark-haired fae with golden-brown skin.

Gareth stared at him, his goblet falling from nerveless fingers to splash wine across the flagstone floor.

It's him. The one who took Niall.

Gareth hadn't seen the bastard for two centuries, but he'd never forget the fae who'd ruined his life.

CHAPTER THREE

The fanfare announcing Eamon's arrival with the Queen sounded as Niall scurried across the deserted throne room and hid in the shadows of the Great Hall's archway.

There. Gareth was unmistakable. He still had the same mop of honey-gold curls as when he and Niall had been lovers.

Unfortunately, Gareth was staring at Eamon as though he were wishing for a sword instead of the harp slung across his back. Before Niall could get up the courage to enter the room, Gareth bolted out of the Hall toward the Keep door, with another man—probably his brother, Lord Cynwrig, judging by the sword strapped across his back—at his heels.

Unable to face shouldering his way through the throng in the Great Hall, Niall retreated into the throne room to take an alternate route to the front door. This corridor wasn't empty though. Several knots of courtiers had beat him there, all gossiping in not-so-low voices.

As Niall hurried past them, he caught snatches of gossip:

"Did you see—"

"The bard ran away. I told you he would—"

"—hates all Unseelie."

"—insult to the new King."

"—won't play for the Convergence. The spell is sure to fail."

Hates all Unseelie? Gareth? Surely that was in the past, when Seelie and Unseelie had played at war for something to do other than gossip and go on pointless hunts. Gareth had never seemed prejudiced, although they'd never discussed Faerie specifically, not with Niall masquerading as human. What had changed since Niall had seen him last?

Niall slipped behind a tapestry in time to see Gareth storm across the entry hall with Lord Cynwrig not far behind. *Goddess, he's still so beautiful.* The wild curls, the clear blue eyes, the tall slim body not overly developed by weapons training.

"Gareth. Hold up. You promised—"

Gareth whirled to face his brother. "Do you know who that is?"

Even from his hiding spot, Niall could hear the fury and agony in Gareth's expressive voice. He could never hide his feelings when he spoke—his face could be as calm as a lake, never giving anything away, but his voice—and his music—always revealed his true feelings.

"He's Eamon, the Prince Regent, the Queen's betrothed," Lord Cynwrig said. "You met him before."

"When I met him, he didn't look like *that*."

"You object to his appearance? Why? I know you have an aversion to the more grotesque of the Unseelie, like many of the high fae—"

"It's not that. He's the one."

Lord Cynwrig frowned. "Which one?"

"The one who—" Gareth's voice caught on a half-sob. "—who took Niall."

Niall reared back, pressing against the stones regardless of the pain in his half-healed wounds, his breath hitching in his chest. Gareth had seen Eamon that night? He'd seen Niall walk away without a last word, a last kiss?

"Are you sure? Eamon was cursed many years ago."

"Did he ever tell you why?"

"Only that his father the King considered him disloyal and uncooperative. He didn't go into details."

"As far as I'm concerned, he deserved any curse the old King wanted to heap on his head. He kidnapped Niall. Took him to the Unseelie realm where I couldn't follow. Killed—" Gareth turned for the door. "Maybe if the King had been some other Unseelie, I might have— But not him. Never him. Never."

Gareth couldn't breathe, couldn't think. How could his brothers ally themselves with the one who'd killed Niall? Who knew how many other humans—or fae, for that matter—the bastard had stolen from friends, from family, from lovers? He was a monster on the inside as surely as he'd been monstrous on the outside when Gareth had last seen him two weeks ago in the Stone Circle. Goddess, if anyone deserved that kind of curse, it was *him*.

"I have to get out of here, Alun."

"You can't."

Gareth blinked at Alun's uncompromising tone. "Don't you understand? I can't play for him, for them. My throat would close up, my fingers be too clumsy. If the new King were anyone else, I might have been able to force myself to play for a court full of Unseelie swine as long as I could have hidden in the minstrels' gallery. As long as I didn't have to be among them." *Where they might touch me. The same ones who enslaved Niall. Took him from me. Hurt him.*

"Ah, not so hasty, boyo. He'd have begged to be hurt by them in the end. That's how glamourie *works, innit?"*

"Shut up," Gareth said through clenched teeth.

Alun stared at him for a moment, his lips parting in shock before his face turned wooden. "I will not."

"I didn't mean you. I meant—"

"Gareth." Defeat infused Alun's tone, something Gareth had never heard before. "I've granted you license, space in the past because I knew you were hurting, none better. But in this, you have to rise above your own past slights. For the Convergence spell to work, all fae must be in Faerie."

"Really? How does that work for the Disappeared? The Cornish, the Manx, the Bretons. Where are they in this glorious feast of harmony?"

"You needn't be sarcastic. I'm not sure about the Disappeared, but Fionbarr doesn't seem to think that matters."

"Then perhaps you should have Mal's pet druid check Fionbarr's work."

Alun scowled. "Don't let Mal hear you talk about Bryce that way. I thought you'd left off being an arsehole to both of us. Wasn't that what you promised not an hour ago?"

Gareth ran his hands through his hair—the curls Niall had loved so much. "I know. I'm sorry. Sometimes it's just—"

"This is one of your triggers. I understand."

"Don't try your psychobabble on me, Alun. This isn't the time."

"Isn't it? You need grief counseling more than any of my clients. I never pushed you in the past because I didn't have a lot of room to talk, but now—"

"Now that David healed you," he sneered.

"Now that I realize how destructive that grief was," Alun corrected, "I'm able to say to you—you need to let him go. You've held on to him for as long as I held on to Owain, and it's doing you no good. You won't get him back. He's gone, Gareth, just as Owain is gone. It's time for you to accept it and move on."

"It's easy for you to say."

"On the contrary, it's the most difficult thing in the world. But I haven't done right by you in allowing you to wallow in your grief and hatred. Mal and I both—we've been enabling you for centuries. We need to help you in a different way."

"What do you therapists call that? Tough love?"

"No. We call it facing reality." He gripped Gareth's shoulder. "We're here for you. To help you however you need."

"In that case, I need to leave and not come back."

Alun shook his head with a wry smile. "Nice try. But I told you—no more avoidance."

Gareth wrapped his arms across his stomach. Avoidance sounded far better than a tumble into this pit of hopeless fury. "I think you'd prefer my avoidance. Because if I perform now, feeling as I do, what do you think will happen to the King Presumptive, let alone the rest of the Unseelie in that Hall? They'd all drop like stones. Or else turn to stone."

"No," Alun barked. "You cannot."

"The problem is that I *can*. I've got Gwydion's fucking harp." Gareth slapped the case slung over his shoulder. "I can do almost anything."

Alun huffed out an exasperated breath. "I'm aware that you are able. I meant that you cannot give in to your personal feelings today. This is bigger than you. Bigger than me." His grip tightened on Gareth's shoulder. "Bigger than Niall."

Gareth pulled away. "Nothing is bigger than—"

"Stop right there. One person, no matter how important, how beloved, isn't an excuse for condemning all fae. For condemning Faerie itself. Fionbarr said that your presence is critical, as is Mal's and mine."

Gareth drew a shaky breath and blew it out. "Please, Alun. Don't make me play tonight. I'll march in the bloody procession. If I must, I'll stand in the Circle for the sake of the spell. I'll even watch the Queen mate herself to that—that—"

"Careful. You're in his Keep."

"To *him*. But I won't go to the handfasting ceilidh, and I sure as all the hells won't perform for it."

"I'll grant you that. But Gareth . . . next week, when the band is in Portland for that concert? You're coming to see me in my professional capacity. Because it's time for you to heal. All right?"

Could he? Anything would be better than this swirling chaos in his mind, the rage feeding the Voices, who in turn fed the chaos. Maybe a little Outer World psychology was what he needed to get rid of his thrice-damned disembodied hitchhikers.

"Think again, boyo. We're with you for good."

Niall cowered in his dusty refuge until Gareth and his brother retreated into the Great Hall again. The gossipmongers were right. Gareth hated with a passion rivaling any Unseelie—a passion directed primarily at Eamon.

It wasn't Eamon's fault. It had been Niall's own folly in believing he could talk Tiarnach into a sensible nonviolent solution. The King would probably have forgotten Niall's very existence if he'd just stayed safely banished in the Outer World. After all, what did the bloody bastard need one son for, let alone a spare, since he intended to rule forever?

Niall had never been able to figure that one out. Most of the Seelie Sidhe, so he'd been told, hadn't been the product of copulation at all. Some kind of spell of the elder gods as part of the creation of Faerie. Sacrifices and rituals and the right phase of the moon and *poof*—instant high fae.

Tiarnach had gotten his sons the old-fashioned way—by kidnapping a female and rutting until he'd impregnated her. Eamon's mother had been a *Gwragedd Annwn*, a Welsh lake maiden, who'd disappeared the third time Tiarnach had struck her. She'd been luckier than Niall's human mother, who'd been trapped with the monster until she died on Niall's eighth birthday. Their mixed blood had been one of the many reasons the high sticklers—especially the Irish who claimed Tuatha Dé heritage—had despised them both.

Gareth's anger seemed rooted in his belief that Eamon had abducted Niall—which was untrue. He'd merely been escorting Niall back into Faerie, since the terms of his banishment prevented him from entering on his own. If Niall told him the truth, would Gareth's anger fade? Or did he have other feelings about the Unseelie aside from that? After all, they had tried to murder him multiple times before Niall's unfortunate wager with Tiarnach, which was one of the reasons Niall had never confessed his true nature.

Would that deception, that first lie, make a difference if he were to reveal himself to Gareth now? Would Gareth be overjoyed because Niall wasn't dead—or angry and revolted because Niall wasn't what he'd seemed, had never been what he'd seemed, but was instead a part of the hated enemy? He might never want Niall again, and Niall didn't know if he could bear to be near him and not touch him.

I thought I lost him once, because of Tiarnach. I can't bear to lose him because he can't love me for what I am. Better to stay hidden, in his cold and lonely quarters, in the corner of the kitchen, with the comfort of the lesser fae's industry to soothe him. *Maybe someday I'll be able to face him. But not today.* Not with Gareth's anger still simmering. Not with Niall still so broken by his captivity.

Better to wait. Until I'm recovered. Until he's not so angry. A small voice whispered that he'd never be ready, but Niall ignored it.

He skulked back down the hallway, keeping close to the wall. It wasn't necessary—the corridor was empty now, all the previous gossipmongers returned to the Great Hall with the feast about to begin. But after so many years encompassed by stone, Niall felt more secure with it at his back. He wasn't sure he'd know how to live in the open again.

A vicious draft hit him as he reached the archway leading to the throne room, and he shivered, wishing for a thicker cloak or another shirt. Another *whoosh* of cold air hit him halfway across the empty throne room, and with it the tramp of many feet.

Shite. Was this what Eamon had warned him about—Fionbarr escorting Tiarnach and Luchullain to the dungeons? He couldn't bear to face Tiarnach. Not now. But he couldn't hope to escape the way he'd come—no time.

His gaze snapped to the huge tapestry hanging behind the throne. The One Tree, with the male figure standing in front of it, the Unseelie crown on his head. For as long as Niall could remember, the figure had looked like Tiarnach. Since his return, though, it looked like Eamon.

He scuttled across the room, low and quick, as he'd learned to do in the forge, and ducked behind the tapestry. There wasn't much room back here—barely three feet between the back of the tapestry and the stone wall.

He hunkered down, making himself as small as possible, and just in time. The *chink* of metal from chain mail grew louder, passing in front of the throne. Niall held his breath.

"My throne." Tiarnach's voice was querulous, but unmistakable. Niall clenched his fists and pressed them against his thighs to fight off the desire to leap out and throttle the bastard. "What has that traitorous whelp done to my tapestry?"

"Trust you to worry about a thrice-blasted tapestry." Niall didn't recognize the voice, but it must have been Luchullain. He sounded nearly as fed up with Tiarnach as ever Niall had been.

"A lot you care. If you'd have done your job properly, he'd never have gotten near the throne."

"And if you had done your job properly, my hand would still be on my arm, so don't—"

"Peace, Your Majesty, Lord Luchullain. We must pass through quickly."

Hmmm. Awfully polite guards. But then, they'd no doubt had millennia of experience with Tiarnach's uncertain temper. Niall couldn't blame them for hedging their bets.

"Is he in there?" Tiarnach said, clearly not obeying because he sounded as if he were directly in front of the throne. "Feasting as if he has a right to wear the crown? He'll be sorry when—"

"Do you *ever* shut up? Goddess strike me blind, if I had to be shackled to an Unseelie arsehole, why couldn't it have been one with better conversation?"

"Fine words from you," Tiarnach sneered. "I liked you better when you were mute. One more way my son has betrayed me."

"If you please, this way." The guard's voice held an edge of worry. *Suppose that's natural when your charges behave like spoiled children but have the potential to take your head off.*

Niall frowned, puzzled. Wasn't the mage . . . Fionbarr, that was it . . . wasn't he supposed to act as escort as well? Although perhaps he was there and simply not as loquacious as the prisoners.

The group finally moved off, though, Tiarnach and Luchullain still bickering. Niall stayed where he was until he was certain the guards had had time to escort their prisoners to the dungeons and install them safely behind fae-resistant bars.

CHAPTER FOUR

Remaking Faerie. Gareth had to believe that a new Faerie would be better than the old one, a place where no one would ever endure his own brand of pain. He'd advocate for that. Make sure the Queen and the new—he had to swallow against a surge of nausea—King enacted the restrictions he'd always wanted against interspecies dalliances.

"Bit of a hypocrite there, aren't you, boyo? You've spent dunamany years wailing about the loss of your human because somebody else took him first."

This time, Gareth couldn't tell the voices to shut up because it was true. He'd *never* approved of fae kidnapping humans and keeping them in Faerie until they grew bored, then releasing them into the Outer World again to suffer because they couldn't find anything there they recognized. Friends and family would be long dead and gone, their home crumbled to dust.

But then he'd met Niall—wild and free and more than a little bit wicked, enticing Gareth to break out of the shell he'd built for himself, overshadowed as he'd been by his brothers, constrained as he'd been by his training. Gareth had never even had a lover before, but Niall had made him *want,* had given him everything he'd never known *how* to want.

But anger and resentment would never bring him back. Nothing would. Perhaps Alun was right and Gareth needed to find a better way to honor his fallen lover. If participating in this thrice-damned ceremony, seeing the Queen mate herself forever to the Unseelie swine who'd shattered Gareth's dreams—if that was what it took to make sure nobody else ever suffered as he had done, as Niall surely had done, then he'd do it.

And then he'd never set foot in Faerie again.

He stole behind the dais at the far end of the glade and set the harp at the base of a willow tree. He didn't worry about anyone snatching it who shouldn't—the harp had its own protections. It would rest here until it chose its next player.

He returned to the edge of the crowd in time to greet Mal.

"You ready there, brother?" Mal slapped Gareth on the shoulder. "Procession's about to begin, and guess what? You're on point."

"Me? Why? I thought the Queen—"

"Nah. She's bringing up the rear. Probably to make sure we all keep in line. I think you're supposed to play the processional."

Gareth shook his head. "No. I told Alun I'll be there, but I won't perform. I can't."

Mal tilted his head, his brows bunched in consternation. "I'm not sure you'll be given much choice, mate. I think that Fionbarr bloke told her bridal Majesty that it was a part of the spell. That's why she asked you to bring Gwydion's harp."

"'Ask'? She *told* me to bring it and I agreed. I never said I'd play it."

"I think it's assumed that if you're here with an instrument, a performance will follow."

"Then they can bloody well assume something else and find some other sucker to do the honors. Hells, the spectral trumpets can do anything I can do."

"You sell yourself short. But whatever. I'm sure she'll make her displeasure felt if it's that all-fired important." Mal gestured for Gareth to precede him to the front of the milling crowd of Seelie fae, who'd all made the trek to the Seelie ceilidh glade after the feast.

"What's the point of staging this stupid procession anyway? Couldn't we have just *processed* from the Keep instead of coming back here first?"

"Ah well. Separation of bride and groom and all that. Plus, not everyone was invited to the feast—and not everyone who was invited attended." Mal nodded at a knot of Seelie fae who weren't precisely humanoid, yet still ethereally beautiful, with flowing green hair and brown skin the color of burnished oak. "Yon dryads refused. Although their objection may have been to entering a building with a stone floor, where they couldn't feel the earth under their rather grubby little toes. And there were others . . ." Mal heaved a sigh. "Let's just say you're not the only one with *feelings* about the Convergence, either here or on the Unseelie bench."

"Bench?"

"Sorry. Bryce has been forcing me to watch bloody American football."

"How's his apprenticeship going?"

Mal grinned. "Journeyman now. Isn't that a pisser? Less than a month gone and he's already passed his O levels. He's a sharp one, my bloke."

"I'm—I'm sorry I wasn't very kind to him when I met him before."

Mal's grin dimmed. "Yeah. Not too happy with you about that, I can't lie. But he's a forgiving sort, as long as you don't threaten his bloody wetlands or mix your recycling, so I daresay if you grovel sufficiently, he'll give you a pass."

"Thanks. I'll—I'll try to grovel at the first opportunity. I'm . . ." Gareth looked back over the throng of Seelie fae—tall, short, radiantly pale to midnight dark, but all undeniably beautiful, at least by the standards of the spell that bound the Seelie sphere. Would he miss this?

"Admit it, boyo. You'll miss being the star of this particular show."

No. No I won't.

"I'm not coming back."

"Coming back?" Mal raised his eyebrows. "You mean here? To the ceilidh glade? Skipping the party, are you? Don't blame you. Wish I could. Don't have much heart for it without Bryce."

"No. I mean to Faerie. Once this is over, I'm leaving and I'm never coming back, no matter what the Queen decrees. I can't be part of a world where I owe allegiance to a King who stands for everything I hate."

"If the Queen orders—"

"I'll refuse. If she exiles me, curses me, so be it. But I've lived in the Outer World for most of the last two hundred years. I'll make it my only home from now on. There are ways to excise the One Tree from our fae souls." Gareth shrugged. "I'm sure I could find someone to rid me of it."

Mal grabbed his shoulders. "You can't mean it. Alun and I were blocked from the One Tree for a time, but its seed was still there in our hearts. Cut that out and you'll die."

"We all die eventually. The One Tree makes us feel like we're immortal, but it's only an illusion, as false as any *glamourie*. It's my choice, Mal, and I choose to become mortal."

"A mortal with Gwydion's bloody harp and a bard's magic," Mal growled, his fingers digging into Gareth's flesh.

"I'll leave the harp behind for the next bard."

"There isn't a next bard. You're it. The last."

"That's what everyone's always said, but how the hells do they know? I hid my potential for long enough. Maybe when they redraw the boundaries of the kingdom, they'll find another one lurking under a convenient rock. And who's to say if my bard's powers will remain after the link is severed?"

"You can't just . . . just *renounce* your nature, and furthermore, I don't believe anyone could cast that kind of spell."

"I'll wager a druid can."

Mal paled, releasing Gareth and stumbling back. "Don't ask that of Bryce. Please."

Gareth smiled wryly. "You may think he's the only druid in the worlds, but there are others. David's aunt, for one. I'll have her make me mortal and then I'll live out my life as a rock musician, aging until I look like Keith Richards at his desiccated best."

"Don't joke, Gareth. Does Alun know of this plan?"

"Not yet. But I've got brother-ordered therapy in my future, so I'm sure it will come out. I'm sure he'll try to talk me out of it —"

"Bloody right, he will. So will I."

Gareth grasped Mal's forearms. "Please, Mal. This is all I can bear. Alun wants me to heal, and this is the only way I know how to do it. I can't live forever with this . . . this hole in my heart, the one that makes me want to scream every time I open my mouth. The hole will never vanish, but at least I can make 'forever' a less distant shore."

Mal's throat worked convulsively. "Shite." His voice emerged as a croak. "If you—"

The spectral trumpets sounded as Alun strode toward them, fae parting before him like a wave. "It's time." He gripped both their shoulders. "We're remaking the world, brothers. Let's make sure it's one we can all live with."

With Alun next to him, Gareth found it easier to march out of the glade and through the woods, the trees moving aside to allow the crowd to pass. Gareth, with his bard's sense of the shape of Faerie, could feel it turning under his feet to feed them onto the plateau crowned with the Stone Circle. Sometimes Faerie adjusted its internal geography for its own ends, the elastic size of the ceilidh glade being a case in point.

This time, it seemed as if Faerie wanted to shorten their journey. Either Faerie was onboard with the Convergence, or else it just didn't want so many feet trampling the paths and disturbing the trees.

They spilled out onto the plateau, and it expanded to accommodate more and more bodies as the Unseelie hordes—*no, I have to stop thinking about them as marauders*— emerged from the trees on the other side of the Circle.

The Stone Circle itself—the outer circle of menhirs, capped with massive lintels; the inner horseshoe of trilithons; the altar at the north point of the compass—was still empty, as if everyone was waiting for some signal before passing its perimeter.

Gareth sidled closer to Alun, a Daoine Sidhe warrior jostling his hip. "Should we enter?"

Alun shook his head. "Not yet. Fionbarr, the mage who's casting the spell, will be first inside. Once he's at his place by the altar, then we can proceed. He'll set up a perimeter spell to allow the appropriate people inside."

Mal's eyebrows shot up. "Only certain fae allowed in? Seems a bit exclusionary for a Convergence spell, eh?"

"I think it's more a logistical question." Alun nodded at the crowd, which continued to pour out of both sides of the plateau. "I don't think the Stone Circle can hold all of us."

Alun was right about that. Faerie may adjust itself to suit its needs, but some things were fixed because they were anchors to the Outer World, keeping Faerie stable. The Circle was one of them. Although the geography around it might change, the Circle itself never changed shape, size, or location. Although it was bloody huge, it couldn't accommodate all remaining Celtic fae. Gareth hadn't realized there were so many of them left.

"Maybe you need to pay more attention during your command performances, boyo. Then you'd see beyond your own nose."

Maybe. But as the crowd stabilized—not growing any larger, though still seething and adjusting itself around the Circle—Gareth was instead surprised that there were so few of them. If this was the entire population of land-based fae, the years had been unkind to all of them. He wondered whether the water-based fae, commanded to attend in the river that wound through the woods, and in the lake at the base of the tor, were similarly decimated.

Across the empty Circle, a tall fae in a long midnight blue robe decorated with silver crescent moons—*shite, cliché much?*—

strode past the north-most menhir and took his place behind the altar stone. He raised both hands, one of which held a long knife, its blade glinting silver in the setting sun. It made Gareth shiver. The mage looked more like someone about to conduct a blood sacrifice than perform a healing spell so powerful that it could mend Faerie itself.

Fionbarr—Gareth assumed that was him, since no other pretentiously-robed twit joined him at the altar—shouted a string of words in Gaelic, and a faint greenish shimmer sprang up between each menhir, enclosing the Circle in a ring of energy that raised the hair on Gareth's arms.

"Shite," Mal muttered. "I hate those bloody power barriers."

Judging by the way the crowd murmured and shifted, they weren't too thrilled with them either. By now, the separation between Seelie and Unseelie wasn't as clear as everyone jostled to get their own square foot of personal space. About a quarter of the way around the plateau, a group of lesser fae—brownies and bauchan, by their size and skin variations—got pushed behind a cadre of Daoine Sidhe, as if the Sidhe were taking precedence here as they tended to do at court. Somehow, that didn't bode well for the new, inclusive Faerie.

As the Sidhe lords swaggered their way past the barrier into the Circle, Gareth's attention snapped to a group of lesser fae, mostly brownies and bauchan. But in their midst, a taller man hunched over, as if he were trying to hide amongst the shorter beings around him. That alone would have made him stand out, but there was something about him—was he Unseelie? Sidhe? He didn't fit those signatures.

Shite, was he *human*? What was a human still doing in Faerie? Hadn't the soon-to-be King sworn to eradicate the practice—after he'd destroyed Gareth's life with it?

Then the human straightened, and Gareth got a good look at his face.

Niall.

Gareth's heart stalled, then took off at a cadence that rivaled Hamish's most manic beat.

Niall still here? Still a captive after all this time? *Still alive?*

"Gareth?" Alun took his arm. "What's wrong? You look as if you've seen a ghost."

Not a ghost. Thank the Goddess not a ghost. But if Niall didn't get out of Faerie right now, before the thrice-damned Convergence spell completed, he'd be a ghost before night fell.

Not if I can help it.

Gareth took off, shouldering past the fae who were surging forward into the Circle. They blocked his way, blocked his view of Niall. Behind him, Alun called his name, but Gareth ignored him.

I'm not letting that Unseelie bastard take him from me again.

As the only high fae amidst a cluster of brownies and bauchan, Niall stood out—or rather, stood head, chest, and shoulders above them. Peadar and Heilyn and the other lesser fae on the Keep staff clustered near him, which in a way was gratifying, yet in another way pathetic. He was pleased they trusted him, but pitied them for believing he had any power whatsoever to protect them. In fact, they had more power than he did right now. He might as well be fully human with his god-delivered wounds only half-healed.

The cluster of redcaps at the edge of the plateau stirred and muttered as a cadre of Seelie Sidhe swaggered past them into the center of the Circle. *Privilege is still reserved for the high fae.* Apparently Fionbarr's spell wasn't as egalitarian as Eamon had hoped. Maybe Niall should have petitioned to elevate the lesser fae when he'd had the chance.

After the Sidhe passed, Niall checked on the redcaps again, to see if any of them was having the irresistible urge to take a swing at one of those entitled backsides. The redcaps hadn't changed their surly attitude, but beyond them, Niall spotted something that made his blood run cold, then hot.

In the trees beyond them stood a trio of trow guards, their crossbows strapped to their backs, and between them stood Tiarnach and Luchullain.

Danu's tits. I didn't realize they had to be here. When Eamon had broken the news, he'd made it sound as if the men would be safely underground in the Keep dungeons. Maybe Fionbarr wasn't so powerful a mage that he could extend his reach from the Circle to the Keep.

So far, Tiarnach's attention seemed riveted on Eamon, his emaciated face twisted with a rictus of hatred, eyes fairly blazing. He hadn't noticed Niall—although that wouldn't last for long, not with Niall standing out like an oak in a peat bog.

Niall tried to hunch forward, reduce his height, but even if he dropped to his knees, he'd still be taller than Peadar and Heilyn. He glanced around, searching for an escape route, Fionbarr's spell be damned. If it could encompass the woods where Tiarnach stood, then Niall could damn well hide there too—as far away from Tiarnach as was possible.

He began edging backward through the crowd, the lesser fae huddling against each other as he passed, those who didn't know him well cringing away from him as if he might do them harm. Considering the treatment most of them had received under Tiarnach, he could hardly blame them, but it cut nonetheless.

He wanted to tell them he was one of them, but he wasn't. He, who had once been a child of two worlds, was now a child of none. No matter what Eamon claimed, Niall had never had a place in Faerie that wasn't tainted by his blood. How likely was that to change after the Convergence?

He'd nearly reached the tree line without attracting Tiarnach's attention when he heard a voice—*the* voice. The one that had haunted his dreams for years.

"Stop!" Gareth's shout rang out over the buzz of muted conversation on the plateau and acted like a freeze ray on Niall.

It also locked Tiarnach's gaze on Gareth.

"Niall?" Gareth's voice broke on Niall's name.

No. Please. Not here. Not now. Niall pretended he didn't hear. How could he face Gareth and confess that their entire relationship had been a lie? That Gareth had mourned for the very Unseelie whose unthinking words and careless wager had been the cause of a vendetta that had cost him so much?

Niall broke for the trees, but hadn't made it two feet before Gareth caught his arm. He jerked it away, but Gareth stepped into his path.

"Niall. It's all right. You don't have to run. It's me."

Niall sucked in a breath. After all this time, to be this close to Gareth, yet know he was everything Gareth hated. "I—" He glanced around wildly.

Gareth's face crumpled. "Don't you . . . don't you remember me?"

Niall froze. *Was this the answer?* Another lie, but if it kept the big one a secret, if it kept Gareth away from him until he could figure out how to tell him the truth, he'd take it. "I'm sorry. I have to—"

"Damn them. They took you away from me, but they took me away from you too."

"I don't know what you mean. I must get back to the Keep. I have duties—"

"You don't." Gareth swiped a hand under his eyes, his mouth firming into a grim line. "Not anymore. You never belonged here and they were wrong to kidnap you. Besides, this gods-bedamned spell will *kill* you if you stay."

I still appear human. He doesn't know. "I can't go. Eamon—"

"Don't mention his name," Gareth snarled. "He's the cause of this. He's the one who should die, not you."

"No!" Niall staggered back until he ran into the trunk of the oak. "Never say that. He's—"

"He's Unseelie. I know you never wanted to hear those songs, those tales, of the evil the Unseelie hordes wrought in Faerie, in your world too. They're the cause of every despicable thing in this world or yours. The reason so few of us are left."

Niall shook his head. The anger infusing Gareth's voice was enough to set his own pulse pounding, to make the surrounding lesser fae shift and mutter uneasily. As a bard, Gareth had to be careful that his own emotions didn't bleed out from his voice to the audience.

He wasn't being careful now. If Niall didn't get him out of here, Gareth's anger could infect the whole crowd, and the ceremony would go tits up before Eamon was ever officially crowned. And with the old King waiting in the wings—literally—to take advantage of the opportunity?

No. He couldn't let that happen. Their people—even the surliest and most isolationist—deserved a better king than Tiarnach had ever been. He had to keep Gareth calm.

"I— You're the bard, aren't you? The Seelie bard."

"Yes." Gareth nodded, eager hope replacing the anger. "That's right. Do you remember seeing me perform?"

Niall shook his head. "No. But I've heard tales."

"I used to sing to you." This time, his voice was sad, and more than one of the lesser fae whimpered. "Don't you remember?"

"No. I'm sorry. I—" Over Gareth's shoulder, Niall met Tiarnach's malevolent gaze. The bastard grinned and motioned to one of the trows, who unstrapped its crossbow. The huge guard lifted the weapon to its shoulder, aiming directly at Gareth. "No!"

Niall pulled Gareth further into the trees, out of the guard's sightlines. "You're right. I want to go. Take me out of here. Take me home."

"Your home won't be there. Time has passed—"

"I don't care. Take me with you. Now."

Gareth blinked, joy infusing his expression. "I've wanted nothing more for over two hundred years. This way."

He took Niall's hand and led him through the trees at a run, laughing joyously.

Niall's felt slippers weren't made for pounding down rocky paths; by the time they reached the bottom of the hill, they'd probably be worn through. Brambles slapped him, striping his face with fire, but that would be nothing compared to what would happen when he stepped across the threshold.

Could he bear it? Perhaps not. Perhaps it would finally kill him, but at least Gareth would be out of Tiarnach's reach. Eamon could finish his ceremony, mate his Seelie Queen, and take care of the realm as he'd planned, even if he had to do it without Niall's help.

Keeping Gareth alive. That was all that mattered—all that had ever mattered.

CHAPTER FIVE

The feel of Niall's hand in his as they wound through the woods was almost more than Gareth could handle without breaking into song. *Not the time. Need my breath for running.*

They burst out of the trees at the top of the tor leading down to the threshold that Gareth used to pass from his home in LA into Faerie. But standing in front of the threshold, arms crossed over their massive chests, morning stars and flails in their fists, were a trio of trows.

Apparently the Queen and her monster intended to enforce their wedding invitation, at least where Gareth was concerned. But there were other gates, to other places, many of which Gareth had used when he'd been summoned to Faerie in the midst of one of the band's tours.

But none of those held any kind of lure—for one thing, there was no immediate aid there—not in Tokyo, or Aberystwyth, or Boston, or Edinburgh. He glanced back at Niall, whose mouth was pinched with pain and whose shoulders sagged with fatigue. Those places all might be unexpected destinations, ones that Eamon might not think of guarding, but none of them held the help that Niall obviously needed.

But one place did—Portland, where his brother-in-law David, the only known *achubydd* in existence, lived, and where Mal's lover, the journeyman druid, was more than competent enough to drive off any attack with evil intent.

"This way."

"I don't think I can go—"

"Don't worry. You're with me. You're safe now." *At least as safe as I can make you.* "I'll take you somewhere he can't find you."

No matter what Alun claimed about the spell, the absence of one more fae when the Disappeared were still outside couldn't really matter. Besides, if it came down to choosing Niall versus choosing Faerie, Gareth's decision had been made two hundred years ago.

But he still needed backup: when it came to protecting Niall, Gareth had no desire to sing solo.

Niall crashed down the hillside, clutching Gareth's hand for all he was worth. At the moment, it might be the only thing keeping him upright. The rasp of his shirt and the violence of their flight had dislodged the bandages on his back, and he could feel the wounds seeping.

But so what? Gareth was alive. Alive and holding his hand. *Holy Goddess.* How had he gone from total despair to soaring hope in the space of twelve hours?

But that hope was tempered with dread too. The trio of guards stationed at the foot of the hill—and why were they there anyway?—were thundering on an intercept course to where Gareth was heading.

Gareth stopped within inches of plowing into a stream. He glanced down at Niall's feet. "Those don't look waterproof."

Niall held up one foot, clad in its felt slipper. "They weren't rock proof either, but I managed to run down that bloody hill, didn't I?" In truth, the soles of his feet were nearly as tough as boot leather, since he'd been barefoot on rough stone for over two hundred years.

"All right then. We have to cross the stream. Keep hold of my hand and step where I step."

Niall actually knew this drill as well as Gareth did—Faerie was always bounded by water, and any non-fae who sought entrance had to do so in the footsteps of someone with access. But he didn't want to bring that up now—if ever—and in his present state, he might effectively be non-fae anyway. *Wish there was some way to test that. I really want to know.* Some way to test it without telling Gareth the truth, anyway. Although once his back healed, chances were good that he'd not be able to hide it anymore.

With the trows roaring behind them, Gareth stepped into the stream. Niall followed, the icy water soaking through his felt slippers and wicking up the legs of his breeches. He clenched his chattering teeth and kept his attention resolutely on Gareth's feet. *Step. Step. Dodge the rock. Step.*

From the sound of it, the guards had nearly made it to the edge of the stream. While no Unseelie could unlock a Seelie gate, they could take advantage of an already open one. If Gareth and Niall didn't exit before the trows splashed in, they could follow across, all the way to the Outer World.

But just then, Gareth took a last step onto a muddy bank, pulling Niall out of the water and into his arms with one final yank.

The first step outside the threshold nearly brought Niall to his knees. With his first breath of Outer World air, air he hadn't breathed in over two hundred years, the *ethera* clamored for his attention in disbelieving joy at his return, like a child whose father suddenly appeared with sweeties.

:Here! Look! Now!:

The images they threw at him overwhelmed him, overloading his senses.

Then there was that other matter.

Only a few years into his captivity, when he'd still harbored some small hope of finding Gareth, he'd actually managed to escape. He'd followed the trickle of Outer World air up a path so narrow and through a tunnel so tight that it scraped the skin off his chest. Up, up, up, and damn the burn in his legs and the agony of the half-healed lashes on his back. Gareth was up there, life was up there, the world of his mother, the world of his lover. But when he'd finally burst out of the last cavern, he'd been in a place he'd never seen before. Not Wales, not England, not Scotland, not Ireland.

With that first breath, the *ethera* had swarmed him, caroling *:New World!:* and the wounds on his back had flared to agonizing life as if he'd just received the beatings of all the years anew, the cool moist air burning like fire in the newly opened wounds.

He'd collapsed onto a bed of pine needles with the sound of axes and the scent of woodsmoke in his nose. Tiarnach's guards had found him there and taken him back to his cave. Govannon had forged his leg and arm shackles that very night.

That was nothing compared to this time, because now he had nearly two hundred years' worth of annual floggings to relive in that instant. He dropped to his knees, his vision whiting out.

"Niall?" Gareth's voice came from so far away, as if Niall were still at the bottom of the cavern, trying desperately to reach the surface.

On one agonized cry, he collapsed forward onto his face, and with Gareth and the *ethera* frantically calling his name, he fell into the dark.

CHAPTER SIX

"Niall! Goddess, please . . . Niall?" No response. Was he even breathing? Then Niall's fingers spasmed, digging into the mud of the bank, and he moaned, long and low, like a wounded beast.

Gareth had never witnessed the return of a kidnapped human to the Outer World. Could this be normal, or a residual spell of some kind, like the one that had stolen Niall's memory?

He'd heard whispers that the *glamourie* keeping the victim in thrall to his captor included a sort of magical chastity belt that made contact with other fae painful or revolting. For how annoying would it be to go to all the trouble of enticing a human to your bed, only to have him stolen by a court rival?

Rain pattered in the trees overhead, with an occasional plop onto Gareth's shoulders. A heavy drop fell onto Niall's back and Gareth reached out to brush it away, only to freeze as a wet patch bloomed on Niall's brown woolen cloak, growing too fast and too *red* to be caused by a few scattered raindrops.

"Now you've done it, boyo. The Unseelie kept him alive so you could kill him your own self."

"No! He'll be fine. He has to be." Gareth glanced around wildly, but of course nobody was near. The point of the gate was to be remote and unobtrusive, blast it to all the hells. He needed his brother-in-law, and he needed him *now*.

David was the last known *achubydd* on the planet—a member of a meta-supernatural race whose healing powers among supes were near-miraculous. He couldn't do as much with humans, but he was a nurse. He'd help, if only Gareth could reach him.

Whenever Gareth ventured into Faerie—as infrequently as he could manage—he couldn't take his cell phone with him, any more than he could take any base metal or synthetic-fiber clothing. The nearest phone was at the Audubon Society center, nearly two miles away—and judging by the fading light, they'd be closing soon in any case.

Then he heard faint voices from the Wildwood Trail at the base of the hill. He smoothed Niall's hair with a trembling hand. "Hold on, *cariad*. I'll be right back."

He raced through the trees, nearly taking a header when he stumbled on an exposed root. *I have to catch them. They could be Niall's only chance.*

"What makes you think they'd help you, boyo? You wouldn't be thinking of using the glamourie *on them now, not with your high and mighty views on coercion?"*

"I'll do what I have to." For Niall.

He paused for a moment to straighten his clothing and run fingers through his hair so he'd look less like a wild man. He forced a smile onto his face and stepped out of the trees just before the hikers rounded a bend in the trail.

They returned the smile—this was Portland, after all—and would have passed him by. *Not this time.* He hummed under his breath, and the couple halted, their attention focusing on him as he'd intended. "Excuse me." He sang more than spoke, weaving his bardic spell around them. "I've lost my cell phone. May I borrow yours for just a moment?"

"Of course," the man said. He and his female companion both smiled dreamily, holding out their phones, and chorused, "Take mine."

"Thank you." Gareth accepted the man's phone and dialed David quickly, the sooner to end the spell that roiled his belly with revulsion. *And the Unseelie claimed using* glamourie *on humans wasn't wrong.*

"Hello?" At the sound of his brother-in-law's usual breezy tone, Gareth breathed a sigh of relief.

"David. Thank the Goddess you're home."

"Gareth?" Immediately David's tone changed from welcome cheer to apprehension. "What's wrong? Is Alun—"

"Calm down, Dafydd *bach*. When last I saw him, Alun was well. But I need your help. I've got Niall with me—"

"Niall? Wait a minute. *Your* Niall? The one that—"

"Yes, that Niall."

"Holy cats. You must be freaking *stoked*."

Gareth couldn't argue with that. "You could say so. But there are . . . complications. He's ill. Unconscious. We're at the ford by the Faerie threshold in Forest Park. Can you—"

"Sit tight. If he's out cold, we'll need muscle. I'll grab Bryce and be right there." David disconnected the call. One thing about the man—he didn't faff around when he had a mission.

Gareth returned the hiker's phone, thanking him again and sending the two on their way with a sprightly marching tune before hurrying back to Niall.

"Excellently done, boyo. Gwydion himself couldn't have managed better."

"Oh shut up." He settled next to Niall, heedless of the mud soaking his pants. Stroking Niall's hair, he murmured, "Be easy, *cariad*. David is on his way, and he'll set you to rights, never fear." David drove like he approached life in general and Alun in particular: in a headlong rush, taking no prisoners. He was a force of nature. And considering Niall's condition, a force of nature was exactly what they needed right now.

Niall was fading in and out of consciousness. One minute he was stretched on a field of snow, freezing and shaking like an aspen leaf. A blink, and then he was strung up next to the fires of the Abyss, Govannon's lash striking him as he nearly bit through the leather strap in his mouth, Tiarnach gloating from the passageway to freedom, shouting, "Again! Again! Again!"

"Again what? What can I get you? Something to drink?" He didn't recognize the soft, concerned voice. *Not Tiarnach, thank the Goddess.*

His eyelids fluttered open. He was on the snowfield again—not snow, but pristine white sheets on the most comfortable bed —*:Sleep Number!:*—he'd ever lain on. "Gareth?" he croaked.

"No. I'm sorry, but he had to go to a band meeting, although I had to threaten him with bodily harm to do it." A slender man with light brown hair and kind gray-blue eyes sat next to him, dipping the mattress. "I'm David, Gareth's brother-in-law. Alun's husband."

"Alun. Lord Cynwrig, do you mean?" Niall blinked his bleary eyes, trying to make sense of David's aura.

David chuckled. "Here in Oregon, he's just Dr. Kendrick, psychologist, but if you've spent the last however-many years in Faerie, you couldn't know that."

He must still be delirious, because the colors in David's aura were clearly impossible. "You can't be."

David frowned. "Our marriage is perfectly legal, I assure you."

"I know." *:Marriage equality!:* Closing his eyes against another bout of chills, he blurted, "*Achubydd,*" then cringed at the slip. But David was clearly American, and *achubyddion* had been extinct since the country's infancy, so he'd not know—

"Oh that. Yes, I am."

Niall's eyes flew open. If he touched David in his desperate need to ease the pain, not only could David suffer—even die—but he'd know the truth about Niall's nature. *Gareth* would know the truth. He made a futile attempt to scramble away, but the flare of agony in his back robbed him of strength and breath.

David slapped the mattress. "Stop. Honestly, you're as bad as Alun, and he *knows* that healing doesn't have to be lethal to an *achubydd*. Besides, since you're human, I can't—"

"I don't care. Please. Stay back."

"Fine. I won't touch you, if that's what you're worried about, but you have to stay still. Frankly, I don't know how you can even *think* about moving with wounds like that."

Niall shook his head, clutching a pillow softer than a cloud. David huffed an exasperated breath and stood up, propping his hands on his narrow hips.

"Look, Gareth will *kill* me if anything happens to you, and then Alun will kill *him* for killing me, and Mal will probably attack *Alun* for killing Gareth, so unless you want to unleash a Kendrick family bloodbath, will you please just rest for a minute while I get another dose of medicine for you?"

Niall nodded miserably, closing his eyes as the sound of David's footsteps retreated down the hallway. He truly hadn't expected to survive that first step outside, let alone find someone who might actually be able to heal him enough to make him ambulatory. That's all he really needed, because once the god-wounds were gone, he'd be revealed as Unseelie. Then Gareth would be more likely to kill Niall than David or Eamon.

Eamon. The binding stone.

When Niall had plunged into the woods with Gareth, he hadn't given a thought to the stone in his pocket. Danu's tits, he'd bolted with half the ingredients for the bloody Convergence spell. Didn't this prove what the whole Unseelie court had thought of him his entire life? Unworthy. Disloyal. Treacherous.

He couldn't give two shites for what most of them thought—he'd done his best to live down to their expectations, after all—but he'd never intended to treat his brother with the same casual opportunism. He needed to get that stone back to Eamon, but . . . *My pants. Where are they?*

Panic flared in his chest. A sheet was covering his legs and arse, but he could tell he was completely naked. He hoped like all the bloody hells that brisk, efficient David hadn't tossed the pants out, or Goddess forbid, washed them. Who knew what plunging the binding stone into Outer World water and soap would do to it?

He eased himself to his hands and knees, crawled to the edge of the bed, and gingerly sat down, needing to recover from even that small movement. *At least Govannon never beat my arse.* Small favors. His gaze caught on his wrist—they'd been raw from the revenant of the shackles when he'd passed out. But now they looked about as well as they had in the Keep. Hunh. Whatever medicine David had used on him was damned effective. *As long as he didn't touch me.*

The room was dim, a lamp on the bedside table turned low, blinds covering the windows. He reached over and flicked the lamp to a higher setting, breathing a sigh of relief when he saw his pants draped over a chair. He snagged them, and thanks to the Goddess the stone was still in the pocket. He dug it out and glanced around the room.

Where to put it? The tall bureau or the closet would make the most sense, but Niall didn't think he could make the trip across the room. Stuff it under the mattress? No, then it would be in danger when the sheets were changed. He eyed the lamp, with its stepped brass base. If it were hollow . . . He tipped it up. Yes! He set the stone under it and settled it back on the table.

"You should be lying down."

Niall startled at David's voice, wincing at the fire in his shoulders, and stole a glance at the other man, who was studying him with his head cocked to one side. Niall couldn't tell whether the speculative look on his face was well-deserved suspicion or a prelude to humoring the madman.

"I need to use the—"

"Toilet?"

"Yes."

"All right. Let me help you up."

"No! You can't—"

"Look, I can totally touch you without activating the *achubydd* mojo, you know. It's not involuntary."

"It's not?"

"Brother," David muttered, then circled the bed to help Niall to his feet. As they shuffled across the room, David said, "It's interesting that you'd know about *achubyddion*, or recognize one if you saw one."

Bugger. This amnesia shite was tougher than it had seemed. "We had— That is, there were several *achubyddion* in the Keep. For a while. They had the same . . . feeling."

"Until they were drained to death, right?"

Niall nodded miserably. He'd known about the pathetic little harem that Tiarnach and his top advisors had kept locked away in the east tower. He'd railed against it, of course, with his usual rebellious rhetoric, but he'd never done anything about it. Never tried to help them. He'd never tried to help anyone until Gareth. "Yes."

"Well, that was just stupid. Honestly, the fae have *no* imagination or empathy. I wonder sometimes how they've lasted so long." David's gray-blue eyes clouded over, and Niall could almost see the tenor of his thoughts flit across his open, guileless face.

We're not lasting as well as we could, are we? And Niall's flight with part of the damned spell might seriously bollux up Eamon's last desperate gamble to fix that.

David ushered him into the bathroom. "I'll be out here. Holler if you need me."

Niall didn't waste any time. David's medicines were effective, but not miraculous, and he wasn't certain how long he'd be able to handle being upright.

David was waiting outside the door and assisted him back into bed, then pulled the sheet up over Niall's bare arse. "So, Niall. I'm curious."

Niall peered up at him. "Curious?"

"Mmmhmm." David shook his floppy bangs out of his face. "Here you are, in my house, and since I've been to Faerie, I know it doesn't sport low-flow toilets—*any* toilets for that matter—or, you know, electricity. So why aren't you more freaked out by the changes? And how did you know how to work that lamp?"

Niall blinked. *Shite.* He hadn't even thought about it—just known what to do, thanks to the hints from the *ethera*. "I—I don't know, exactly."

David snorted. "And that's another thing. Language has changed a lot in the last two hundred years. Why are you speaking like any other Portland hipster?"

"Uh . . ." *If I had truly been kidnapped, wouldn't I be feeling a bit angry now? Sure, go with that.* "How am I supposed to know? Perhaps it's part of a . . . a spell. Maybe Ea— the prince was kinder than you give him credit for."

David's eyes narrowed. "I'm making no assumptions here. We can let it go at that, but somehow, I think there's something you're not telling us. Now, let's take a look at your back, shall we?" When Niall recoiled, David gave him an exasperated look. "I promise I won't touch you, although why you should be so freaking worried—"

"These wounds—they'd kill you for certain."

"Really? Why do you think that?"

"Because . . . because they were inflicted by a god."

David's eyes widened. "A god? One of the elder gods Alun is always on about? Really?"

"Yes. Govannon. The smith god, who tends the forge at the Abyss."

"Holy cats. You mean there really *is* a 'flaming Abyss' like Mal is always swearing by?"

Niall nodded. "In the underworld."

"Wow. This is—" He shook his head. "You know, being married to a Sidhe lord, working with the supe communities, you'd think I'd get used to this stuff. But every time I think I've got it nailed, something else pops up."

Niall cringed. "Druids? You know druids?"

"My aunt is one. So is my brother-in-law's sort-of fiancé."

Niall's heart plummeted. "Gareth is . . . engaged?"

"Gareth? Are you joking?" David laughed. "He's been so obsessed with you, I don't think he's registered the fact that other men even *exist*. No, I mean Mal. In fact, he and Bryce live next door." He jerked his chin at Niall. "Bryce is the one who gave me the potions to treat your back."

"What?" *Druid poisons?* Shite, how could he get them off? He tried to lever himself to his knees again, only to cry out at the pain.

"Hey hey hey. Calm down." David held up his hands, palms out, and Niall froze in place, trembling. "Bryce is a totally modern kind of druid. He doesn't believe in the old-school 'no-pain no-gain' mantra, and if you've been listening to fae propaganda for the last couple hundred years, forget it. We can talk more about that later, but the point now is that between my nurse's training and Bryce's druidry, we were able to come up with a treatment that helped you."

"You didn't touch me?" Niall clenched his fists in the sheets. "You swear?"

David crossed his arms and glared down at Niall. "Jeez, I *told* you. No, I did not. I *never* use my *achubydd* energy unless the patient agrees to it first and truly wants it. Otherwise I don't get the right feedback. Besides, it never works the same way on humans. Although," he tapped his lips with one finger, "since the wounds were inflicted by a god, that might be a different thing. It might be interesting to try—"

"*No!* Absolutely not. I won't risk it."

"Fine. Then it's time for another dose of Bryce's superhealing potion, so lie down and shut up."

Niall settled onto his stomach. "Will it . . . will it hurt?"

David rolled his eyes. "This from the man whose back looks like a Body Worlds exhibit. No more than anything else, and considerably less than a traditional druid remedy, so stop being a big baby and let's get on with it."

Niall sighed. "Fine. But how can you apply the potion without touching me?"

"A wonderful little thing called a spray pump." A click and a hiss and Niall felt a cool mist settle onto his back, making him twitch like a horse under the bite of a fly. Although it soothed the fire in his wounds, the shivers returned in earnest.

"I'm sorry. You're cold." David bustled about and added a blanket to the sheet. "I can only cover your legs and your—behind. Your back has to stay uncovered until the potion sets."

"I understand," Niall said through clenched teeth. "Promise me you won't tell Gareth. About Govannon. He can't know."

David started pumping the potion again. "Why not? I don't see what difference it makes if he knows how you were injured. I mean it's not as if you can *hide* the results." Another pump. "Are you sure you don't remember him? You said some things while you were delirious—"

"He's the only bard in Faerie. He's famous. I've heard *of* him. Everyone has."

"Well . . . that's a point, I suppose. He's pretty well known around here too. His band is—" David shrugged and offered an apologetic smile. "Sorry. I shouldn't chatter on. Alun says I could talk a dragon out of its hoard."

Niall chuckled just as another bout of chills set his teeth clattering. "I don't mind. What about Gareth's band?"

"Oh, they're amazing. They're called Hunter's Moon."

"Hunter's Moon? Appropriate."

"Appropriate? Why?"

"Because of Herne. The horned huntsman. When the full moon floats in the October sky, so soon after sunset, it's the prime time for hunting. Herne—" Niall broke off as another round of shudders racked his body. "When it coincides with

Samhain—what the Welsh call Calan Gaeaf—it's the perfect night for Herne to take his pack out and hunt down traitors and conspirators."

"Oh. The *Cwn Annwn*, right?"

"How do you know about them?"

"They sort of chased me once."

Niall stared at David in disbelief. "They chased you and you lived to tell the tale? That *never* happens. Once Herne sets his pack after prey, they never fail to bring it down. Permanently."

"Well, Herne wasn't there that night. So maybe that's why they didn't follow us over the threshold."

"You were lucky."

David sighed, a dreamy look on his face. "I know. It was the best first date ever."

Niall blinked. "You got chased by the *Cwn Annwn* on a *date*? And you *liked* it?" Maybe convincing Gareth to hold up a carriage with him on their first meeting hadn't been quite as outrageous as Niall had always believed.

"Well it was the company, you know, not the running for our lives thing. But still."

"Did you—" Ah, shite. Niall bared his teeth in a grimace as the mist that had been so cooling suddenly burned like acid.

"Niall? Are you— Holy cats. I've got to call Bryce. Hold on. I'll be right back."

Niall fisted his hands in the sheets, his fingernails piercing the soft fabric. How could he be so cold yet his back be on fire? He had to— had to—

He buried his head and screamed into the pillow.

Chapter Seven

After the band toured the venue, Gareth wanted to head back to David's house to check on Niall, but Hamish insisted they all needed a drink—that Gareth owed the rest of the band a drink and some conviviality after being such an arsehole lately. Since David had promised faithfully to text if Niall woke up or took a turn for the worse, Gareth agreed. Niall was his main concern, of course, but his band was his family too.

"One drink," he said as he followed Hamish into the shifter bar tucked unobtrusively in Portland's industrial district.

"Too right." Tiff shared a nod with the bartender, holding up five fingers and pointing to the left-most tap. "It's fight night downstairs later. We don't want to be here when that crowd shows up."

"Speak for yourself." Hamish bounced on his toes. "In fact, I'm off to put my name down for a bout or two."

"Hamish." Josh's voice held a hint of reproach. "Not the night before two shows."

"Ah, shite. You're right. Afterward though, for sure." He grinned before bounding away.

Josh watched him go, a troubled look on his face. "One of these days, he'll find someone he can't beat. Then what?"

"We find a new drummer?" Spence draped his arm across Josh's shoulders, but Josh pulled away with a frown.

"Don't joke about that. Why does he have to fight anyway?" The three of them watched Tiff thread her way onto the dance floor and pick up the beat, several other dancers drawn immediately into her orbit. Josh sighed. "Never mind."

Spence nudged Gareth toward the tables. "Snag us a spot, Kendrick, and don't drink all the beer before we get back." He pulled an unresisting Josh onto the dance floor.

Gareth nodded and headed toward the corner booth, trying not to feel out of place—and not just because he was the only fae in a bar full of shifters. Everyone here understood a language that had been foreign to him for most of his life—the language of attraction, the dance of sexual allure and completion.

How many times had he listened to Mal tout the pleasures of the flesh? Before Gareth had met Niall, Mal had been explicit, as if he'd thought it his duty to tutor Gareth in mechanics and technique. After Niall had been taken, the instructions had been more general—as if Mal were proposing the only practical way to stave off loneliness.

Mal didn't understand that Gareth had never felt he was missing anything by not falling into bed with anyone who gave him a come-hither glance, let alone a blatant invitation. He'd never wanted that—and had never felt the lack. His passion was channeled into his music, and he felt complete. Or mostly.

It wasn't until Niall that he'd found someone who touched that part of him that his brothers were so eloquent about. He didn't want just anyone to fill his bed, to fill his body. He wanted Niall, and only Niall.

When Niall was gone, he could no more have replaced him than he could change his skin like a kelpie.

The server delivered their pints at the same time Hamish returned. He plopped down next to Gareth. "So you didn't say. How'd it go? Convergence all converged? Her Majesty safely spliced to the monster?"

Gareth drew his glass toward him, but didn't drink. "I don't know."

"What do you mean, you don't know? Wasn't that the whole point? 'All fae must be present' and yada yada yada. 'No non-fae allowed and stay thee the hell out of Faerie, you shifter scum.'"

"I never said that."

Hamish shrugged and took a long swallow of his beer. "Didn't have to. That's the attitude we always get whenever we show up for a gig in Faerie."

Gareth blinked. "You what? When? I never noticed—"

"Of course you never noticed. You were too busy being the surly bard, ticked off because you didn't want to be there. Didn't ever occur to you that those poncy Sidhe bastards didn't want *us* there either?"

"Sorry. I guess I've been . . . well . . ."

"A self-absorbed git?"

Gareth snorted a laugh. "That bad?"

"A talented self-absorbed git, so we made allowances, because what rock musician isn't a self-absorbed git from time to time?"

"Well, I did the same thing this time, I suppose. I scarpered before the main event."

"Why's that?"

"Because the Queen's monster turned out to be *my* monster."

"You had a monster on the side? You've been holding out on us. I thought your one and only bloke was human."

"I mean the monster that took Niall away. The one that stole him from the Outer World."

Hamish's spit-take sprayed beer all over the table. "Shite." He grabbed a handful of napkins from the dispenser and mopped up. "The Queen's marrying the arsehole who killed Niall?"

"Not exactly. I mean, she's marrying him all right. But he didn't kill Niall." *Only killed his memory of me.* "In fact, that's why I came back. Niall was there. I brought him with me before the gods-bedamned spell could kill him for good."

Hamish goggled. "Fuck me sideways. You *found* him? The bloke you've been pining after for longer than I've known you?"

"Yeah. Want to know the pisser though?"

"Go on. What could be better?"

Gareth smiled wryly. "He doesn't remember me."

"Amnesia? Ah, come on, mate, you're shitting me. That never really happens. It's nothing more than a plot point in a movie or a dime novel."

"First, novels don't cost a dime anymore. Second, we're talking about fae enchantment. He could have wiped Niall's memory without breaking a sweat."

Hamish ran a finger through the condensation on the side of his glass. "Are you sure . . . Now don't go off on me, mate, but are you sure the memory was there to begin with? Maybe *your* memory was the one that's faulty. Didn't you say you were dodging Unseelie assassins at every turn back in the day? I mean, maybe one of them landed a blow you never registered."

Gareth froze with his glass halfway to his lips. "No. I don't believe it. There were too many memories. Years that we spent—all the times I met him at one eisteddfod after another."

"That's what I mean. Always at those bloody music festivals. You know better than anyone how music can cast a spell. Maybe somebody slipped you a musical mickey and you never noticed."

Gareth set his pint on the table carefully, fighting the urge to fling it at Hamish's head. "It's not possible. Nobody, not even a high mage, could use music to ensorcell me. I'm the last bloody bard. My magic trumps theirs."

"If you say so. So what are you gonna do now? You're not gonna cast him out to flounder about on his own, right? That's what you lot used to do in the old days. Why you're always on about how criminal it was for that bloke to take him in the first place. You planning to do the same?"

"No. No of course not. But if he doesn't want me—"

"Look, mate. Unrequited love . . ." Hamish's gaze followed Tiff on the dance floor. "You think I don't know how much it sucks? But you know what's worse? Not making the effort. Don't, for shite's sake, *stalk* the poor bastard, but show him you care, yeah? How did you first catch his eye anyway?"

Gareth smiled into his beer. "I was onstage. Singing a song I'd written about one of the famous highwaymen who was ranging the country at the time. Robbing corrupt nobles and returning the money to the townsfolk."

"A robbing hood kind of bloke, eh?" Hamish said with a cheeky grin.

"*Robin* Hood, you wanker, and yes. Niall was there, at the back of the crowd. And afterward . . . well, turns out *he* was the highwayman in question."

"Get out. How'd you find that out?"

"He took me with him that night to rob a coach."

It had been the second-to-last night of the eisteddfod, Gareth's last night, since he never stayed long enough for the prize-giving. He'd noticed the dark, handsome man with the flashing grin and the confident swagger before; somehow he always seemed to be there, at the back of the crowd, whenever Gareth performed. Yet even through the mass of other people, Gareth could pick him out as clearly as if he were standing alone in a sunlit meadow.

When he'd slipped away after his performance, Niall had been waiting.

"It's customary, is it not, to offer a bard a pint after a worthy performance?" Niall's voice held a hint of an Irish lilt, which, for a Welsh fae who'd never forgotten the cruel treatment of Branwen ferch Llŷr by the Irish King Matholwch, should have been off-putting. But instead, it was one more thing—one more *forbidden,* and therefore exciting, thing about Niall.

"Are you offering then?"

"I am and all. Yon inn serves a decent brew, and if we hurry, we'll be able to quaff a few before the rest of these thirsty buggers snabble the lot."

The taproom at the inn was busy but not overly crowded, and Niall led the way to a table in the corner which had been occupied when they'd entered, but which was miraculously free by the time they reached it.

The barman brought them two pints with only a glance from Niall. "Evening, John. Keeping all right?"

"Ach, Niall. That bastard of a baron has nearly stripped us bare again. Taxes." The barman snorted. "You ask me, them taxes is going to buy another trinket for the blighter's jewelry box, while half the town is nigh on starving."

"Is that so? Well, we'll have to see what we can do about that." He took a sip of his ale. "Ah. Always the best around, John. You never disappoint."

"Obliged to ye, Niall."

"By the way, this is— What was your name again, boyo?"

"Cynwrig. Gareth Cynwrig."

"Gareth then. Gareth's a rare bard, John, and we wouldn't want his throat to get too parched, now, so keep them coming, aye?"

"Welcome to ye, bard. If the ale's to your liking, perhaps you'd favor us with a tune?"

Gareth smiled at man. "It would be my honor." He could sing his latest song, the one that would have won him the eisteddfod chair if he'd been unscrupulous enough to pit his bardic magic against human musicians. But here, he could repay the barman, and maybe catch that look of admiration in Niall's eyes again before he had to move on.

After the song, though, Niall welcomed Gareth back to their table with an arm slung across his shoulder. "That was grand, boyo. But are you after a spot more excitement tonight?"

Gareth swallowed. *Is he going to kiss me? Do I* want *him to kiss me?*

But instead of the expected kiss, Niall led him behind the inn to the stables. *Is he going to do* more *than kiss me?* Gareth's mouth went dry with newfound desire. He expected the Voices to mock him for that, since he'd never approached another man, but they were mute, as if Niall's presence—so big and bold and *real*—had muzzled them.

But Niall didn't lead him to the hayloft and the tryst that Gareth was suddenly desperate for. Instead, he nodded to a groom, who led out two horses.

"You can ride, can't you, bard?"

"It's Gareth, and yes, I can ride. Better than you, I'll wager." That was one thing other than music that he excelled at.

"A wager, eh? You've pegged my weakness. I'll never say nay to one of those." Niall grinned as he mounted a black stallion with a blaze on its forehead. "What are the stakes?"

Gareth took a moment to whisper to the chestnut mare the groom handed over to him. She flicked an ear back before pressing her head to his chest for him to stroke her neck and mane. *Stalling.* He could admit it, but if he asked for what he really wanted, and Niall said no, or worse, attacked him for the insult? He mounted, and when he glanced at Niall, his grin had widened, as if he knew what Gareth was thinking.

Gareth took his courage in both hands. *Nothing ventured, nothing gained.* "A kiss."

Niall's eyebrows shot up. "A kiss is it? From some comely barmaid?"

"No. From—from you."

Niall laughed then, a sound that Gareth had longed to try to capture in a melody. "Then, boyo, I hope you outride me for certain." He pulled a fist-sized bundle out of his saddlebag and tossed it to Gareth. "Once we're clear of town, put that on. Wouldn't do for anyone to see that pretty face."

"What about you?"

"I've got my own, never fear. Coming?" He urged his horse to a trot.

Gareth wheeled his own mount and followed Niall out of the stable yard. He'd never stepped a foot out of line before, the responsibility of being the last bard in Faerie weighing him down, reinforcing Arawn's—and later the Queen's—refusal to allow him combat training. His hands were too valuable to risk, they said; his voice too precious to break in a battle cry.

But the excitement surging in his veins tonight set off a whole new melody in his soul—bright and martial and a little bit sly.

His heart beat like a bodhran as they nearly flew through the windy night, Niall's eyes dancing behind his mask, his grin manic in the moonlight when they intercepted the coach.

When the coachman raised his weapon, pointing it square at Gareth's chest, he ought to have been terrified. Instead he'd never felt more alive. *One moment of life before death.*

But the gun misfired, and Niall's order to "Stand and deliver!" met with no more resistance.

The trembling lord handed over his fat purse and stickpin, causing a twinge of guilt in Gareth's chest. Thievery—the Voices were dismissive of it, all of them having been thieves or worse themselves. For that reason alone, Gareth disapproved on principle.

But then Niall led him back to the village where the lord had just been to collect taxes, returning the money to the villagers, and their gratitude, the lessening of desperation in their faces, wiped out any regret.

Niall had given the stickpin to Gareth, along with the promised kiss. Gareth had had the sapphire made into an earring that he still wore to this day, but the kiss was the greater treasure.

That night, Niall had made love to him for the first time, adding yet another thrill to a day that'd been brim full of firsts.

"Oi. Gareth." Hamish clunked his glass on the table, jerking his head at the discreet door in the corner of the bar. "You'd best be off before the fight crowds arrive. Wouldn't want to offend your fae sensibilities."

"Shut up." But Gareth slipped out of the booth nonetheless, even though the rest of the band hadn't yet left the dance floor. David hadn't texted yet, but Gareth couldn't stay away any longer. He had to see Niall, make sure he was all right. He tossed a few bills on the table to cover their tab. "See you at rehearsal tomorrow." He raised his hand in farewell to the others as he left the bar.

The drive back to Hillsboro was interminable despite the lack of traffic this late at night. When he got to the house, he'd barely parked the car in the garage before he was out of it, the last minutes of separation suddenly too much to bear.

He breathed a sigh of relief as he closed the front door behind him. Then he heard the murmur of voices from the guest room. Niall was awake? Had he gotten worse? Why hadn't David called him?

He strode down the hall and stopped in the doorway, anger warring with anxiety. Niall wasn't speaking—in fact, his eyes were closed, tremors shaking his body as he moaned. David and Bryce were standing at the foot of the bed, frowning at Niall's back, which seemed worse than it had been not two hours ago when Gareth had left.

Anger won out over anxiety. "You promised me you'd call if he worsened," he whispered fiercely. "I'd call this worse."

David glanced up, his cupid's bow mouth forming an O of surprise for an instant before he blinked. "Calm down. We're just about to apply a more potent remedy."

"You should have called."

Bryce dug something out of one of the many pockets in his canvas vest. "You'd have gotten here at exactly the same time, so I don't see the problem."

"The problem," Gareth said as he advanced into the room, "is that I should have been here."

Bryce glanced at Gareth irritably, the harsh words Gareth had flung at Mal the night the Unseelie King was deposed obviously still hanging between them. *Those words would have been harsher if I'd known that the Unseelie monster Mal had been abetting was the one who'd kidnapped Niall.* "You're here now, so don't get in the way."

Gareth circled the bed and sat on the edge of the mattress. He couldn't help it—he had to touch Niall, at least a little. Surely it wouldn't matter since Niall was unconscious and would never know. Very gently, he laid his fingers over Niall's where they rested on the sheet.

Bryce snorted, but Gareth ignored him. Sometime in the not too distant future, he needed to sit down with Bryce and clear the air. He still wasn't entirely onboard with Mal's relationship with a druid—nobody knew better than Gareth that relationships between fae and other species rarely ended well, although in the case of a fae/druid pairing, it was the fae with more at stake.

"Why should that matter to you, boyo? Aren't you the bloke who wants all fae to suffer?"

Not all fae—only the Unseelie. And definitely not his brothers.

Bryce handed David an ampoule of some cloudy liquid, which David inserted into a spray pump. David moved to the side of the bed opposite Gareth and used the device to mist Niall's back with the potion. The skin on Niall's back twitched.

"You're hurting him. Druid potions—"

"I *told* you. Bryce doesn't believe in the cathartic healing power of pain. The potion is cold and Niall is reacting to it, that's all. He's pretty out of it anyway, so even if it stings a little, he won't know."

"He might. You don't know—"

"Gareth." David's tone was laced with exasperation. "Do you want him to get better or not?"

"Of course I do!"

"Then stop being obstructionist."

Gareth gazed at Niall's tousled hair, his dark curls spilling across the pillow, stroked Niall's fingers and sighed. "I'm sorry. I— I just feel so helpless. I want to *do* something."

"Then why don't you sing to him? Something soothing so he can rest more easily."

"I . . . can do that, I suppose."

"Good thing you're cooperating for a change," Bryce grumbled as he gathered packets of herbs from the top of the dresser.

"Bryce." David's voice held a warning this time. "You need to behave too. I don't allow anyone to distress my patients—even if they're not conscious enough to know about it."

Bryce huffed, then ran his fingers through his hair, sending it spiking every which way. "You're right. I'm sorry. I'm just— Well, the portents are really weird right now. I'll be much happier once Mal and Alun get back."

David's lips compressed into a line. "You and me both."

"I'll check back in the morning, but call if you need anything." With one last glower at Gareth, Bryce walked out of the room.

Gareth laced his fingers with Niall's, and when Niall's tightened on his, a tiny thread of joy wound around his heart. He settled down with his back against the headboard and began to sing a Welsh lullaby. When that made Niall stir restlessly, earning Gareth an admonitory glare from David, he switched to "Bridge Over Troubled Water."

He knew he should sleep. He knew he should rest his voice; he had a concert in less than twenty-four hours. But screw that.

Niall needed him, so he sang. Simon and Garfunkel. Fleetwood Mac. Five for Fighting. All the popular Outer World standards.

When he ventured into one of Hunter's Moon's songs, though, with their roots in Celtic folk music, or one of the old ballads he used to sing when he and Niall had been lovers, Niall would thrash and moan. So Gareth sang his way through songs Niall had never heard until the dawn bled through the blinds and Niall finally opened his eyes.

Chapter Eight

Niall was in the underworld again, strung up next to the flames while Tiarnach strutted across the cavern. Not content with simply having Niall flogged, he had to *talk* at him too. Perhaps he believed it worsened the punishment—the anticipation of knowing the blows were coming, but first having to wait in suspense for the usual pointless demand.

"He dallied with not one, not two, but seven this year, both fae and human, and some that were neither. What say you to that?"

Every year it was the same—Tiarnach spouted tales of Gareth's adventures in the bedchamber of one Seelie lord after another, or affairs in the Outer World that would put a satyr to shame. But it had never made a dent in Niall's resolve. *Better that than dead.* If Tiarnach realized that Niall actually treasured those stories that proved Gareth wasn't mourning a relationship founded on deception, perhaps he'd never speak again.

But Niall, who'd given up any hope of clemency long since, couldn't forgo those nuggets of information. He let Tiarnach natter on, pretending indifference.

"Nothing. Let's get on with it, shall we?"

The wildness in Tiarnach's eyes, the way his hands writhed in the ermine trim of his velvet cloak, should have warned Niall this wasn't a normal visit, but he'd gotten so resigned to Tiarnach's rants that he simply nodded to Govannon to place the leather strap between his teeth and braced himself for the first blow.

Tiarnach continued to march back and forth, his steps keeping pace with the stroke of the whip. Niall counted them off in his head, but when Govannon would have stopped at the expected number, Tiarnach cried, "Again!" over and over, until Niall collapsed, hanging from his manacles, legs unable to support him.

Still Tiarnach didn't call a halt—Govannon laid down his whip himself. "I'll not be your executioner. If you want to kill him, you'll have to strike the blow with your own hand."

Tiarnach advanced and gripped Niall by the hair, wrenching his head up. "For the last time, will you kill the bard?"

Niall spat the strap out of his mouth. "No. Never."

"That's what I thought you'd say, you stubborn, insolent fool." Tiarnach's eyes burned with fury as he glared at Niall. "I grew tired of waiting. I killed him myself."

Niall's breath caught on a sob—he couldn't help it—and Tiarnach finally smiled in triumph and let go of Niall's hair. "Leave him there overnight. Let him consider what his actions have cost."

But Govannon must not have obeyed, because he wasn't shackled to the wall, the agony in his back nothing to the pain in his heart. Someone stroked his hair, held his hand gently, as an angel crooned to him of comfort and happiness and love.

He sighed, the words a healing salve to body and soul. When he blinked open crusty eyes to an expanse of white pillowcase, the hand holding his was real, the voice not that of anything as ineffectual as an angel, but—

Gareth. The ceremony. The escape. The *lie.* Goddess strike him blind, what had he done?

He whimpered, and immediately Gareth was there, blue eyes full of concern and affection that Niall didn't deserve. "Hey. You're awake. You were unconscious all night long." He squeezed Niall's hand. "I was so worried."

"You needn't be. I was . . ." Shite, what *was* he? He vaguely remembered a conversation with David, when he'd seemed to be recovering, then suddenly the pain had rebounded. But now? He flexed his back muscles tentatively. Not yet fully healed, thank the Goddess, so he still appeared human. But better. As if the wounds were healing normally. "I'm fine." He withdrew his hand, and Gareth's smile faded. "But I—I need to take a piss."

Gareth's eyebrows popped up and he laughed, which made Niall frown. "Not funny. Fine way to repay hospitality, soiling a bloke's bedding."

"No. I know. I'm just— Never mind. The bathroom is across the hall. Let me—"

"I can manage it." He pushed himself to his haunches, wincing a little, then glanced down at his body. *Naked. All my imperfections on display.* He bolted across the hallway and closed the door behind him.

Fixing all his latest mistakes would take every ounce of his former cunning, but just when he needed it most, his old cleverness seemed to desert him. *Bloody hells. Now what?*

The hollow-eyed stranger staring at him from the mirror over the sink had no answers, but the *ethera* had a suggestion.

:Punt!:

Gareth hadn't missed Niall's full-body blush before he'd rushed into the bathroom. *He still doesn't want to be naked in front of me.* If that wasn't evidence that he didn't remember Gareth, nothing was. In their days as lovers, they'd barely managed to make it to the inn of the day, or to Niall's lodgings, before ripping each other's clothes off. They'd only bothered to put them on to venture out to eat or to appease the servants.

Gareth heard the toilet flush and the water turn on in the sink. *How does he know about bathroom fixtures?* Was the Unseelie Keep equipped with modern plumbing? Hells, for all Gareth knew, they regularly kidnapped construction workers to build onto the bloody thing.

Or it could be magic? *Whatever*.

Niall emerged from the bathroom, scrubbing his hands through his hair, one of David's lavender bath sheets wrapped around his waist. "Danu's tits, whatever David did is bloody remarkable. I've never recovered as fast as—" He glanced at Gareth. "I mean—"

"It's all right. You don't have to go into it." *Yet.* Although Gareth hoped Niall would feel comfortable enough soon to share a little of what he'd been through. Maybe if they talked about it, Niall would start remembering more about their lives, their love.

David bustled in, stopping when he got a look at Niall's back. "Holy cats. Now *that's* what I'm talking about. Nothing like a druid with a chemistry degree, I always say."

Niall tried to look over his shoulder. "It feels better. I checked it in the mirror and it looks better too."

"That's because it *is* better."

"Think I might rate a shirt today then?"

David chuckled. "I think so. I'll put a light dressing on first, and you can borrow one of Alun's nice, soft T-shirts." He studied Niall dispassionately, head tilted to one side. "Your shoulders are as broad as his, I think, and your chest as deep. I'll bring you some of his sweatpants too. They'll probably be a little long, but sweats aren't supposed to be tight."

"That'd be grand. Thanks."

As David trotted out of the room, Gareth leaned an elbow on the dresser. "You know what sweatpants are?"

"I—" An odd look flickered across Niall's face; Gareth wasn't sure how to interpret it. Not guilt, surely? Alarm? Then it was gone. "It must be part of the enchantment, a kindness to make it easier for me to acclimate."

Gareth snorted. "Not bloody likely. Fae can't absorb change themselves—how likely is it that they'd be able to manage it for someone else."

"You mean Seelie fae don't change. Unseelie embrace it."

Gareth frowned. "How do you know?"

"I was there, wasn't I? Got the whole story about the tenets." He tipped his head back to stare at the ceiling, and Gareth couldn't help ogling his bare chest, the dusting of dark hair on his pectorals, the treasure trail leading from his navel below the improbable lavender towel.

It was one of the things that had always fascinated him about Niall. High fae—at least the humanoid Seelie variety—didn't have hair anywhere except on their heads and at their groins—and they certainly didn't have navels. That was the one wisp of *glamourie* he'd allowed himself when he'd been with Niall—he'd given himself a navel so Niall wouldn't recognize him as fae and be frightened or disgusted.

Niall opened his mouth, about to say something else, but David returned with an armful of cotton and fleece.

"Here you go. If you want to take a sponge bath, you can go ahead and do that, but don't get your back wet yet."

"Got it." Niall left, and a moment later the bathroom door clicked shut.

David turned to Gareth, an odd look on his face. "You sang to him for eight hours straight. I don't think you even noticed when I brought you that water bottle."

Gareth shrugged. Truth be told, he hadn't been aware of the passage of time, content to watch Niall sleep, gratified when his song choice caused him to nestle deeper into the pillow with a sigh. "I noticed." He hadn't. "Thank you."

"Don't you have a concert tonight?"

"Ah, bollocks. Yeah. Well maybe I can catch a nap after the rehearsal this morning."

"You're going to rehearse *after* a marathon solo session and *then* perform at a concert? Holy cats, Gareth, how can your voice take it?"

"My voice? That's what you're worried about?" He nodded in the direction of the bathroom. "You should be worried about him."

"Oh I am. But he doesn't have the stress ahead of him today that you do."

"My voice isn't a concern. I'm a bard. My voice never fails. It's part of the package."

"Really? Then why is your energy pattern red and tangled around your throat?"

Gareth's hand flew to his throat. Any distress there had nothing to do with his singing. He was trying not to cry over Niall's continued distance. "It'll be fine."

"At least let me—" David reached out, but Gareth dodged away.

"Don't waste your energy on me. I'll be fine by the time I get to the rehearsal. You just take care of Niall."

"Hmmm." David frowned and stared down at his shoes. "Well, here's the thing . . ."

"What?"

"I'm not going to be here. I've been summoned to appear before the supe council this morning."

"So what? Tell them you can't make it."

David glared at him. "You don't tell the supe council 'Sorry. Can we reschedule?' Some of them have come in from out of the country, and since neither Mal nor Alun are here to escort them through Faerie as a shortcut, they can't just pop home and return when it's convenient for me."

"What about Bryce? He's the one with the potions." He might still be pissed at Gareth, but surely he wouldn't let Niall suffer because of it. "He—"

"*He* is supposed to be there too. It's a joint session with the local druid circle. They want to hear about his methods."

"Come on, David. Niall can't very well stay here on his own. He doesn't know a fucking thing about this world."

"And yet he's managing perfectly well so far." David's tone was dry and a bit mocking.

Bugger that. "What if he has another relapse? How will he—"

"Chill out. He's ambulatory now, so if you don't want to leave him here alone, take him with you."

Gareth blinked. "To the rehearsal? But my bandmates aren't human. The shock of exposing him to more of the supe community—"

"For pity's sake, the man lived in Faerie for over two hundred years, yet figured out how to use an effing bidet on first contact. I kind of doubt you could surprise him, even if Hamish shifts and plays all the songs as a kangaroo."

"All right. But—"

"What's the matter? I though you *wanted* to spend time with him."

"I do."

"Well then. This seems like a perfect opportunity." David's expression softened. "Look. I know you're having a rough time. If Alun forgot me, I couldn't answer for the kind of tantrum I'd throw. But just because he doesn't remember what you *had*, doesn't mean he can't learn what you *could* have now. Let the past go, Gareth, and make a new present. A new future."

Hope coiled inside him. Could it be that simple? Music had brought them together once. Maybe it could do it again.

"You have a point. I'll . . . I'll try."

"Good. Now there are bagels and juice in the kitchen, as well as a pot of coffee."

"Your aunt's special blend?"

David grinned, flashing his dimples. "What else? Consider it my contribution to your reconciliation with Niall." He kissed Gareth on the cheek. "Now I've got to run. Bryce is driving me in his goofy little electric car, so you can use Alun's SUV. I'll see you later."

He zoomed across the hallway and knocked on the bathroom door. Niall let him in, and Gareth heard their murmured conversation for a few moments before David emerged and tossed Gareth a wave on his way out.

Gareth took a deep breath. *You can do this. An invitation. That's all it is.* Why did it feel like a point of no return?

"Ah, that's easy, boyo. Because if he says no, he's turning down the only thing you've got that makes you special."

Niall emerged from the bathroom, clad in Alun's sweats, toweling his hair dry as he walked across the hall. He glanced around the bedroom. "Where's David? I wanted to thank him for what he's done and for the clothes. They beat handspun wool to flinders."

"He ... ah ... had an appointment." Gareth gulped. Goddess, why was he suddenly tongue-tied? "The thing is ... he ... well ..."

"Afraid to put it to the test, boyo? That's clever, that is. Best never take the chance, eh?"

Gareth gritted his teeth against the urge to shout at the thrice-damned Voices. Instead he morphed his grimace into a desperate smile. "How would you like to go to a band rehearsal?"

"Truly?" Niall's grin bloomed. "Sounds bloody brilliant. What are we waiting for?"

Chapter Nine

A chance to hear Gareth play again, perform again? *:No-brainer!:* Niall chuckled at the *ethera's* enthusiastic agreement as he followed Gareth out of the house.

Then, face to—*:Grill!:* —with an enormous black metal box —*:SUV!:*—he balked. Logically, he knew he must have ridden in this monstrosity to get from the gate to the bed where he'd awoken, but to do it consciously?

"Niall?" Gareth peered at him from across the hood of the vehicle. "Are you all right?"

"Do we have to ride in this?"

Gareth shrugged apologetically. "The rehearsal studio is too far away to walk. I suppose we could take the MAX train, but —"

The next house over, the garage door slid up, and a small, silent car glided out, David waving to them from inside on the way past. The glowering, dark-haired, bespectacled man behind the wheel must be the druid. Niall shivered, but then he caught sight of something else in the garage.

:Harley!: the *ethera* caroled.

Niall pointed as the bay door began its descent. "Can you ride that?"

Gareth glanced over his shoulder. "Mal's bike? Yes. But I'm not supposed to take risks on concert days. Besides, your back —"

"Never mind that." He grinned, feeling like himself for the first time in two hundred years. "Come on then. Let's give it a go."

Gareth's eyes widened and his shoulders hitched, but then he relaxed and grinned back. "All right."

He led the way through a side door, locating helmets and jackets for them both. As they mounted the bike in the garage, Gareth gave Niall pointers about the ride that he really didn't need with the *ethera* whispering gaily in his ear.

Then they were off, and it was glorious—wind and sun and a speed Niall had never experienced on his swiftest horse. The ride was over almost too soon, but once they were inside the studio and Gareth had introduced him to the rest of Hunter's Moon, Niall surrendered to a different kind of thrill.

The band rehearsal was bloody *fascinating*. He'd never seen Gareth as anything but a solo performer—just him and his harp or sometimes the lute. But being with his band, working out the balance in a song, arguing over the set list, trading cues with the other musicians, put him in a completely different light. It made him seem . . . human.

"Ah, shite, Gareth. Can't we change this bloody set list?" The drummer—Hamish—bounced on his stool behind the drum kit, flipping a stick from one hand to the other. "You've had us mired in this love-lost-woe-is-me crap for so long I need a Xanax just to rehearse."

Spence, the keyboardist, sauntered out from behind his equipment. "Have you seen the Twitter feed lately? The fans are starting to get whiny. It's been too long since we released something new." He slung an arm across the other guitarist's shoulders. Josh, the guitarist in question, glanced at Niall and blushed, although he looked pleased. Spence shot a sly glance at Niall. "Maybe now you can get out of your funk, Gareth, and you and Josh can get back to work on something that isn't so fucking depressing."

Gareth stayed hunched over his guitar, fingering a few chords, and Niall could tell by the tension in his shoulders that he didn't want to have this conversation. Maybe it would be easier if Niall weren't there. He had learned in his years wrestling with Unseelie politics that difficult negotiations were made more awkward with an observer—especially one who might be construed as critical.

This was Gareth's business, the band's business. Niall should let them have their privacy. He got up from his chair in the corner—a hard, wooden one that was murder on his arse but allowed him to sit forward without pressure on his back—and slipped out the door of the practice room into the hallway.

The rehearsal space had two other studios, but neither of them were occupied at the moment. Niall wandered down the hallway into a small dingy kitchen with a battered table and chairs. It also sported several large, brightly lit machines full of unfamiliar food and beverages.

:Vending machines! Coca Cola! Cheez-Its!:

Niall peered at them, bemused. He wasn't hungry—the breakfast at David's house had been both delicious and filling. *Coffee*. He'd never had any that tasted quite that good. He glanced at the machine on the counter, which had one glass pot with a burnt crust at the bottom. He doubted seriously whether he'd get anything similar here. Maybe he should try the Coca Cola—although he had no idea how to get one out of the machine.

:Money!:

Well, he didn't have any of that, so he'd make do with water.

As he was slurping from his hands at the sink, Tiff, the bass player, walked over and handed him a cup made of paper. "This might make things easier."

He took it, flushing. "Right. Thanks." He might have the information at his fingertips, but changing behavior that had been ground into him over centuries would take time.

Tiff leaned one hip against the pitted counter, toying with the giant hoop that hung from one ear. Her dark hair was cut close to her scalp on one side but hung down to her chin on the other, one long lock—dyed blue—hanging over her eye. "What was Gareth like back in the day?"

"I—I don't remember."

She lifted an eyebrow—which had a smaller hoop threaded through it. "Oh right. Am*nes*ia. Very convenient."

"I'm sorry. What?"

"Look. I've known Gareth since 1969—"

"But that's—you can't have been born back then."

She stared at him, and for a moment, her brown eyes flashed gold. "Let's just say Gareth isn't the only one with a foot in the supernatural. Niall—" She leaned toward him, lowering her voice. "I can call you Niall, right?" Niall nodded, mesmerized by her gaze. "You've spent a loooong time around the freaky-ass shit in Faerie, so you won't be surprised to find out that there are other freaky-ass things in the world, right?"

"Uh—"

"Well, this band is full of freaky-ass, and we're not afraid to capitalize on it."

"And that means?"

"Gareth has been brokenhearted over you for as long as I've known him. If you're pulling an amnesia stunt to keep from having the tough conversation, from having to tell him you don't feel that way about him and never did? If you're too much of a coward to just tell him he was wrong to mourn you all this time, well . . ." She flicked out a finger, and her fingernail grew and grew, losing its purple polish until it was a very long and very lethal-looking claw. "Let's just say some of us might take it . . . badly."

Niall raised his eyebrows. "Is this how you greet all of Gareth's visitors?"

"Gareth has no visitors. That's the point. You're either the best thing ever, or the thing that'll destroy him for good."

"So you're saying I should pretend to remember things I don't, just to make him feel better?"

She scowled. "No. I just mean— Shit. He'll kill me if I scare you off. But tell the truth, man. One way or another. Just don't fuck with him."

Niall nodded. "Understood." He crushed the cup in one hand and tossed it in the bin. "But just out of curiosity—say I never remember. Say I move on. What will happen to Gareth?"

"If I were you, I'd worry more about what will happen to you."

"Yet you just said it didn't matter as long as I didn't fuck with him."

Her scowl deepened. "Damn it. This threatening bodily harm shit is more complicated than it looks."

"How about this? Even if I don't remember, I'll do my best to get to know him now. For all you know, he may not be interested in *me* anymore. It's been a long time. I'm probably a different person." He rubbed his wrist absently where the healing shackle scabs itched. Tiff glanced down at his hand, and her eyes widened. He checked—and pulled the sleeve of the sweatshirt down where it had exposed the scabs.

"Damn," she breathed. "I—I didn't know. I guess you haven't had an easy time of it either."

"No. I don't suppose I have."

"Okay." She ran a hand through her hair. "Look. Sorry. I shouldn't have gotten all up in your grill."

"No, it's fair. You want to support your friend and I respect that."

"But I shouldn't have done it at your expense." She held out her hand. "Truce?"

"Truce." He shook her hand. "Do you suppose it's safe to go back inside?"

"Your guess is as good as mine. If you're around much, you'll find out our rehearsals can get a bit lively."

"Is that what you'd call it?"

She grinned. "Nah. I'd call it a fucking circus, but who wants a quiet life, eh?"

When they stepped inside the studio, Gareth glanced up from where he was scribbling notes and smiled briefly before handing the paper to Hamish. "That's the set list then. Is it sufficiently cheerful for you?"

Hamish shrugged, then passed the list on to Spence. "Beats a poke in the eye with a drumstick, but it could still use a little lightening up. When are you and Josh gonna write something new?"

Gareth glanced at Niall and then away. "You can't force it."

"What the fuck? You're a bard. Isn't that what you do? I thought this stuff just shot out your ass like rainbow farts."

"Nice, Hamish." Spence wadded up the list and bounced it off the drummer's head.

Josh smiled a little tentatively. For a musician, he was awfully shy until he got lost in the music. "There's something we could work on."

"You been holding out on us, Joshie?" Spence kissed his temple. "I didn't know you'd written something solo."

"Well I didn't. And it needs work. There's something . . . missing. It's hard to define, but I think it would be a perfect close to the first set." He picked up his violin. "This is a little rough."

"Don't worry about it, mate," Hamish said. "I don't care if it limps along like a wounded wildebeest, as long as it's new."

"Okay." Josh took a deep breath and launched into a reel that could have been played at the eisteddfod where Niall had first met Gareth. In fact . . . Niall frowned. It sounded almost familiar. Not the whole thing, but a phrase here and there, as if he'd heard bits of it from another room.

He looked at Gareth—who'd gone stark pale, muscles bunching in his jaw.

"Stop. Stop now." He strode forward and snatched the sheet music off the stand in front of Josh. "How dare you—"

"Hold up, there." Spence stepped forward, in front of the cowering Josh. "Out of line, Kendrick."

Josh's eyes were huge in his thin face. "I'm sorry. You left it in the notebook in the studio last week. I thought you were ready to—"

"No. I'll never be ready." Gareth wadded up the papers and slammed them into the bin. "And you had no right to play that without asking."

Josh hugged his violin to his chest. "I just wanted to surprise you. It's the start of a good piece, Gareth. We could work on it. I've already got some ideas for lyrics—"

"I said no." Gareth snatched up his guitar. "We'll end the set with 'Clancy's Fancy,' just as we'd planned."

The other band members glanced at one another, but made no move to pick up their instruments. The tension was thick enough to slice with a blunt sword. Niall knew how much Gareth's music meant to him. He couldn't let Gareth bollux up this relationship. And Josh—poor bloke looked as if somebody had just drowned his dog.

But the music, that aborted song, tugged at Niall. As the band members glared at one another, tension so palpable it almost colored the air, Niall drifted unnoticed toward the trash bin as if in a trance and pulled out the paper, smoothing it until he could read the words scrawled at the top of the music. *Lover's Reel.*

The memory tumbled over him—lying in the bed at an inn in Aberystwyth, with Gareth, naked, sitting cross-legged next to him, his harp in his lap. He'd smiled down at Niall.

"I'm writing a song for you."

"For me? Nobody's ever thought I warranted a song before. A bit of doggerel, mayhap, and here and there a curse or two."

Gareth played a snatch of the tune—sprightly and martial, with a hint of slyness. "Maybe nobody's ever loved you like I do."

The memory punched Niall in the gut. It had been the first time Gareth had told him that he loved him. But he'd never heard the full song. Gareth wouldn't play it for him until it was finished, and before he'd finished, Niall had been chained underground.

Maybe he could do something to defuse this imminent implosion. For Josh. For Gareth. For all of them.

Niall ran a finger over the writing. "I remember."

Gareth's head cranked around. "What?"

"You were writing this for me. You played me a bit of it once. In an inn." He glanced at Gareth, who was gazing at him with a mixture of hope and despair. Niall shot him a cheeky grin. "You were naked at the time."

Gareth laughed as if the sound had been wrenched out of him. "I was. So were you."

Niall walked across the room and pressed the pages to Gareth's chest. "I think you should play it. Don't you?"

Gareth placed his hand over Niall's for an instant before taking the papers. *Don't go too far. He'll still hate you when he finds out the truth.*

Gareth studied the notes marching across the page—incomprehensible to Niall, but a native tongue of everyone in the band. "Maybe. But Josh is right. It's missing something."

"So finish it. It's what you do, right?" Niall glanced around at the other band members. "It's what you all do."

Josh nodded, and Hamish whooped.

Tiff just picked up her bass. "Then I suggest we get down to it. We've got six hours before sound check, and if we're going to slot this in, we need to move our fucking asses."

CHAPTER TEN

Gareth could barely contain his excitement as he and Niall left the rehearsal studio. Niall remembered him! Or at least remembered something about him, about their relationship. Gareth had poured everything he had into prepping "Lover's Reel" for its debut tonight, and the rest of the band picked up the song like they'd been playing it for years.

Although Josh was right—something was missing. He wasn't satisfied with it. But it was good enough for tonight.

Because Niall had remembered.

He was about to put on his helmet when Niall touched his arm. "If you have time, let's not go home straightaway. Take me someplace else first. Someplace you love."

Gareth smiled tentatively. "I don't live here, you know, so I don't know the city the way someone like David would. But there's a spot on the way home where we could stop for a bit. A rose garden." The two of them had spent several days in the gardens at Wrexham once. Perhaps it would jog another memory.

"Sounds grand. Shall we?"

As they flew down the freeway on Mal's bike, Gareth had to force himself to concentrate on the road rather than the welcome pressure of Niall's arms around his waist. He was both sorry and relieved when they pulled into the parking lot at Washington Park.

He led Niall to the gazebo overlooking the fountain. Niall settled on the bench somewhat gingerly.

"Are you all right?"

Niall glanced up at him, his shoulders lifting in a deep breath. "Yes. Just thinking."

Gareth sat down next to him. "Are you . . ." *Don't push. Don't push.* But he really wanted to know. "Do you remember anything else? Anything besides the song?"

He smiled wryly. "Sorry." He looked out over the garden, which wasn't exactly at its best in late October. "It's a good song. I'm glad you've decided to play it."

"Thanks to you. If you hadn't stepped in . . ." He looked down at his hands, clenched between his knees. "I nearly lost it with Josh."

"Nearly? I think you were there and beyond. Poor blighter looked ready to weep."

Shame scalded Gareth's throat. "I shouldn't have done that. Josh is . . . well, he's sensitive. He's an introvert, which is odd for his kind."

"His kind? You mean a violinist?"

Gareth chuckled at the teasing edge in Niall's voice, but he still couldn't look at him. He focused a flock of starlings dancing in the sky. "No. I probably shouldn't tell you this—"

"Why not? I can't exactly run away. Not like I've got anywhere to go."

Guilt curdled in Gareth's belly. It was Eamon's fault for ripping Niall out of his life before, but Gareth had done the same thing when he'd urged Niall to escape from Faerie with no plan in place for what to do next. "Not because I think it'll scare you. You were always fearless."

"Me? You sure you're not confusing me with one of your other lovers?"

Gareth cut a glance at Niall. "I don't have any other lovers."

"Not now, maybe, but—"

"No. I mean ever. Not before you, and not since. You were the only one. *Are* the only one."

"Ah, shite, Gareth," Niall muttered.

Goddess bless, that made him sound pathetic, didn't it? Over twenty-five hundred years old, and he'd only ever had one lover. Mal probably laughed himself sick over that on a regular basis. "Anyway, I mean you're human, and usually we're not allowed to divulge this to humans. But since you already know about supes—"

"If you mean your bandmates are a little on the bent side, Tiff already let that one out of the bag. She's a shifter. A big cat, right?"

"She told you?" Gareth shook his head. Tiff liked to skate on the edge, but risking a violation of the Secrecy Pact was courting disaster.

"More like she showed me. In the nature of a warning I believe. Your bandmates have got your back, boyo."

Gareth winced at Niall's use of the word, the same one the Voices always used on him. Although the way Niall used it was more like a benediction. With the Voices, it was contempt. "As long as I don't act like a total arsehole like I did today. And with Josh, of all people. As I was saying, he's an anomaly. He was a lone wolf."

"That's not such an oddity. Most of us have times we'd prefer privacy."

"No. I mean he was literally a lone wolf. He's a werewolf, and he was living packless, which is virtually unheard of—at least when it's by choice. But he's like me—he never wanted the pressure to find a mate, to pair up, to explain to anyone why he doesn't feel sexual desire like others do."

"But he's with Spence, right? Seemed like it anyway."

"I can't answer for how Josh and Spence conduct their relationship in private, but for me—well, I felt sexual attraction and desire exactly once. With you."

Niall turned a troubled gaze on him. "But David told me you're opposed to alliances between supe and non-supe races—or even between supe and supe, if they're not in the same camp, so to speak. Did I . . . back then, did I compromise your values? Make you *less* somehow? Is that why you could justify a relationship with a . . . a human?"

"Aye, that's the question, isn't it, boyo? Let's hear you defend yourself to him."

Gareth gripped the edge of the bench. "I wasn't always this adamant. I mean, I wasn't a fan of crossing class or affiliation lines because the conflict between Seelie and Unseelie, between Irish and Welsh, between high fae and lesser fae . . . well, they never turned out well for one party or the other, and often resulted in full-scale war. Look at the last of the Oak Wars. And farther back, in the days of the elder gods, the Irish and Welsh nearly wiped each other out because of Matholwch's treatment of Branwen, and then Evnissyen's murder of his own nephew."

"Ancient history doesn't have a lot of relevance here, does it?"

"It wasn't ancient for me, not back then. The Unseelie had been targeting me for years, although they had remarkably bad aim if they were trying to kill me." They'd certainly caused him heartache enough nevertheless. "They always seemed to miss me and hit whoever or whatever I was with. My favorite greyhound. My horse. My groom."

Niall shifted in his seat, and Gareth thought he heard him curse in Gaelic.

"So I should have known better than to get involved with you. Just being near me put you in danger, but I thought I'd evaded them. They hadn't made an attempt for over a year when we first met. And I . . . well, like I said, I'd never felt anything like that before. It was easier than I'd expected to put aside my own principles when it was for my own benefit. Then they took you. And it was my fault."

"How could it possibly be your fault?" Niall's voice was rough with some kind of emotion. Anger? It was no less than Gareth deserved.

"If I hadn't been with you, if they hadn't realized you were important to me, they'd never have targeted you."

"Listen, Gareth." Niall gripped Gareth's arm, sending a shiver of desire through him. "You can't blame yourself. I'm not a nice person, or I wasn't anyway, and I certainly haven't had much chance for self-improvement lessons in the last little while."

"I imagine not."

"But although I don't remember all of what we were together, I know what I was on my own. I was a thrill-seeker. I never counted the cost to others in pursuit of adventure. I didn't *think*—not about consequences."

Gareth covered Niall's hand with his own and squeezed. "You never did realize your own worth."

"Oh I pegged my worth at its precise value, trust me, and it wasn't anywhere close to the cost you've obviously paid."

Gareth frowned at the seriousness of Niall's tone. "What are you saying?"

"What I'm saying," Niall said, his eyes somber, "is that maybe you shouldn't wait for me to remember anything else. This might be your chance to see that you've put your trust in the wrong person all these years. To realize I'm not worth it. To move on."

Gareth took Niall's hands in his. "You are worth it, Niall, and if I haven't moved on by now, I doubt I'm likely to do it in the future. Can't you give us a chance? You've remembered one thing. Maybe you can remember something else. And even if you don't, we can make new memories, can't we?"

"Danu's tits. Gareth—"

Gareth placed his fingers over Niall's lips, his breath catching for an instant at the sensation, especially when Niall's mouth moved under them in a smile. "Let's table the discussion for now." Niall studied him for a moment, then nodded. Gareth stood and held out one hand. "So. Do you want to come to a rock concert?"

Niall stared at him for a moment, then laughed helplessly and took his hand, allowing Gareth to pull him to his feet. "You couldn't keep me away with an army of trolls and a bludgeon."

Despite the exhilaration of the motorcycle ride, Niall's heart was as heavy as his feet as he trudged into David's house.

Gareth had known he'd been targeted by the Unseelie court, but he didn't know why. What would he do, how would he react, when he found out that the reason was because Niall was a gods-bedamned idiot who didn't know how to keep his mouth shut?

David and Bryce were in the living room, although they didn't appear to be chatting—only huddled in the corner of the sofa (in David's case) and propping up the mantelpiece (in Bryce's).

Niall turned to retreat into the bedroom, his back twitching with the need to scratch the itchy scabs, but before he could escape, David stood up. "Niall. Wait a moment, please. We need to talk to both of you."

Gareth set his helmet by the door. "What's wrong? Have you heard from Mal or Alun?"

David shook his head. "Not a peep. And it's waaaay past time when they should have been back. Alun's missed an important session with his PTSD group without even notifying them. I mean, I notified them, of course, when it seemed like he wouldn't get back in time, but he *never* misses that."

Bryce stalked to the middle of the room, his hands shoved in the pockets of his pants—well, in one set of pockets. There were at least two other sets scattered elsewhere. His hair looked as if it had been styled with a pitchfork. "I've been working on water scrying. I'm not that great at it yet, but even though I'm still an amateur, I can tell something's wrong."

Gareth frowned, and Niall could tell that the wild joy that had infused him back at rehearsal—when he'd literally *willed* the band to learn that song—was bleeding out. "It's a druid spell. They don't mesh with Faerie magic. Everyone knows that."

Bryce glowered at Gareth. *Oi. No love lost between these two. Wonder what that's about?* "With all due respect, that excuse is one that has prevented innovation and enlightenment for generations. If you had bothered to talk to Mal or me after your dramatic exit last September—"

"Bryce." David put a hand on Bryce's arm. "Not now, okay?"

Bryce clutched his hair with one hand and tugged at it. *Ah, so that's where the hairstyle comes from.* "Sorry. But I have no patience with close-minded, biased attitudes, and from what you and Mal have told me, he's been holding on to a fuck-ton of them forever."

Gareth squared his shoulders, brows pinched together. "You talk about me behind my back?"

"Can't very well do it in front of your back, since you're never here. Christ, first you're mad at Alun and don't speak to him for two hundred years. Now you're mad at Mal because he had the presumption to fall in love with someone you don't approve of. Which is total *crap* because you violated your own rule anyway, didn't you?" Bryce jerked his head toward Niall. "Yet you have the unmitigated *gall* to give Mal shit about his choices."

"You have no idea what agreement Mal and I have reached."

"As of yesterday, before he left for Faerie, that would be none. I know you hadn't spoken to him and he was devastated."

Gareth snorted. "Mal? Mal is never devastated. Besides—"

"Is that another thing that 'everybody' knows? Because I'll tell you right now, you supercilious jackass." Bryce strode across the room until he was inches from Gareth and poked him in the chest with one stiff finger. "He's operated under your shadow and Alun's shadow for his entire life, and you probably never even guessed. You took him at face value, just like everyone else, never asked him how he really felt or what he really wanted."

Gareth slapped Bryce's hand away. "I suppose what he really wanted was to get fucked by a druid."

"What he really wanted," Bryce said through clenched teeth, "was to be more than the spare champion or the bard's brother. He wanted to be himself."

"For your information," Gareth said, his tone low and intense, "I spoke with both of my brothers before the Convergence feast, and we're fine."

"Are you? Then why aren't you more concerned that they still haven't returned from the ceremony? The one that *you* bailed on, right in the middle? The calculations for that kind of spell are massive and precise. Didn't they tell you your presence was required?"

"Yes. And I *was* present. I just left."

"Before the damn thing completed! You escaped with no thought for anyone but him." Bryce flung out a hand, pointing at Niall.

Shite. Bryce was cutting a little too close to Gareth's bone. Niall might be the . . . the—*:Poster child!:*—for rebellion, but he'd also learned the hard way that some fights couldn't be won without compromise—or by paying a two hundred year price for obstinacy.

Gareth's fists clenched at his sides. "He was the one who needed rescuing. Everyone else could take care of themselves."

"Ordinarily, yes." Bryce's voice gained in volume, and David shared a wide-eyed, panicked stare with Niall. "But we're talking about a spell that *remakes Faerie*. Do you have any notion what that means? The foundation of your world was about to get demolished and rebuilt."

"And Niall wasn't part of it. If he had stayed, he'd have died. Alun told me so—only fae allowed on pain of death. I couldn't . . ." Gareth's voice, his bard's voice, always so smooth and sure, broke. "I couldn't let him die again."

Goddess, why hadn't Niall learned more about that damned spell when he'd had the chance? He'd *looked* at the documents, but he'd been so distracted that the details hadn't registered. He'd done the same thing Gareth had done—or thought he'd done. He'd pulled Gareth out of Faerie so he wouldn't be killed. The difference was that Gareth had actually been in immediate danger. Niall had not.

Gareth might have endangered all of Faerie for a lie—and Niall had let him.

Bryce shoved his glasses up the bridge of his nose. "We're talking about the lives of all fae in existence—including your brothers. I don't buy that one person's life is worth all of theirs." He glanced at Niall. "No offense."

Niall called on his old brash attitude, the one that had allowed him to face down Tiarnach, that had sent him on countless Outer World adventures, and raised an eyebrow. "None taken."

If something was wrong in Faerie, that meant Eamon was in danger too. Eamon and Peadar and everyone—other than Gareth—that Niall held dear.

He pushed that thought aside. He needed to know what Bryce feared, what plans he and David might have to fix the problem. Maybe, despite wanting desperately to stay with Gareth until he found out the truth, Niall needed to leave his own desires behind.

He stepped forward to stand shoulder to shoulder with Gareth. "From what I gather, you're concerned that something's wrong in Faerie. Have I got that right?"

Bryce nodded. "Yes."

Gareth turned to Niall, taking his arm. "You don't have to deal with this. You're still recovering."

"It's all right." Niall patted Gareth's hand. "After our little jaunt today, I'm feeling quite the thing." He turned back to Bryce. "So if you're worried about what's happening in Faerie, why not go back there and find out?"

Bryce scowled. "Not even David can cross the threshold without a fae escort."

Neither can I. Not until these wounds heal completely. This could be the hard part, but Niall had to succeed, to return the binding stone. Eamon's life could be at stake. *Faerie* could be at stake. And as little as Niall had appreciated the politics and endless jockeying for power, there were many things in Faerie that he loved. And to have all that removed from existence—well, everyone would all be diminished, wouldn't they?

"Seems like we've got a fae escort, though, don't we?" He turned to stare steadily at Gareth.

Gareth's hand tightened on his arm. "No. I won't."

Bryce's face took on an alarming red hue. "You—"

David stepped in, putting a hand on both Bryce and Gareth, and even Niall, with his reduced perception, could see the soothing golden energy flowing out from David's core. *Hunh. I never knew* achubyddion *could heal mental stress as well.* "Let's calm down and think about this, shall we?" His breath sped up and he turned a bit pale. "Niall, why don't you tell us what you —what you—"

"Grab him!" Niall shoved Gareth. "He's about to faint."

Both Bryce and Gareth lunged for David, whose eyelashes fluttered as his eyes rolled back in his head. They eased him down on to the sofa.

"Shit," Bryce muttered. "We weren't giving him the right feedback. He was trying to calm us down and we were resisting. Alun is going to have us both for *lunch* if he finds out."

"You mean *when* he finds out." Gareth smoothed David's hair back from his forehead. "I'm not going to lie to him. Not about something as important as David's well-being."

"It'll only be *when* if we can get them back." This time Bryce's tone was much less accusatory, almost despairing. "Please, Gareth. I think something is really wrong."

Niall walked over and gripped Gareth's shoulder. *I shouldn't. It's only going to make him feel worse once he finds out the truth.* But Niall needed to store up these touches, these moments, for when they were forever out of his reach. "Gareth. You're the only one who can do the trick. Come on. If you're so sure nothing is wrong, no harm, right? You'll be able to nip across and back in no time."

Gareth gazed up at him, his eyes troubled. "And if something *is* wrong?"

Niall shrugged. "We'll ford that stream when we come to it. Let's take the first step, eh?"

Gareth took a deep breath and nodded. "All right."

Bryce clenched his eyes shut behind his glasses. "Thank you." He stood up. "I've got a kind of *achubydd* Gatorade potion for David that'll set him right again, although our gratitude for keeping us from throttling each other will probably do more to restore him. We should be able to go in half an hour or so."

Gareth turned to Niall. "It won't take long. You weren't conscious when we brought you here, but it's not more than a twenty-minute drive. I'll be back in plenty of time for the concert."

Niall crossed his arms. "You make it sound as if I'm staying here."

Gareth's brow wrinkled. "Of course you are. You're barely healed enough to walk around, and it's not like you can do anything. I'm not about to let you back into Faerie."

That's what you think. "Give me a minute or two in my room and I'll be right as rain." Not that he needed to rest, but he had to retrieve the stone from its hiding place. "Don't worry. I know my limits."

And stepping through the portal, leaving Gareth behind, would stretch them to the breaking point.

Chapter Eleven

Gareth stomped down the Wildwood Trail, brushing irritably at the drooping fir branches. "I don't know why you can't wait until tomorrow, after the concert. It's not as though Alun and Mal haven't stayed away more than one night before."

David pattered along at his side. "Yes, but Faerie was never getting an extreme makeover before. Come on, Gareth. It can't hurt you to check. We wouldn't ask you if either one of us could do it."

Gareth glanced back at Niall, who was keeping a safe distance from both David and Bryce, who was bringing up the rear. And since David was sticking to Gareth's side like a cute but annoying burr, that meant Niall was keeping his distance from Gareth too.

Gareth pushed aside another surge of guilt. He'd been so sure he was rescuing Niall from captivity and torment—and considering his wounds, it was true. No matter what else happened, Gareth had to believe that had been the right thing to do. But if Niall never warmed to him again, if Gareth had to learn to live without him when he was *right there*—

He'd probably be spending way more time with Hamish in the future. Maybe he'd see if the fight pens would accept a fae.

He leaned down to murmur in David's ear. "I wish we could have left Niall behind though. Do you really think he's up to this kind of hike? Just yesterday, his back looked like raw meat."

David glanced behind them. "He insisted. And he's an adult, Gareth. It's his choice whether to accept our advice or not." David's gaze met Gareth's. "Just as it's his choice whether to accept you."

"I know. But—"

"Don't worry." David patted his arm. "When Alun gets back, he can put on his therapist hat and start the old head-shrinking routine. I mean, think about what those wounds mean. If anyone has some trauma to overcome, it's Niall. If nothing else, he can join the human PTSD group. Although . . ." David tilted his head, gazing at the trees overhead until he stumbled over a root that laced the path.

Gareth caught him before he fell. "What? You've thought of something."

"Way back when I was first temping for Alun, I . . . um . . . got hold of your solo CD."

Gareth's hand tightened on David's arm. "How— Goddess, that wasn't supposed to go anywhere. I only made it as a sort of catharsis and gave it to Mal so I wouldn't have it around."

"Well he gave it to Alun. And I . . . um . . . found it. I played it in the lobby while the PTSD group was waiting for their session."

Gareth released David and ran his hands through his hair. "Oak and bloody thorn, I was playing Gwydion's harp. Tell me you weren't inside a circle."

David scrunched up his face. "Weeelllll . . ."

"Goddess strike me blind. They all were forced to dance, weren't they?"

"Yes. And, um, me too."

Gareth snorted at that image. "I'm not the only one who'd be struck blind then. I'm surprised you didn't set their treatment back months."

"Hey! I'll have you know that night was a *breakthrough*. For me and Alun, it was totally awesome." David blushed, and Gareth wasn't sure he wanted to know any more about what kind of breakthrough was involved. "But it made a difference to the group too. I mean before, they hadn't even looked at each other, let alone smiled or talked. But afterward . . . Well, they weren't all heading out for a beer together, but they were interacting. I think your music helped them. What if your music could help Niall too?"

Gareth stole another glance at Niall, who was peering into the woods, a frown creasing his brow. Was that a grimace of pain? It was hard to know. "Do you think so?"

"He got orders of magnitude better overnight when you were singing to him. It wasn't only Bryce's supercharged potion."

"Maybe that was just your imagination."

"Gareth, I'm a nurse. I'm trained to notice this kind of stuff. He got better faster when you sang. In fact, afterward, I'm not sure the potion did anything other than keep everything from getting worse. Have you ever tried to weave a healing spell with your music?"

Not since he'd healed his own broken hand—and gotten outed as a bard. "I never try to do anything at all except play and not hit a wrong note."

David glared at him. "But is that because you *can't* or because you *won't*? I know all about your passive-aggressive stance with the Queen."

"I am not passive-aggressive."

"What do you call it then? You show up when ordered and do the bare minimum of what's required. Maybe it's time to let loose and see what you could do if you *try*."

"Even if it does help heal his back, that's no guarantee it will heal his mind too."

"Don't be so modest, boyo. You can do anything you want. Remember those lessons? You could make *him love you."*

Gareth slammed that thought down *hard*. The coercive nature of music . . . what Gwydion hadn't taught him, the Voices had filled in with glee. Gwydion himself was a stellar role model;

he'd started a war and assassinated a king just so his brother could commit a rape.

Gareth had done everything in his power to distance himself from that side of his spectral tutor. But if it could spare Niall pain? He'd dust off the memories and see where they led.

They reached the spot where they split off from the path, heading toward the threshold ford, and stopped to let Bryce and Niall catch up. Bryce strode over to them, but Niall hung back. Gareth sighed.

Bryce peered up the hillside. "I don't like it. We're not supposed to leave the path, otherwise we risk damaging the park's ecosystem."

"When we were here for the Midsummer Revels," David said, "Mal led the way and the trees sort of . . . moved aside for him. I don't think we left a mark."

Now *that* Gareth knew how to do. "Don't worry. I've got this." While Mal had probably just called on the One Tree to convince the forest to let them pass, Gareth never asked the One Tree for anything if he could help it. But one thing he *had* learned from Gwydion other than how to keep his instruments in perpetual tune had been the secret of getting the trees to walk.

He glanced at Niall. What would make him smile? Niall had always loved a jest. Maybe he wouldn't understand this particular joke, or at least wouldn't understand the reference, but the subtext in the song, in Gareth's voice, would be the same.

He started to sing "I Talk to the Trees" as he struck off the path.

Bryce snorted, and David rolled his eyes and said, "Seriously?"

And Niall—Niall grinned at him in the old way, the way that had made Gareth follow him anywhere.

Once they'd passed through the woods, Gareth stopped next to the ford. The weather had taken a turn for the chilly. Was that why Niall was huddled in his sweatshirt, visibly trembling, or was it something else? *I should have found a heavier coat for him.* The creek burbled over the rocks, a little swollen perhaps from recent rains, but otherwise perfectly ordinary.

Let's get this over with. Gareth took a deep breath and let it out on a low hum. He stepped onto the first stone, but when his second step should have taken him to another stone as the creek expanded into Faerie, instead he stepped onto the bank, skidding in the mud, his arms windmilling to keep his balance.

He frowned and met David's worried glance across the water. "Sorry. Must not have been concentrating. I'll try again." He leaped over the creek to the starting point—it wasn't that wide in the Outer World—then positioned himself. This was the right place, he was sure of it. He could even still see the spot in the mud where he'd dragged Niall clear of the water on their crossing, when he'd turned to block the trows from following.

"Ah, shite." He'd locked the door with one sustained note. Was that the problem? Well, he'd just have to unlock it and hope the guards weren't still lurking on the other side.

"What's wrong?" Bryce's voice still held an edge of anger. Thank the Goddess David had stepped in earlier. For all his fine words to David about never using his music as a weapon, Gareth had been tempted when Bryce had called Niall's rescue into question. He'd been on the verge of hitting his brother's lover—if not with his fist (he had a concert to play later after all), then with a tune that would've made him double over in pain.

"When we crossed before, I shut down the gate to keep a couple of guards from following us."

"Wait." Bryce took a step forward. "You never told us someone chased you. Didn't that ring a few warning bells? If all fae needed to be present, maybe they were just doing their job, trying to keep you inside."

"Trust me, they weren't doing any job of Eamon's," Niall mumbled.

Gareth didn't want to hear any more of what Niall thought of Eamon. "Now that I remember, I'll just undo the lock." He sang the counterspell, this time *forzando*. However, instead of the second stone, he ended up on the other bank again. "I don't understand. I can feel the resistance, where the threshold should be, but I can't interact with it."

Bryce frowned. "The One Tree won't respond?"

"I never connect with the One Tree. Not anymore."

"Is this more of your rebellion against the Queen, now that we know she's really the One Tree?"

Gareth scowled at Bryce, who scowled right back, his arms crossed and his boots planted wide on the other side of the creek. "It has nothing to do with that." In fact, he'd refused the One Tree connection ever since the Queen had refused to help him recover Niall, long before Bryce's discovery that she was the avatar of Faerie itself.

"In that case, don't be so fucking stubborn. Use the connection and get it over with."

Gareth jumped the creek again. "I don't see what—"

"Please, Gareth." Niall's plea, low and urgent, stopped Gareth before he could go toe-to-toe with Bryce. "If we caused a problem, we need to fix it. For the sake of Faerie."

"So altruistic. Is he begging for the sake or Faerie, or the sake of his ravisher?"

Gareth clenched his fists. Why was he still hearing the thrice-damned Voices? He'd never heard them before in Niall's presence.

"Maybe because he's not truly yours anymore, boyo."

"All right. But it's been a long time."

Bryce canted one eyebrow. "Hedging? Because from what Mal says, it's instinctive. Part of your DNA."

"Whatever." But the worry in Niall's dark eyes made Gareth's resistance seem petulant and petty.

He faced the stream again and closed his eyes, calling on the place just below his heart where the link to the One Tree nestled in every fae.

It wasn't there.

His eyes flew open. Was this his own doing? Because he'd denied the One Tree, denied Faerie for so long, had it decided to return the favor? He tried again, reinforcing the call with a hum. This time he could detect something, but it was faint and twisted as if the normally shining thread were tangled and dulled.

Nevertheless, he latched onto it. Trusting it to guide him, he stepped into the creek. The stone wobbled under his foot, but then steadied. He took the second step, forming the image of the threshold in his mind as he hummed a martial tune under his breath, and his foot landed on a stone. *Thank the Goddess.*

He opened his eyes, and for a brief moment, he saw the tor with the Stone Circle on its crown. But when he took the next step, he was ankle deep in frigid water with nothing but the park in front of him.

He returned to the bank, shaking water out of his trainers, and shook his head. "I can't. I'm sorry."

"No!" Niall rushed forward, splashing into the creek and glaring wildly around. "It must be here. We have to go back."

"How about that, boyo? Is that the reaction of a bloke who's ready to give his ravisher the boot and come bounding into your bed again?"

"Shut up," Gareth growled.

Bryce pressed his lips together, looking incredibly grim and far more druid-like than Gareth had ever given him credit for. "Let's go home then. We need to talk."

Niall kicked himself for losing control in the park, but with the binding stone all but burning a hole in his pocket, he'd given in to his desperation and guilt. Now Gareth was looking at him with decided suspicion, David with disappointment, and Bryce with speculation.

Of course, that could be his own paranoia talking. If he were them, that's what he'd be thinking. But settled here around the wide oak table in Bryce's dining room—which looked exactly like David's in reverse, other than the furnishings—he tried to put his remorse aside and focus on a solution.

Gareth was pacing back and forth across the kitchen floor —*:Cork!:*—his hands slicing the air to punctuate his words.

"It's the Unseelie. It has to be the Unseelie. Why would they want to submit to the new rules? They always do exactly what they please, with no regard for how it affects anybody else."

David gathered several ceramic mugs in brilliant rainbow hues onto his fingers like rings and brought them to the table. "Isn't that a little harsh, Gareth?"

"No. It's the precise truth. That's one of their tenets. They're motivated entirely by self-interest."

Bryce dodged past Gareth with the coffeepot and poured them each a cup. "If you could leave your prejudices behind for half a minute—"

"They're not prejudices. They're facts. Faerie is governed by the rules of the original spell, and the tenets of the courts—"

"Are a lot more flexible than you give them credit for. It's all a matter of perspective. Of the way you justify your actions."

Gareth scowled at Bryce. "That's exactly the kind of argument I'd expect from an Unseelie. Self-justification is their way of life."

"I thought you just said they didn't care about anyone else. Why would they need to justify themselves?"

"And *that* is the kind of argument I'd expect from a druid."

"Enough!" Bryce slapped the coffee pot onto a ceramic trivet. "Blame is irrelevant. What we need to do is figure out what the underlying problem is—if there even is one—and form a plan to remediate it."

"Spoken like a college professor," Gareth mumbled.

Niall glanced from one man to the next—a druid, an *achubydd,* a Seelie fae bard . . . *and me, the dog in the manger*. As far as any of them knew, he was the only one without a stake in the game. They didn't know Eamon was his brother, didn't know Faerie was his home. Although they might suspect he hadn't relinquished his ties to Eamon—*:Stockholm Syndrome!:*—they didn't know for certain. And Niall wasn't about to tell them, not with Gareth certain the whole thing was an Unseelie plot.

For all Niall knew, it *was* an Unseelie plot. The presence of Tiarnach in the woods—with guards who did his bidding rather than restraining him—was troubling. What if Eamon hadn't ordered him to be there? What if there were other factions with a stake in the outcome of the Convergence, their own reasons for wanting it to fail? *:Hidden agenda!:*

Niall barely restrained himself from rolling his eyes. As much as he appreciated the way the *ethera* made him at home in the Outer World so quickly, the random communications—*:Instant messaging!:*—were extremely distracting.

He shifted in his chair, and David immediately focused on him.

"Is your back bothering you? Is it time for another dose of the potion?"

"No. I'm fine." Physically anyway, but trying to untangle potential Unseelie conspiracies made his brain spin.

"Have you remembered something else?" Gareth's tone was hopeful.

Niall shook his head. "Nothing." He cradled his coffee cup in his hands. "What do you suggest, Bryce?"

"First—" Bryce took a sip from his own cup. "Christ, that's good, David."

David dipped his chin. "You always say that. Thanks, but it's nothing. Please go on."

"Right. First, I need you two to tell me everything you remember about the ceremony up to the point where you bolted."

"We didn't—"

"Gareth." Niall cocked an eyebrow. "We bolted. Wouldn't self-justification be an Unseelie trick?" *:Cheap shot!:* Fabulous. Now the *ethera* were rating his remarks. What next—sex tips? *:Lubed condoms!:*

Bugger.

Gareth carded his fingers through his curls, sending them awry, more than ever like a golden halo. "A point, I suppose. All right. I've told you everything already."

"Are you sure?" Bryce asked. "Any detail might be relevant, no matter how small."

The binding stone seemed to pulse against Niall's thigh. Even if it was a key to the ceremony, or at least Eamon's handfasting, if he couldn't return it, there was no point in revealing its existence and enduring the awkward questions about why Eamon would have entrusted it to him.

Still, there was some information he could share. He cleared his throat. "There were some fae who hung back in the woods. I think they were probably among the ones who are most opposed to the Convergence."

Gareth stopped pacing and sat down heavily at the table. "Why didn't you say so before?"

"It didn't seem relevant. There were so many on the plateau. I thought maybe they just didn't want to be part of the crowd. I mean, *I* didn't."

Bryce leaned forward. "Did you recognize them?"

Niall avoided Gareth's sharp gaze, looking directly into Bryce's eyes with the false sincerity he'd perfected in the days when he'd hidden the worst of his rebellion from Tiarnach. "No."

Bryce slumped in his chair. "Damn it."

"I'm sorry." Gareth stood. "I have to go now or I'll be late for our sound check. We can talk later."

"I'll be with the druid council, but if either of you remember anything—anything at all—for God's sake, call me immediately."

CHAPTER TWELVE

As Gareth prepared to leave for the concert, he wavered between cautiously optimistic and flat-out panic-stricken. What if he'd caused Alun and Mal to be trapped? Despite his feelings about the Queen's alliance with Eamon-the-kidnapper, Gareth didn't want to be the cause of the death of everyone he knew. Especially now that Niall was safely out of the crosshairs.

Gareth would push aside his bias against the druids—as difficult as that might be—because if Bryce was able to find out what was happening in Faerie, or find a way for Gareth to get inside, resisting because it was a druid plan would be bloody idiotic.

"You really want to cozy up to the blighter who ties up your brother and buggers him regularly—just like yon human and his paramour?"

Gareth froze in the act of putting on his shirt. He'd known it was likely—that Niall had not only been kidnapped by Eamon, but raped by him as well—but he'd done his best to deny it.

"Ah, come now. What other reason do fae ever snatch humans? What good are they besides arses to shag?"

"Shut *up*!" Gareth yanked savagely on his shirt, sending a button flying off onto the floor. Shite. He didn't have a lot of spare clothing here since he'd expected to go home to LA after the Convergence. He'd expected a lot of things that hadn't happened—he'd expected Niall to remember him, for one thing.

But he'd never expected him to still be alive. That had to be the most important thing. Niall was alive. Niall was safe. Even though the Convergence wasn't something he'd have chosen, what possible difference could it make to him since he wasn't planning to return to Faerie again?

Once they had the issue of the portal alignments resolved, once Mal and Alun returned, Gareth would absolutely concentrate on winning Niall back. He'd done it once. Surely he could do it again.

But now he needed to focus on his job, because if he did intend to make his permanent home in the Outer World, he couldn't afford to bollux up his career. It made him appreciate humans a bit more—or anyone who only had the option of a living in a single realm. If you fucked up your life, you had to . . . well . . . live with it.

He dug his last clean shirt out of the bag he kept at Alun's house for emergencies. It wasn't exactly something he'd choose for performances—a collarless button-front shirt in black with silver pinstripes. Tiff would no doubt give him grief for looking like an office drone. Hamish would just say he looked like a wanker.

But then Hamish never wore anything other than a tank and shorts. He always said he got too overheated under the stage lights otherwise. He also claimed he worked harder than the rest of them.

He certainly bounced about more—Josh was nearly stationary, communing with the music with either guitar or violin; Spence was constrained by his keyboard rig; Tiff took her job laying down the bass line too seriously to leap about. *Probably comes from being a kangaroo.*

Hamish's hopping was another part of Hunter's Moon's percussion—a counterpoint that was lost in their recordings. That was one of the reasons their concerts were so popular—because the visual experience gave a whole other dimension to the music. Gareth spent his time as front man looking out into the crowd as he sang, and their reviews always mentioned the way his gaze mesmerized the audience, how everyone in the venue felt he was looking directly at them, singing directly to them.

That's because he was. That was one of the gifts of the true bard—connection to the listener on every level. It was one of the reasons—other than the problem of the fairy circle—that Hunter's Moon never played stadiums. They kept to more intimate venues—venues where Gareth could still see the faces (albeit tiny) of the people in the back row.

He finished getting dressed and was about to run a comb through his hair when Niall peeked into the room.

"Am I— That is, is it still all right for me to come to the concert tonight?"

Gareth hesitated in the act of rolling up his shirtsleeves. "Do you still want to?"

"I do. I loved the rehearsal today. I was looking forward to hearing a true performance. But if you don't want me to come —"

"Of course I do. Why wouldn't I?"

Niall shrugged. "I don't know. You seemed a little different when we got back from the park. Distant."

"I'm sorry. If I did, it was because this whole Convergence thing has me completely bonkers. Setting aside the fact that my brothers might be in some kind of danger, I hate the whole idea. Well, you've heard my opinion of the Unseelie." He smiled and shrugged. "I haven't made a secret of it."

"That's for bloody sure."

"But that has nothing to do with you." Gareth took a breath. *Now's the time to find out. Find out exactly what happened to him.* "Niall . . ."

Niall looked up, his eyebrows raised. "Yes?"

"I have a question for you. Something that might upset you. But after your reaction today, I really want to know. You can tell me to vanish into the maw of all the hells if you want, but—"

"Go ahead and ask the bloody question, all right?"

"Did Eamon . . . well . . . did he . . . force you?"

Niall's eyes widened, and a look of revulsion skittered over his face. "Bloody hells. No, he did not forcibly bugger me, nor did anyone else. Happy?"

"Actually, yes." He took a step forward, gratified that Niall didn't shy away from him or flinch as he had before. "I hate the idea of anyone hurting you. The fact that you were beaten is bad enough. If there's been other kinds of abuse—"

"Leave it, Gareth, all right? Eamon didn't touch me. I never saw him after I was— He didn't. Nobody did. You say you haven't been with anyone other than me? Well in the last two hundred years, I haven't been with anybody at all. So we're even."

Gareth wondered why that didn't make him feel better. Yes, he was glad that Niall hadn't been brutalized in more ways than his wounds betrayed, but the notion that he'd been as lonely as Gareth had been himself? That hurt his heart in an unexpected way. Not that he'd have suffered in precisely the same way—his loneliness was general while Gareth's had been specifically for Niall.

That didn't make Niall's experience any less devastating.

Niall met his gaze steadily. "But I'd take it as a favor if we never discussed that again."

Gareth nodded. "Agreed. Now are you ready for the concert?"

Niall ducked his head, scuffing his borrowed sneakers on the carpet. "I'm not exactly dressed for the occasion." David had found another pair of sweats to replace the ones that had gotten wet earlier, and dug out one of Alun's old henleys.

"Don't worry about that. There's no dress code at these things. The fans wear all kinds of clothes." He grinned and tried to put a teasing note into his voice. "Some less than others."

As he'd hoped, Niall looked up, that old sparkle in his eyes and his mischievous smile in place. "That kind of crowd, is it? Or are you that kind of band?"

"You'll never know unless you come along and find out."

"All right then. Let's get on with it."

Gareth led the way down the hall, picking up his guitar case and retrieving his jacket from the coatrack. "I've arranged for you to have a backstage pass. You can hang with us in the green room before the show, then watch it from the wings. Unless you'd rather be out front. The show's sold out, but our manager always holds on to a few house seats until right before curtain."

Niall looked almost panic-stricken. "Not one for crowds these days. Backstage sounds brilliant."

Excitement bloomed in Gareth's belly, more than the usual preshow anticipation. Niall would be there while he performed. For the first time in two centuries—if you didn't count rehearsal—he'd be able to glance over and meet Niall's gaze as he sang, as he played. He remembered that they were closing the first set with "Lover's Reel," and maybe if he played it for Niall, *to* Niall, Gareth could find the missing piece, the thing that would make the song whole and perfect.

And maybe Niall would remember more. *Maybe he'll be one step closer to remembering he loved me.*

If Niall had felt out of place at the rehearsal studio, that was nothing compared to being the one person without a purpose backstage at the concert. He stayed in the green room while the band ran their sound check onstage. Gareth had told him he could watch from the wings, but with the crew—*:Roadies!:*—still running cables and stacking equipment, he didn't want to get in the way or distract the band from their jobs.

He huddled in the corner, wishing he'd brought an extra coat. The air conditioning was cranked up back here, despite the chilly weather outside. When Hamish erupted into the room, he noticed it right away.

"Cold, mate? It'll get better presently. They keep it refrigerated for us because we get so bloody hot onstage under the lights."

"Ah. Makes sense."

"You'll feel it too, if you're to watch from backstage." Hamish grinned and downed half a bottle of water at one go. "We generate heat to spare."

Tiff brushed by him and checked her eyeliner in the mirror. "He's modest too. You might not have noticed that about him."

Niall chuckled. "Yes. Very retiring sort. Performing must be a right chore for him."

"Not me." Hamish finished his water and tossed the empty into a green bin with a triangular logo on the front—*:Recycling!:* "Josh still vomits before every show though."

"Hamish!" Tiff punched him in the biceps as she passed on her way out of the room. "That's Josh's business."

"His and Spence's."

"Exactly. Not yours. And not any str—" She cast a furtive glance at Niall. "Anyone else's."

"Not a stranger's, you mean." Niall gave her a two-fingered salute. "Guilty as charged. But it's not my place to judge."

She nodded once and continued out the door. "Pee before you go onstage."

Hamish rolled his eyes. "I'm not a bloody toddler."

"No. You just behave like one. Who knows when you might embrace the rest of the behavioral package."

She disappeared, and Hamish screwed up his face in something halfway between a smile and a scowl.

Niall shook his head. "Does she always give you this much shite?"

"Yeah." He sighed. "Isn't she great?" He wandered toward the door.

"Where are you going?"

"To take a piss, of course. I've had my marching orders. Later."

Niall half expected to see Gareth, but apparently he was already in consultation with the sound engineer. The band's manager—a tall, thin person with a shock of rainbow hair who caused Niall to do a double take because of their resemblance to nongendered fae—gave Niall a sharp look but didn't otherwise comment on his presence.

In fact, nobody paid him much attention at all—very similar to his last weeks in the Keep, with the exception that the kitchen had been much warmer and less sterile, and the company considerably more friendly.

Shite, was he actually missing the Keep? What a comedown for the scandalous prodigal prince, who'd always seized every opportunity to escape.

After an announcement that the house was open, the band filed back into the room, Spence with his arm around Josh as usual, Josh looking a mite green around the gills. Gareth made his way over to Niall and sat next to him.

"You doing all right?"

Niall nodded. "Feeling a bit out of place"—*:Fifth wheel!:*—"but I'll manage. You all ready for the show?"

Gareth nodded, gazing around at the rest of the band. "Yeah. This'll be a good one, I think. I can always tell by their energy."

Niall glanced at the other band members. They might be in separate corners—Spence and Josh standing close, foreheads touching, murmuring to one another; Tiff leaning against the wall, eyes closed, fingers making patterns on her thigh as if it was the neck of her bass; Hamish tossing a drumstick, bouncing on his toes—yet somehow they seemed part of a whole anyway, almost as if Niall could see the threads connecting them to one another.

And Gareth held the ends of those threads. Niall remembered the way Gareth shone onstage, the way others were drawn to him, helpless moths to his brilliant flame. He suspected that the success of the concert rested more on Gareth's mood than anything, because a bard's mood could influence everyone within range of his voice. For the band, who experienced it at close range all the time? It must be almost automatic.

Niall remembered his own reaction to Gareth, onstage and off. That had never gotten old, never been taken for granted.

And then it had been taken away.

The band's manager opened the door and popped their head in. "Five minutes, everyone."

Gareth flashed a thumbs-up in acknowledgment and motioned his bandmates to the center of the room. "Okay, mates. This is it." With their heads together and arms around one another, their connection was even more evident. Gareth murmured something to them that Niall didn't catch.

"And break!" Hamish called.

They parted, heading out the door, Gareth bringing up the rear. He stopped in the doorway and looked back at Niall. "Come on then. I've got a stool set up for you backstage. Best seat in the house."

"Are you sure? I won't be in the way?"

"Nah. They're mostly set now anyway. Unless—" Gareth's smile faltered, and Niall's heart clenched to see the uncertainty in his face. "I mean, you don't have to watch if you don't want to."

Niall forced himself to grin and rose to join Gareth. "Wouldn't miss it for the world."

Gareth's smile returned. "Excellent. This way."

He led the way down the corridor and through the stage door, guiding Niall to a stool just offstage. The rest of the band was already there, and Niall could almost feel the energy vibrating in the air between them.

The house lights dimmed. Hunter's Moon surged onto the stage in the dark. With three rimshots and a long note from Josh's violin, the stage lights flared to brilliant life and the crowd roared.

If Hunter's Moon in rehearsal had been amazing, Hunter's Moon in performance was nothing short of a revelation. Niall was mesmerized by the interplay of the band with each other—manic Hamish, sly Tiff, quiet Josh, intense Spence—and Gareth. Bloody brilliant Gareth.

He shone. Sparkled almost. His grin flashing, curls flying. The electronic instruments and the presence of the other musicians muted his bard's power, but it was there nevertheless.

The audience felt it. The band felt it. And Niall most definitely felt it.

The band swung from their opening instrumental piece into a song about love lost—one of those that Hamish must have been complaining about, because Gareth's voice, with Tiff on backup, was enough to bring a duergar to tears. Niall caught himself dabbing at his own eyes because it was obvious that this was a song from Gareth's heart, Gareth's experience.

This is how he felt after I left.

Goddess, how could Niall have done this? He'd never intended to fall in love. Had never intended to make Gareth love him. It had all been a lark at first, no different than any of the other tricks he got up to in the Outer World. Rob a stagecoach. Smuggle brandy from France. Aid in a revolution—on both sides.

Eliminate the Seelie bard.

He ought to have left before things got so serious between them. Then Gareth wouldn't have had this heartache following him down the centuries. Wouldn't have had to mourn a lover who had never been more than an imposter, whose entire relationship with him had been based on a deception.

Gareth would never have been put in danger, and Niall would never have had to endure his incarceration. Everyone would have been better off. Yet Niall could never regret falling in love with Gareth.

For loving him still.

Onstage, the band swung into "Lover's Reel," and Gareth locked gazes with Niall. Niall could almost read his mind: *This is for you.*

Even though he couldn't tear his gaze away from Gareth, Niall sensed when the crew in the wings near him began to sway and then dance; could see peripherally that the audience was doing the same. Even the band was moving—Josh swaying, his eyes closed as his violin sang; Spence dancing behind his keyboard; Hamish bouncing higher than usual; Tiff moving her feet in counterpoint to her bass line.

I can't resist him. Not anymore. I'm no more immune to his allure than anyone else.

If what he'd endured already had been worth the price, then surely succumbing now—taking this second chance to love him again—surely it would be worth whatever happened later. He was different now. Gareth was different. Even Faerie was different, or would be once the Convergence was complete.

Who was to say that a broken Unseelie prince couldn't find happiness with the last true bard, a lord of the Seelie court? Stranger things had happened.

Although no matter how Niall racked his brain—in the small amount of space not taken by Gareth's music—he couldn't think of a single one.

I'll worry about it later. For tonight, I'll live for us.

CHAPTER THIRTEEN

They had to do two more encores than usual. The audience wouldn't let them go, and frankly, the band didn't want to leave either. After his big mistake during "Lover's Reel," when he'd let his emotions cloud his common sense and played directly at Niall, unleashing his bardic powers and forcing everyone to dance, Gareth had contained himself. He'd only glanced at Niall from time to time, forcing himself to look away from Niall's smoldering gaze and interact with the audience.

Oddly, it hadn't been that difficult. He'd felt Niall's presence there, knew he was watching, and that spurred Gareth to perform better than he had for years. Not that he ever stinted in performance. He owed it to the band and the fans to give his all. But tonight was something special, because tonight Niall was there.

The band bounded offstage, for once Josh just as lively as Hamish, and boiled down the hallway, whooping with joy. Gareth, out of breath and flying on postshow adrenaline, stopped next to Niall.

"Well?"

"Bloody brilliant."

Gareth beamed. "You think? I hoped—"

"Oi, Gareth," Hamish called. "Green room now."

Gareth shrugged apologetically. "Sorry. We've got a postshow ritual. It won't take long. Since we've got another show tomorrow night, we don't have to strike our instruments or clear out the dressing rooms."

"It's all right. Do what you need to do. I'll wait."

"No way. You come along." Gareth waggled his eyebrows. "There's champagne in it for you."

Niall grinned. "Well then, lead the way."

Gareth was tempted to grab Niall's hand, but he didn't want to push things—yet. Although he didn't quite trust himself not to jump him once they got home. He hadn't been this high after a performance for a while, and he needed something to bring him down.

They walked into the green room just as Hamish popped the cork on the champagne. Before they drank it, though, they guzzled water like dying camels. Niall retreated to the corner again, watching them with a bemused smile, although when his gaze caught Gareth's, there was a definite spark.

Hamish held up the champagne bottle by its neck. "Here's to Hunter's Moon and the best damned show we've ever had."

Spence, with his arm across Josh's shoulder, grinned and flipped Hamish off. "Speak for yourself, douchebag. *All* of our shows are the best we've ever had."

"Aw, come on, mate. Admit it. This one was special."

"I admit nothing. But if you're pouring, I'm drinking."

Everyone had a plastic glass full of champagne as they laughed and joked and came down from the high of the show. Niall took his own glass over to the corner, not intruding on the band's camaraderie. Every time Gareth caught his gaze, Niall smiled at him, but made no move to join them.

Finally, Josh nudged Gareth with an elbow. "Go on. He's the reason you were on tonight. You played for him. We were onstage, sure, and the audience was incredible. But for you, it was all him, wasn't it?"

Gareth frowned at him. "Did I— I didn't mean to let you down."

"You didn't. It's just that your energy came from somewhere else tonight. I don't begrudge it. None of us do. So go talk to him."

"Forget that," Spence said. "Take him home and take him to bed."

"Shh." Gareth glanced at Niall, but he didn't seem to have heard Spence's less-than-quiet comment. "It's not like that. He's not ready. If he still doesn't remember—"

"I don't think it matters if he doesn't remember." Josh gave Gareth a little shove in Niall's direction. "Tonight you made a new memory. Work with it. We'll see you at the sound check tomorrow night."

Gareth let himself be pushed—not that he wanted to fight it. At the moment, there was nowhere else he'd rather be than with Niall. After every one of Hunter's Moon's concerts, he'd always felt a certain desolation when the performance high wore off and he was on his own, alone in his house in Laurel Canyon or wherever they'd stopped on tour. Tonight, he wouldn't be alone. He couldn't take Niall home to LA, but at least they'd be under the same roof, even if they weren't in the same bed.

"So . . ." He fetched up next to Niall, hoping he appeared casual as he downed the last of his champagne and tossed the cup in the recycling bin. "Are you ready to go?"

"If you are. Hamish said the band was heading out to a bar. I don't want to stop you if you want to go along."

"No. I'm ready to call it a night. We've got another show tomorrow and I didn't get a lot of sleep last night. Unless you want to go out?"

"Not me. I'm a more sit-by-the-fire kind of bloke these days."

Gareth smiled at him and grabbed his jacket. "I think that can be arranged."

When they got back to David's house, the windows were dark, as were Bryce's next door.

"Bryce and David were heading off to that druid confab. I guess it's still going on." Gareth pulled the SUV into the garage, and the automatic door slid shut behind them. "I'm not sure if that's a good thing or a bad thing."

"I'm inclined to think good. At least it means they've got something to talk about, right? If there was no news, they'd be home by now."

"I suppose you have a point."

They walked into the kitchen, and suddenly things got awkward. They were alone in the house, with nobody to observe them or judge them or insulate them from each other. While an hour ago, Gareth would have sworn this was what he wanted, now he wasn't so sure. Then he remembered: there were only two bedrooms. He wasn't about to sleep with his brother-in-law—assuming his brother didn't suddenly come home anyway—and Niall hadn't exactly invited him to share the guest room bed.

True, there had been those smoldering looks during the concert, a certain heat and tension in the car as they'd driven home, but now Gareth wasn't sure what to do. If he moved too quickly, assumed too much, he might ruin everything. But what if Niall wanted him to make a move?

Then there were Niall's injuries. Would they allow him to do anything amorous, even if he wanted to?

I'll never know if I don't do something.

"So . . . do you want a snack? Something to drink?"

Niall tilted his head, studying Gareth from under quirked eyebrows. "No. I'm fixed, thank you."

"Right. Then . . . I'll bed down on the sofa. If Bryce were home, I'd see about staying with him—"

"Bryce?" Niall snorted. "The two of you can't speak two sentences to one another without a catfight. What's that about anyway?"

"He's a druid."

Niall's eyebrows traveled halfway up his forehead. "That doesn't explain anything."

"Druids and fae—traditionally we don't mix. And his relationship with my brother is . . . complicated."

"What relationship isn't? Show me an uncomplicated relationship, and I'll show you two people in matching comas."

"I'm also not pleased because their relationship was founded on a treasonous action by Mal: conspiracy with the Unseelie. With Eamon, actually. The two of them had no business facilitating Eamon's plot."

"But it was a good thing, surely. It deposed the Unseelie King."

"You know about that?"

Niall gave him an exasperated look. "It was hard to miss."

Gareth flushed. "I suppose. But one of the things that came out of that other than the seed of the Convergence was the knowledge that fae were created by the elder gods to be subservient to druids. And that a bond can be formed between a druid and a fae that puts the fae in the servant role."

"And you object to your brother submitting to another man?"

"I object to any kind of coercive relationship, to any kind of power imbalance. You should know that better than anyone."

"Should I?"

"That's what happened to you. You were forced into a situation that stripped you of choice. How can that be good?"

Niall ran both hands through his hair. "You know what? I think that poor dead horse has been sufficiently flogged, don't you? Do you suppose we can lay the beast to rest?"

Heat washed up his chest. "Right then. I'll just . . . get the sofa ready."

Niall advanced on Gareth, one slow step at a time. "Why?"

"Because . . . because I'm tired?"

"Are you? Even if you are, there's a perfectly good bed right down the hall. Although it does have a distinct disadvantage."

Gareth swallowed. "It does?"

Niall nodded, his eyes dark and intense. "You'll have to share it with me."

As much as Niall remembered from their time together, regardless of what he claimed, the one thing he truly couldn't recall was their first kiss. Considering what a wild, reckless care-for-nobody he'd been back then, chances were their first kiss—Gareth's first kiss ever—wouldn't have been as tender, as careful as it should have been had Niall known the truth.

As much as it shamed him, he wasn't sure if it would have mattered even so. He'd been living the Unseelie creed to the fullest back then, searching for the next thrill, the next mark, the next situation he could send spinning into beautiful chaos with himself at the center of the storm.

With Gareth, he'd landed in the eye of that storm, the danger he'd craved wrapped up in the forbidden nature of their relationship.

Gareth edged closer until his breath ghosted against Niall's cheek. "That sounds like more of an advantage to me."

Niall's own breath seemed trapped somewhere under his heart. He twined one of Gareth's curls around his finger, and Gareth stilled but for the quick rise of his chest. Gareth had drawn him then as he did now. If Gareth had asked, would Niall would have abandoned the Unseelie code for his sake?

How could I? His nature was bred in his bones, the stamp of his gods-bedamned father as inescapable as the shape of his nose or the color of his eyes. But once, during that brief time with Gareth, he'd *wished*—Goddess, how he'd wished—that he was capable of that kind of change.

He tugged on the curl. "I don't remember our first kiss. Was it gentle? Tender? Reverent?"

Gareth smiled crookedly. "You know, I'm not entirely sure myself. I think you may have kissed me behind the stables after we held up the coach and distributed that baron's gold to the villagers. If that's the case, I doubt tenderness was the order of the day."

"Adrenaline-fueled, eh? Those tend to be less nuanced. No matter. Since neither of us remember, then, let's make this one count as the first."

Gareth's pupils were huge, nearly merging with the dark ring around his iris until only a narrow band of blue remained. "You're so beautiful," Niall murmured. He traced Gareth's top lip with his finger and was rewarded with a gasp. "I may remember nothing else, but I remember that. And your hair . . ." He laced his fingers through the honey-brown curls. "I love your hair."

Gareth let out a soft half-laugh, although it seemed like he had to search for the breath for it. "You always said that."

I did. Because it's true. "You'll have to remind me of everything else I always said. Everything you said to me. Everything I did to you, or that you did to me. I want to know about it all. From what *you* remember." Because then Niall would have the memory of what Gareth had felt then, even if his feelings changed completely when he learned the truth.

"Does the past really matter? There are things there that you don't want to share." Gareth traced Niall's cheek with a gentle finger, and Niall shivered. "And there are things I don't want to share either."

"Really? What?"

Gareth chuckled for real this time. "Didn't I just say I didn't want to share?"

Niall shrugged. "Can't blame me for trying it on, eh?"

"You always said that too."

"Shite, I was a right bastard, wasn't I?"

"No." Gareth cupped Niall's jaw in both hands, the calluses on his fingers rough against Niall's skin. "You weren't. You were lovely. Everything about those times was lovely." He closed his eyes and pressed his lips together for a moment, but Niall could still see them tremble. "Goddess, Niall, I've missed you so much. You've no idea."

Oh I do, my darling. I do.

While Gareth's eyes were still closed, Niall leaned forward until his mouth was a whisper away from Gareth's. "Then let's waste no more time. New memories are better for us both."

He pressed his lips against Gareth's, gently, with every bit of the tenderness and care he ought to have shown all those years ago. Gareth's lips parted under his, but Niall didn't take the bait and deepen the kiss. Not yet. This was about firsts. About exploring. About learning the shape and softness and texture of Gareth's lips. This was about restraint, not abandon. About sipping from the cup, not gulping.

Because Gareth was worth every moment and more. In the not too distant future, Niall might be denied this privilege; he needed to store up every sensation now, while he had the chance.

So he teased out the first kiss to two, three, a dozen. Still only the feel of lips on lips. Some soft as the brush of a lark's wing. Some firm and insistent, but always, always reverent and so, so thankful for the gift.

But then Gareth must have lost patience, because he growled deep in his throat, a sound that made Niall's already hard cock throb in his unfamiliar underdrawers. He grasped Niall's jaw more firmly and angled his head, fitting their mouths together and laving Niall's lips with his tongue until Niall gave in—*how can I not?*—and opened for him.

Only his hands on Gareth's hips kept him standing as his knees turned to water. The taste of Gareth's mouth, still sweet with champagne, was achingly familiar even after all these years. Niall matched stroke for stroke, call with response, as willing—no as *eager*—to give as to receive.

Gareth pulled back, breathing hard—as was Niall, for that matter—and pressed their foreheads together. His curls tickled Niall's face, and Niall wanted to shout with the sheer joy it. He'd always batted Gareth's hair out of his face when Gareth rested his head on Niall's chest after lovemaking. In his years in the forge, he'd regretted that. He'd have given anything for that gentle torment. Now he had the chance for it again.

But would it be fair to take it now, allow an intimacy that should contain nothing but truth, when such a huge lie still lay between them?

Two lies, if it came to that, and a number of smaller deceptions and half-truths. Now that Eamon and his bride were about to change the nature of Faerie, Niall actually had a chance for a future with Gareth at the new court. Or even here, in the Outer World, where Gareth had a life and a career and Niall had champions in the very air.

But if they were to succeed, this new relationship had to be clean and free of past deceptions. Niall had to trust Gareth—that his feelings for Niall were strong enough to overcome any sense of betrayal. And that Niall would be able to convince Gareth that Seelie and Unseelie weren't as inimical as he believed.

"Gareth. There's something I must say. I—"

Gareth stopped him with another kiss, this one so full of passion that Niall moaned into his mouth. *Passion.* It had always been the tenet that had gotten him in the most trouble.

When Gareth pulled back and Niall opened his mouth to try again, Gareth put a finger across Niall's lips. "Shh. No talking. We're making new memories, remember. No apologies. No regrets. No talking about the past. New memories." He stroked down Niall's chest to his groin and cupped his bollocks, giving them a squeeze. "Now come to bed."

CHAPTER FOURTEEN

All the way down the hall—which felt like a journey of miles instead of yards—Gareth vibrated like a plucked guitar string. Niall's hand was in his, warm and firm. How many times had he woken from a dream, believing he'd found Niall at last, only to discover it wasn't true, his heart plummeting like lead?

But this time—this time it was real. He knew it, because this time he wasn't completely overjoyed. This time, they both had baggage on board that hadn't been there before.

When they'd first met, Gareth had been so turned inward everywhere but onstage. Mal had accused him of locking everyone out, but really it was the opposite. He was trying to lock himself in so he didn't fly apart at the Voices' poisonous prompting.

Niall had opened him up at the same time he'd held him together.

Gareth paused, the guest room door suddenly looming as if it were the maw of the underworld. So many years he'd dreamed of this. What if it had all been for nothing? What if when he had his chance to make love to Niall, he remained as unmoved as he had been by everyone else before and since?

Or worse, what if Niall decided Gareth wasn't enough, couldn't measure up to whatever had made Niall follow Eamon through the threshold and then kept him in the Unseelie realm for centuries? He'd been tortured, yes. But had there been some other reason for him to stay there, to not try to escape and return to Gareth? Someone he missed—that he loved more?

"Gareth." Niall's voice, although it carried a rough burr as if he'd broken it through screaming, nevertheless stroked Gareth's nerves like velvet. "We don't have to do anything you don't like. If you'd rather—"

"No." Gareth shook his hair back and brought Niall's hand to his mouth for a kiss. "If you're ready, I am. I've been waiting for this for two centuries."

"You missed sex that much?"

"No." He dropped his gaze to their joined hands. "I missed *you.* I know you don't remember, that you didn't miss me, but —"

"Shite," Niall muttered. He put a finger under Gareth's chin, raising his head until their gazes met. "Don't think about that, all right? New memories. Starting here." He leaned in for a gentle kiss. "Starting now."

He tugged Gareth into the room and then dropped his hand. Gareth would have protested the loss of contact, but Niall removed his shirt and Gareth's breath stalled in his chest. Then he shucked off his sweatpants, and Gareth had to steady himself against the wall.

He'd seen Niall naked when he and David had stripped him to treat his wounds, but at the time, Gareth had been nearly frantic with worry, and only David's practical, matter-of-fact nurse's attitude had kept him grounded. Besides, Niall had been unconscious, and Gareth had never been attracted to bodies alone. It hadn't been Niall's body that had drawn him in—although he'd appreciated his beauty, and later reveled in the sensations of touching and being touched. It had been the way Niall's personality, his life, had felt almost too big to be contained in even a body as fine as his.

As a musician, it was Gareth's job, his calling, to understand beauty and sorrow and joy, transform them and deliver them to his audience. But no beauty had ever touched *him* the way his music seemed to touch others, not until Niall.

So now, the sight of Niall's skin affected him on both a physical and a visceral level. His cock hardened in response. *How many years since it's done that?*

Then Niall bent over to turn down the sheets, and Gareth saw the scars peeking out from under the dressing on his back.

Niall's body was like the moon: His chest was all smooth skin and sculpted muscle. His belly was taut, with a dark treasure trail arrowing to his groin. But his poor back . . . It had been the same as his chest before, all honey-gold skin and flexing muscle. But now it was as scarred and pitted as the moon's hidden dark side.

Niall looked up, and his smile faded when he got a look at Gareth's expression. "It's too much for you, isn't it? The ugliness?"

"Not that. No. You could never be ugly to me. But, Goddess, Niall. How much you suffered under that bastard—"

Niall took one giant step forward and stopped Gareth's diatribe with a finger across his lips. "We're not thinking about that. We agreed. Nothing in the past. If my body disgusts you, that's one thing. I won't ask you to force yourself. But if your only concern is my comfort?" Niall threaded his fingers in Gareth's curls and snugged his naked body against Gareth's unfortunately clothed one. "You're all I need for that."

This time, the kiss was more heated. Gareth grasped Niall's forearms above the shackle galls and held on while his skin tingled and his cock hardened, a thrill buzzing in his veins greater than anything he'd ever felt onstage.

Niall didn't pull away from the kiss, but he pushed Gareth's jacket off his shoulders and fumbled with the buttons of his shirt.

Gareth broke the kiss this time, suddenly remembering that he'd been drenched in performance sweat not two hours ago.

"Goddess, I'm sorry. I must stink. I should shower. You don't want to smell me—"

Niall grinned. "Are you barmy?" He nuzzled a spot under Gareth's ear and inhaled. "That's the perfume of an artist. Honest sweat, earned in your true calling. It's intoxicating. Besides, we'll both be sweatier and smellier by the time we're done here—at least if we do it right. Showers can wait."

He leaned back and began unbuttoning Gareth's shirt, a frown of concentration pleating his forehead. "This is our first time, remember? I should take care of you. If I had done it right before—" He glanced up, his cheeks unaccountably pink. "And since I don't remember, I can't say. But if I'd known it was your first time ever, I'd have made sure our first time together was a slow build. A tender rush. Like this."

He slipped his hands under the collar of the shirt and eased it off Gareth's shoulders and down his arms. "I'd have taken the time to learn what you liked, what touches made you gasp, where my tongue made you moan. But since I didn't then, I'll do it now."

He licked a slow path from Gareth's collarbone to his sternum. "You taste like salt and music."

Gareth laughed, but caught it when Niall circled his nipple and nipped it lightly.

"I'd have drawn you to the bed," Niall said, his lips grazing Gareth's skin, "like this." He stood up and captured Gareth's hands, then walked backward until his calves hit the mattress. "Although I think I'd have made you take off your pants, so I could watch." He grinned. "I believe I might have mentioned that I'm not a nice person." He sat on the bed and leaned back on his hands, legs splayed—naked and gorgeous and a more than a little bit wicked. Gareth couldn't breathe, let alone move. Niall tilted his head, eyebrows quirking. "Well?"

"I'm not sure—" Goddess, he sounded more like a bullfrog than a bard. He tightened his belly and tried again. "I'm not sure I remember how. Maybe you should . . . tell me."

This time, Niall's grin went past wicked and into delicious sin. "Play your pants like you play your guitar, my bard. Slide." Niall ran two fingers up his own cock, bollocks to tip. "And pluck." He added his thumb and gave the head a twist, his eyes heavy-lidded. "And strum." He grabbed the shaft in his fist and gave it one swift stroke. "Now you."

Gareth swallowed against his mouth gone dry. "Slide." He eased down the zipper on his jeans, reveling in the way Niall focused on his every move, lips parted. "And pluck." He popped the button so the pants sagged on his hips. "And strum." He tucked his hands into the waistband and shucked them to his feet in one go.

Niall groaned. "Goddess strike me blind, Gareth."

The same sense of power that possessed him in performance, when he knew he held his audience in his palm, filled Gareth like warm honey. He toed off his shoes and kicked off his pants, then swaggered forward until his legs bracketed Niall's, his hips level with Niall's head.

He smoothed Niall's hair off his forehead. "Now what would you have done?"

"Well . . ." Niall's breath gusted warm against Gareth's cock —they both shivered. "If I hadn't passed out already from sheer lust, I'd have laid you down on the bed."

"Like this?" Gareth swung his leg over Niall's lap so he could crawl up the mattress, slowly, Niall's gaze on him like a fire in his blood. He flipped over onto his back, head propped up by a pile of pillows. From this angle, he could see the ruin of Niall's back, his dark side, but it didn't matter. Those scars were part of Niall now. "Or have I done it wrong?"

"Oh no," Niall growled. "You're perfect." He scrambled onto the bed and kneeled astride Gareth's thighs, gasping as their bollocks collided. "I'd have held you . . . like this." He wrapped his hand around Gareth's cock, causing Gareth to whimper. "And this." He lined his own cock alongside it. "And then we'd move together."

Niall's eyes were half-lidded, his breath coming in gasps that matched Gareth's own as he rocked his hips, sliding his cock against Gareth's in the tender prison of his fist. "I'd have made sure . . . that you . . . unnngh!" Niall gritted his teeth, and his motion stopped.

Gareth flexed his own hips and wrapped his hand over Niall's, swiping his thumb over the head of Niall's weeping cock. "I would have too. Exactly."

"It's been too long, Gareth, I can't hold out."

"Then don't." He rocked against Niall, faster, faster. "It's our first time. It won't be our last."

Niall threw his head back, eyes clenched, and spent—over their joined hands, over their cocks, over Gareth's belly. At the sight, Gareth's own release sparked low in his spine and, vision whiting out, he came for the first time in two hundred years.

With Niall warm against his chest, Gareth sighed. He'd slept well for the first time in forever and he didn't want to move—he might never move again.

"You may not want to move, but you think he won't? Didn't promise anything, did he?"

Damn and blast. He'd been so sure that once he and Niall were together again, the Voices would shut the hells up. Why had that happened before, but not now? Were they right—that Niall was planning to bolt again? Had Niall really *wanted* to go with bloody Eamon all those years ago?

After all, he'd tried to cross the threshold in the park.

He's here. We're together. Consequences could take care of themselves.

As Niall stirred against his chest, Gareth was careful to stroke only his arms, his hair, the back of his neck. *His arse*. Goddess, Niall was still beautifully made, despite the marks of his captivity. His biceps were, if possible, even larger and more defined than Gareth remembered.

Gareth dropped a kiss on Niall's hair and was rewarded with a chuckle that vibrated his bones and thickened his cock. Goddess, he hadn't had the least inclination to bed anyone since Niall had disappeared, but now he was ready to go again. Apparently a good night's sleep would do that.

Or else I only needed the right person. Like Josh.

Niall raised himself up on his elbows and gazed down at Gareth, a smile playing on his full lips—lips that were still a little red and swollen from their kisses. "I must be crushing you. You've not put on any more weight since—" Niall's eyes widened, panic flickering across his face.

But Gareth's heart bounded in joy. "You remember? You remember what I looked like then?"

Niall rolled off of Gareth onto his side and propped himself on one elbow, tracing patterns on Gareth's belly with the fingers of his other hand. "Told you I remembered that song—and you singing it naked."

Gareth scrambled up and sat gazing down at Niall, capturing his roving hand in both his own. "Yes, but is there anything else? Did . . . what we just did . . . anything jog free?"

"I thought we agreed—only new memories."

Gareth sighed. "I know. But something in me really wants to believe that I wasn't so forgettable."

Niall clenched his eyes shut for a moment. "Shite." He opened his eyes again and pushed himself up so he faced Gareth on the mattress. "You are more memorable than anybody in the world."

"Except to you." Goddess, could he sound any more sullen?

"You know. You know he remembers his captor perfectly. What does that say about you?"

Niall waved it away. "Don't judge by me. I told you, I'm not the best measure of a man."

"If we—"

"Gareth!" Bryce's voice echoed down the hall, followed by the slam of the front door and the murmur of David's more modulated tones. "Where the fuck are you?"

Gareth grinned wryly at Niall. "I've heard that Bryce was shy and retiring before he met my brother. Sometimes I wish he was still the same." He turned his head so he wouldn't shout into Niall's face. "Be out in a minute. Keep your drawers on."

When Gareth would have slid off the bed, Niall grabbed his hand. "But that's all you wish, right? Only that he wasn't so bold?"

"What do you mean?"

"You don't wish he'd never met your brother, do you? That Mal was still alone?"

Gareth opened his mouth to retort, but thought again. Did he? Mal had never shown the least desire to settle down before Bryce, flitting from one bed to the next—usually in the Outer World. Gareth had kept a close eye on him, though, and he'd never dallied with a human more than once.

"He showed more self-restraint than you, boyo. Or maybe you put the fear of the gods into him and kept him lonely so you wouldn't be the only one."

"I didn't."

"'Didn't'?" Niall's eyebrows bunched together. "Didn't what?"

"I mean no. I don't. I suppose— Mal always seemed satisfied with his life before. He was famous for his fickleness, to be honest." But when Gareth had seen him in Faerie before the Convergence feast, he'd seemed. . . content. At peace. Considering that Gareth now had the only one he'd ever wanted—and again, he'd chosen outside of his own species—he could hardly fault Mal for his choice.

"That never stopped you before, though, did it? Face it, boyo. You're a fecking hypocrite and always will be."

Call it a throwback to his old rebellious days, but Niall purposely delayed Gareth from rushing out at Bryce's command, drawing him into the bathroom and sending him into the shower with a heated kiss. Unfortunately, Niall couldn't join him there, blast his still unhealed back. Although he should be grateful for it, as annoying as the awkward sponge bath was. If he'd been healed, he'd never have had a chance for that interlude with Gareth—lovemaking, in keeping with Gareth's worth. Slow, careful, cherishing—the way he should have done it their *real* first time.

By the time they got to the living room, early morning sunlight slicing through the windows, Bryce's pacing had probably worn a path in the wood floor—*:Sustainable! Bamboo!:*—while David was huddled in the corner of the sofa with his knees tucked against his chest.

Bryce glared at Gareth, then his eyebrows climbed up his forehead as he glanced between Gareth and Niall. "It figures."

David looked up and smiled at them, although it didn't completely banish the misery in his eyes. "Congratulations. I guess you worked things out."

Bryce crossed his arms. "I hope it was the most spectacular fuck in the history of the world, because otherwise it wasn't worth it."

Gareth's fists clenched. "Just a gods-bedamned minute—"

Niall put a hand on Gareth's arm. If anyone was going to punch Bryce, it would be him. Nobody talked to Gareth like that. "It's none of your business."

"No? I just got back from a joint session of the supe council, including all the druid circles in the Pacific Northwest. From everything we can tell, that Convergence spell is completely fucked—some twist in the Unseelie side—and unless it's miraculously repaired, Faerie is going to collapse. Implode. And take everyone inside with it." When David's breath hitched on an unmistakable sob, Bryce winced and ran a hand through his hair. "Damn it. Sorry, David. But pretending this isn't a disaster won't help us solve the problem, and we've got a limited amount of time."

Gareth sank down on the ottoman, eyes wide, apparently unable to speak.

Niall turned to Bryce. "How long?"

"Forty-eight hours. Maybe seventy-two if we're lucky. It depends on whether the collapse gathers momentum as Faerie deteriorates or if it's a straight linear progression."

"Then what can we do?"

Bryce fixed his basilisk stare on Gareth again. "Gareth needs to figure out what the hell he did to that gate and open it up again so we can get inside."

"'We'? Druids aren't allowed in Faerie." Gareth looked up at Niall's testy words, confusion in his face. *Shite.* "I mean, that's what I was told."

"Normally no. But that's more a druid restriction, a part of a treaty, so we wouldn't run power-mad and enslave the whole population. I've got special permission to enter, but I can't open a gate. I still need a fae escort."

"I'll escort you," Gareth said. "Of course I will."

"That's mighty big of you, but where? You broke the fucking gate!"

Gareth frowned, and to Niall's relief, he started to get angry instead of devastated. "Wait a minute. Why did we go back to the park anyway? Don't you have a gate down in that swamp of yours?"

Bryce's nostrils flared. "It's not a swamp. It's a wetlands."

"That's not the point."

"That gate is an Unseelie gate, and in case you haven't noticed, we don't have an Unseelie around to unlock it."

Niall shifted uncomfortably. All he needed to do was confess. Get David to heal him, and he'd be able to find the gate.

Gareth stood up to face Bryce. "You and Mal used it before, and neither one of you is Unseelie."

"That's because Eamon gave us a token to let us pass."

"Eamon." Gareth spat out the name as if it were a mouthful of troll piss. "If it's an Unseelie plot, he's probably the mastermind. Trying to take control away from the Queen, just like that wanker Rodric Luchullain tried to do."

And that is why I can't. Gareth would hate him forever. Besides, since the druids had identified an Unseelie plot, if they knew Niall was Eamon's brother, they might suspect him of colluding. Especially since he'd never been truthful about his nature in the entire course of his relationship with Gareth.

"Don't blame it on him," Bryce growled. "Mal said he was totally invested in the Convergence. That's why we helped him depose the old King."

Wait, what? Eamon had never mentioned druid intervention. Then again, Niall hadn't given him much opportunity to discuss the events that had led up to his release from the forges. *I suppose I should be grateful to Bryce for helping to get rid of Tiarnach, but that doesn't excuse his attitude toward Gareth.*

Although Gareth was giving as good as he got. "Then how do you know this isn't *your* fault? An imbalance caused by your actions?"

"Because it didn't start until you two exited unexpectedly. *You* were the catalyst."

"You can't know that for sure. Why are you suddenly blaming me for the whole fiasco?"

Bryce snorted. "That's right. Blame is a prerogative you reserve for yourself. I know all about how you blamed Mal and Alun for not caring enough about you to realize your tutor was a ghost."

Niall's eyes popped wide. *What the bloody hells?* "You were trained by a ghost?" *And I thought enslavement to a god was peculiar.*

Gareth tore his furious gaze from Bryce, his expression softening when turned to Niall. "I'm the last bard, remember? Arawn had to dig up a tutor from somewhere. So he literally dug one up—none other than Gwydion himself."

Shock rocketed down Niall's spine. "Danu's tits. *Gwydion*? And you hate the *Unseelie* for their self-interest?"

"Don't look at me like that," Gareth said irritably. "I didn't pay attention to his political or personal values. Only to the music."

Bryce shouldered Niall aside and parked himself in front of Gareth. "Don't give me that shit. You only *think* you ignored it. But you're doing exactly the same thing that he did."

David lifted his head off his knees. Shite, he looked totally miserable. "What did Gwydion do? I mean who was he anyway? I only know him by his bollocks."

Despite the tension in the room, Niall couldn't help but laugh. "His bollocks?"

David colored. "Not *literally*. I mean obviously not. But that's one of Mal's favorite expletives. What the heck did the guy do?"

Bryce stared Gareth down. "You going to tell him, or should I?"

"How do you know about it?"

"Since I got shanghaied into druid apprenticeship, I've done nothing but study this lore. Apparently, it's the druids' job to know everything."

"So what do you know?"

"He's possibly the greatest magician in Welsh prehistory. The son of the goddess Dôn. A bard. He also started a war between Dyved and Gwynedd so that his fucking whiny arrested adolescent brother could rape a woman whose position depended on her virginity and who had no interest in the bastard."

Gareth face had gone red. "He—"

"He did. You know he did. Then he killed the king of Dyved in personal combat to end the war. How many people died because he decided to satisfy his brother's sexual obsession? He didn't care about any of them. He was willing to sacrifice all the men in two kingdoms just for that one despicable act. And you're doing the same thing."

Gareth's mouth dropped open, and his face faded from ruddy to pale. "I'm not."

"No? You're sacrificing Alun, Mal, your own Queen, all the fae on the entire planet, Faerie itself . . ." Bryce thrust his hand out, pointing directly at Niall, and Niall could swear he felt a spear of energy pierce his heart. "For him."

CHAPTER FIFTEEN

The expression on Niall's face when Bryce made that accusation—Goddess, Gareth hoped never to see that look of horror again. And David—he looked devastated.

"I think I know of one other gate." David's voice was soft but steady. "Alun told me about it. It's an hour or so south, near the Enchanted Forest."

Niall blinked, startled enough that the horror drained from his face. "There's an enchanted forest here? A real one?"

"No," David said. "It's an amusement park. That's just its name."

"Fine." Bryce snatched up his jacket. "Get in the car. We're leaving now."

Gareth collected his own jacket. "All right, but I have to be back for the second concert tonight."

"Then you'd better hurry." Bryce stormed out of the house.

Gareth turned to hand Niall his jacket, but Niall shook his head. "No. I'm not coming."

Gareth's belly curled in dismay. "But—" Hadn't they found each other last night? He'd been so sure they'd finally spilled all their secrets, that even if they couldn't share the past, they at least had a future. "All right."

"How about that, boyo? He's got your measure at last."

Gareth tried to ignore the Voices. Maybe this had nothing to do with Bryce's accusations. After all, Niall was Irish, not Welsh, and he'd lived in the Georgian age, far later than the events of Gwydion's time. He hung up the jacket then turned toward Niall, hoping for a kiss, but Niall had already moved away, dropping down on the sofa next to David, his hands clasped between his knees.

Gareth swallowed his disappointment. "I'll . . . I'll see you later. A couple of hours. Three or four at the most." He hoped. Although even if he managed to get inside Faerie, he had no idea what he could do to fix things.

He left the house and walked next door to where Bryce was already waiting for him behind the wheel of his LEAF.

"So," Bryce said once Gareth had buckled in. "Are we going to argue all the way to Turner?"

"No. I'd just as soon not speak to you at all."

"Christ, Gareth." Bryce took off down the street. "You can't let it go, can you?"

Gareth swiveled in the narrow seat and glared. "Would you? You're taking the piss out of me now because Mal's trapped. Are you going to forgive and forget if you can't get him back?"

Bryce's knuckles whitened on the steering wheel. "Don't say that. Don't even think that."

"Is this a druid thing? What you say comes to pass?"

"No, it's not a druid thing. Call it an avoidance mechanism if you want, but I'd rather not imagine the worst outcome. Besides, you're the one who just sealed the only threshold in Portland with nothing more than a random hum."

"You don't know that."

"Don't I? You tell me why we can't get in then."

Gareth stared out the window at the passing cars. "I can't."

"Nor can I. Look." Bryce took a huge breath and blew it out. "You're what amounts to my brother-in-law. I think we should at least make an attempt to be civil to one another, don't you?"

Gareth shrugged. "I suppose."

"Then *work* with me. Faerie's not the only thing at risk—it's anchored here, in the Outer World. If it collapses, it could send ripples through our ecosystem that we can't begin to estimate."

A frisson of fear cascaded down Gareth's spine. His home. The band. The whole world. Could it be that severe? "I thought you didn't want to imagine worst-case scenarios?"

"There's a difference between borrowing trouble and problem-solving. Does your hatred of Eamon—which, by the way, I think is entirely misplaced—outweigh the fate of everyone else on the planet? He harmed one person—allegedly."

"Allegedly?" Gareth punched the dashboard. "I *saw* him approach Niall. Speak to him. Take his arm. And Niall just followed him through the gate without a backward glance before I could get to him." *I didn't even get to say goodbye.* "Eamon looked at me, though. He knew who I was and he knew exactly what he was doing."

"But Niall has never said a word against Eamon."

"He can't! It's a tyngyd. You should know all about those. Eamon prevented Mal from talking about him when he talked you two into doing his dirty work at the equinox."

"I don't think it's the same. Mal tried to talk about him and couldn't. Niall doesn't seem to want to talk about it, or reveal any information about himself at all. Maybe you're misreading the situation entirely."

"If you'd been tortured for a couple of centuries, would *you* want to talk about it?"

"A fair point. But you've got Niall back. From what we saw this morning, it looks like you've got him *all* the way back."

"We're working on it." Gareth's heart tripped over itself. *Why wouldn't he kiss me goodbye though?* "But it's promising."

Bryce jammed on his turn signal. "Well I don't have Mal and David doesn't have Alun. What's more, they don't have us, and they *need* us. They need our help and they need yours. So what if helping them means helping Eamon too? You are no longer the injured party, Gareth, so get the fuck over it and do the right thing."

After Gareth followed Bryce out the door, Niall stayed planted on the sofa like a lump for a good ten minutes. *An Unseelie gate. In the backyard. Eamon in danger—along with Gareth's brothers and Peadar and every other fae in both courts.*

Although Niall couldn't find the gate and pass through in his current state, if he was healed, he could do it—and he was sitting next to the only known *achubydd* in the world, who could probably do the trick without breaking a sweat.

But if I'm healed, Gareth will know the truth. They'll all know the truth. And then what? Since Bryce had been a party to Eamon's coup, he might grant Niall a bit of credibility. But would David? Even if they listened to him as an Unseelie, would they trust him as someone who'd lied to them since they'd met, concealed information, maybe caused the whole bloody mess by fleeing Faerie in the first place?

Bryce had accused Gareth of putting the good of one before the good of all, as Gwydion had done, but was Niall any better?

David, who'd been silent too, finally sighed and rose from his corner of the sofa. "Would you like some breakfast? Coffee or tea? I can make something."

"You don't have to play the host. I know you're worried. The last thing you need is to concern yourself with a guest."

David pushed his shock of brown hair off his forehead and shrugged. "Doing something, anything, is better than sitting around and brooding. Alun always says—" He pressed his lips together and took a shaky breath. "Alun always says that I'm not capable of sitting still."

"You love him very much, don't you?"

David nodded, and this time a tear escaped, trickling down his cheek. He dashed it away with the back of one hand. "So so *so* much. He can be a stubborn, pigheaded bossypants when he gets on his ethical high horse, always wanting to take everyone's problems on his own shoulders even when they're perfectly capable of dealing them on their own. But he's got the biggest heart of anyone I've ever known. If something happens to him—" David's face crumpled and he turned away. "I'll make some coffee."

He scurried into the kitchen, where he began to bang cabinet doors and run water at full force. It didn't cover the sound of his sobs, however.

Danu's tits, Bryce is right. This was bigger than Niall's own blighted love affair. *Gareth was out of my reach for two centuries, and I had him again last night.* That was more than Niall had dared hope for. Even if Gareth never forgave him for his deceptions, he couldn't stay silent any longer.

He got up and walked into the kitchen, where David was scrubbing the sink with a yellow sponge.

David glanced up and then away, as if he were ashamed of his tears. "Did you decide you want something after all?" His voice wobbled.

"Yes. I do."

"The coffee will be done in a few minutes. Would you like eggs? Toast? Yogurt?"

"I'd like for you to heal me."

David turned slowly, a hint of fear in his blue-gray eyes. "I'm not sure I understand. You realize I can't affect humans the way I can supes."

"I know. But thanks to what you and Bryce"—*and Gareth*—"have already done, my injuries are just down to time, right? So they won't they won't be life-threatening to you. Trivial, almost. Like healing a . . . a . . ." *:Paper cut!:* "A paper cut."

David rolled his eyes. "About a bazillion paper cuts. Assuming the paper was as thick as a horse's leg. But you have a point. It's just extreme first aid now." He tossed the sponge in the sink. "If you're sure."

"I am."

"I should warn you though, I'm not certain I'll be able to do much about the scars. I've never tried to heal something imposed by a god. I wasn't able to do much about Mal's curse when it was the result of one of those bogus fae rules."

"I know. I don't care. I just don't want to be an invalid anymore."

"All right." He marched across the kitchen and pointed to a chair at the table. "Sit down, straddling the chair backward, and take off your shirt, please."

Niall complied, although when the cool air slid over his skin, he shivered. Propping his arms on the chair, he leaned forward. "Like this?"

David *hmmph*ed as he palpated Niall's back with gentle fingers. "Yes. I'll try to make this quick."

"Thorough is better than quick, but only if it doesn't endanger you."

"Got it." David laid his hands on Niall's shoulders lightly—a feather touch—but the warmth flowed over his skin like warm honey, making him twitch and tense.

No turning back now. When this was over, he couldn't hope to hide his nature from Gareth any longer. *It's worth it, though. To save Eamon. The Kendricks. All the lesser fae. Even bloody Tiarnach.* None of them deserved to be victims of Niall's own reckless impulses.

He rested his forehead on his clenched fists. Too bad this didn't hurt more. He deserved to be punished for what he'd done to them all.

David snatched his hands away. "You said you wanted this."

"I do." *I must.*

"Then stop fighting me. *Achubydd* healing is as much about the cooperation of the patient as my own ability or power or whatever you want to call it. If you don't want it, I don't get the feedback I need to replenish my energy, and then *you'll* be the one taking care of *me*."

Shite. Niall stood up and faced David. "Are you all right?" Was he a little pale? Was that pain etched in the corners of his eyes? "If this is going to hurt you—"

"It won't as long as you cooperate. Can you do that? Send yourself, I don't know, healing thoughts?" His eyes narrowed. "Wait a minute. Do you believe you *got what you deserved*?" David's voice rose until he'd have given a druid a run for his money. "That being flogged to within an inch of your life was *justified*?"

Niall turned away, folding his arms over his chest. "It was worth the price. Or at least I thought so at the time."

"You know what? Screw that. Screw that sixty-two ways from Sunday with a six-foot bedazzled ratchet, because *nobody* deserves to be tortured. So give it up, Niall. If you want my help, you have to help yourself too."

Could he do that? Let go of the sacrifice he'd made on Gareth's behalf? *If I do, I won't have anything left of him at all.* But if he didn't, Faerie could be doomed.

He straightened and took a deep breath, squaring his shoulders. "Yes. I'm ready."

"Then sit back down. I can't do anything with you looming in the corner like that. You're as bad as Alun when it comes to doing what you're told."

Niall settled himself in the chair again, remembering what was at stake and forcing himself to . . . to what? Think healing thoughts? *:Mindfulness!:* Shite. "I'll wager I'm worse. I made it a point to always do the opposite of what anyone expected."

"You'll fit right into this family then."

David's hands were gentle on his shoulders again, and Niall closed his eyes, willing himself to ignore the consequences of revealing his deception and focusing instead on saving Eamon. Saving Faerie.

Energy flowed from David's hands, across his back, down his arm and legs, pooling in his wrists and ankles and in the deep welts on his back. He stopped shivering, any residual pain overcome by the soothing warmth.

Goddess, how long had it been since he hadn't been in pain? He almost couldn't remember what it was like. The absence of pain was almost a pain in itself, as if his mind had spent so long compensating that it couldn't process the sudden cessation.

David hummed happily. "This is going a lot better than I expected. All the open wounds are gone and you're giving me the exact feedback I need. Wow. The scarring is even fading. It's almost as if—" David jumped back. "Holy cats. You're fae!" He blinked at Niall, eyes as round a bauchan's. "Did you *know*?"

Niall huffed a laugh. "Yes. I knew. Of course I knew."

David squinted one eye. "But Gareth has no clue. Setting aside how the heck you managed to hide it from him, why did you think it would be a good idea? I mean, seriously? That's kind of a big freaking deal."

Niall yanked his shirt over his head. "How long have you known Gareth?"

"Long enough to know he's been so gone on you he's nearly turned psychopathic."

"And have you heard his opinions on the Unseelie?"

David snorted. "Who hasn't?"

"Then you know why I didn't tell him."

David's mouth fell open. "Shut *up*! You're Unseelie?"

"Yes." Niall grasped David's wrist. "You can't tell him. You can't tell him I'm fae, and you especially can't tell him I'm Unseelie."

David squinched his face. "Seriously? I won't have to. He'll take one look at you—heck, Bryce will be able to see your aura with his druid sight the minute he walks in the room."

"No they won't." Niall pulled the mantle of his human guise over himself like a comfortable old coat. He didn't need the One Tree for this—it was part of his heritage from his mother, just as the communion with the *ethera* of the Outer World was.

David blinked. "Whoa. That's . . . wow. How can you mask yourself so completely? Even Alun can't fake human *that* well, and he's had tons of practice."

"I'm half-human. It comes naturally." Niall pulled on his jacket. "I need to find that gate. Will you lead me to the wetlands?"

"Are you kidding?" David ran to the French doors and wrenched them open. "Let's go!"

CHAPTER SIXTEEN

David shot out of the back door as if he'd been launched from a catapult. "It's down this way. I think. I mean Bryce said it was in the wetlands, but I've never been in there. He's offered to take me in, but—" David shot a mischievous glance over his shoulder. "I got enough of the nature-boy stuff when I was growing up. I never knew it was druid-related. My aunt never told me she was a druid, just as she never told me I was *achubydd*." He slowed, allowing Niall to catch up with him. He had a scowl nearly as prodigious as Bryce's on his face. "When I found out what she'd been hiding from me all my life, I was not a happy little camper, let me tell you. I mean, she put spells on me to *invert* my abilities. I caused riots everywhere I went!"

Niall glanced away. Hadn't that been what he'd done with Gareth? Would Gareth be just as angry as David had been? Although apparently David had gotten over his anger. "Do you still hold it against your aunt?" He followed David onto a raised path that cut through a shallow pond. "For hiding things from you?"

"Oh I got over that. I call her my aunt, but there's no relation really. She took me in and gave me a family. She loved me unconditionally, and I love her." His scowl deepened as he watched a trio of ducks cutting a V across the water. "Although when I found out she'd put herself in danger—she nearly died! —to protect me . . . well." The ducks took flight and David continued on the path. "I still haven't quite forgiven her for that."

Would Gareth feel the same? Would Niall's sacrifice be gratefully accepted and understood, or reviled as a gross impertinence?

David glanced over his shoulder as he led Niall into the woods at the far side of the pond. "Look, Niall. I get that letting Gareth in on your true nature will be . . . awkward, but I have to say that I think continuing to hide it from him is a mistake. I mean, hiding it from him in the *first* place wasn't the best idea anyway."

Niall shoved his hands into his jacket pockets, still astonished when the action didn't set off an ache in his back. "You think I don't know that? I never planned to—" He swallowed convulsively and blinked the moisture from his eyes.

"To fall in love with him?" David's voice was gentle and soothing, and made Niall want to weep even more. Could *achubyddion* heal with voice alone? Niall had never heard of such a thing—although those in the Unseelie harem had little opportunity, or cause, to exhibit such a talent.

"I'll tell him. When I find the right time. I'd planned on telling him, back then." That very night, in fact. He'd amassed all his arguments about why a mating between a Seelie bard and an Unseelie prince, albeit one with a slightly tarnished reputation, would be a brilliant idea.

But before he was willing to put his heart on the line, risking Gareth's refusal, he needed to get his father's consent, and get him to call off the vendetta against Gareth. It had been easier to contemplate his father's apoplectic rage, because that wouldn't be any different than any other interaction Niall had with him, than the chance that Gareth might turn him down.

David picked his way around a boulder mottled with gray and green lichen. "Why didn't you?"

"I was . . . overtaken by events." Niall paused when he picked up traces of bauchan scent, and not just any bauchan, but one he knew. *Heilyn.* Heilyn had been here—not recently, but more than once. "This way."

He took the lead, finally stopping next to a stream. On the far bank, two birch saplings leaned toward each other, branches intertwined. A glimmer of the *other* still hung about the place. "That's it."

"You can tell?"

"Yes. Heilyn's tracks lead straight here, but then disappear abruptly between those trees."

"All righty then. Do your thing. You know, magical appearing stepping stones and all that."

Niall frowned, tilting his head. "I— Something's wrong. Off. Like a hole in an icy pond that's frozen over."

"Isn't that normal? I mean, these things don't just hang open, inviting people to waltz in and out. It's a . . . thing, a process. You have to try, right?" David was bouncing on his toes, anxiety leaching into his tone.

Well naturally. His husband was in there. Of course he'd be worried.

Very well. Maybe the odd feeling was simply the result of too many years spent not using the gates. Niall's memory was normally eidetic—for both information and sensation—but two hundred years as the slave of a god might affect anybody.

He positioned himself on the bank of the creek, directly opposite the birch archway. Closing his eyes, he concentrated on his *calon,* his Faerie heart. It pulsed with life, but it beat erratically. *My body isn't the only thing that's battered. My spirit needs recovery too.*

He called on his connection to the One Tree, the birthright of every fae, Seelie or Unseelie, greater or lesser, and got . . .

Nothing.

No, not nothing. A thread of something, faded, almost like a faint plea for help, a mere shadow of the magic that had always been there before.

Perhaps this was another residual effect of his captivity. He hadn't called on the One Tree often, even before he'd been severed from it in the underworld. Had he lost the trick of it?

He closed his eyes, breathing in the scents of the earth and water and sky. The *ethera* danced around him, awaiting a chance to share their knowledge treasures with him.

Wait. Maybe he could *ask* them. He'd always been a passive observer of their comments, viewing them with amusement or sometimes irritation, as he would a child's patter. But he should know, better than anyone, that simply because an entity had different abilities, it didn't mean they weren't worthy of respect.

He sent out a query: *Your aid?*

Immediately, he was surrounded by a veritable whirlwind of *ethera*.

:Yes!:

The One Tree. Can you reach it?"

The whirlwind lost velocity. *:Not ours.:*

Damn it. Of course not. The *ethera* were of the Outer World. How could he—

:Not anymore.:

You were once of Faerie?

:We are the bridge.:

The bridge? What the hells did that mean. *The gates?*

:Gone.:

Shite. *Forever?*

:You have seen.:

I've seen what? When?

A vision of his quarters in the Keep rose in Niall's mind, his table covered with rolls of parchment. Danu's tits, he was a bloody fool. So intent on pretending to forget that he actually had forgotten.

The Convergence spell. He'd *seen* it. Now if he could only remember the details—

"Um . . . Niall?"

Niall opened his eyes to meet David's concerned gaze. "Sorry. What?"

"Do you realize that your hair has taken on a life of its own? I mean, there's no wind but—"

Niall chuckled as the *ethera* twirled another lock of his hair. "Just some friends." He turned back. "Come on. There's no point in trying to get into Faerie. There's no gate here."

"But . . . but there was. Mal and Bryce used it multiple times."

"Yes, but it's not there now." He motioned for David to follow him back the way they'd come. "Think of Faerie and the Outer World as two spheres. Faerie, as the magical construct, is held within the sphere of the Outer World." Niall sketched a sphere in the air with both hands. "Faerie itself is two interlocking spheres, one Seelie and one Unseelie. The portals are the points where the inner and outer spheres align, and allow passage for someone with the right magical signature. But with the Convergence—" He rotated his hands. "Those points don't line up anymore because the inner spheres are being remade. None of the gates will function until the spell is complete and the alignment points are reestablished."

David's eyes grew round. "You mean it's like a prison. A room with no doors."

"Pretty much. My brother showed me the schematics for the new spheres—"

"Wait. You have a brother too? Does he know something about this? Is he a magician?"

Niall smiled crookedly. "Not exactly. He's the new King."

"Holy *super* freaking cats. I'll bet you dollars to Voodoo doughnuts that Gareth doesn't know *that* little tidbit."

"No. And you can't tell him. Please."

David's steps slowed. "Niall, I really think—"

"I'll tell him. I promise. But I need to find the right time."

"Oookaaay. But you have to talk to Bryce. He was dying to find out about the spell, and you've *seen* it."

They passed under an oak tree, sending a jay squawking into the sky, its raucous call like another accusation. "I know." *I just hope it's not too late.*

CHAPTER SEVENTEEN

If Bryce had been antsy on the ride down to Turner, he was ten times worse on the way back—leaning forward over the steering wheel as if he could push the car up the highway with his will alone. Gareth wished Bryce's electric car made more noise because, with only the sound of the wind and the wheels on the pavement to fill the car, their lack of conversation was pathetically obvious.

Gareth was split on his opinion of the trip. On the one hand, it had been a total waste of time—the gate in back of the Enchanted Forest had been just as nonfunctional as the one in Forest Park. On the other hand—*it's not my fault.* His use of bardic powers to shut the gate hadn't been the reason for the failure.

But now his worry for his brothers took center stage. In the way of younger brothers, he'd always viewed Alun, the eldest, as virtually omnipotent. When Alun had lost his lover, Owain, in that dreadful massacre two hundred years ago, Gareth had taken it as a betrayal: Alun wasn't all-powerful after all. He'd succumbed to the temptation of a cross-species relationship, then hadn't been strong enough to protect his partner. He and Gareth had been estranged for years because of that, and might have remained so to this day if not for David's intervention.

And Mal . . . Mal had always presented a good-time face, trying to jolly Gareth along, dragging him to his favorite Outer

World amusements. At the time, he'd resented being forced to emerge from the dark room of his grief. But it had worked eventually. If it weren't for Mal, he'd never have met Josh in New Orleans in the Thirties. Wouldn't have met Spence in Liverpool in '63. Wouldn't have found Hamish and Tiff at Woodstock.

He owed Mal for his friends, for his band, for his life in the Outer World. And he owed Alun more, because Gareth had been a total prick to him at a time Alun had most needed comfort and support.

Had he been this much of a selfish arsehole back when he and Niall first met? If so, no wonder Niall hadn't looked back. Maybe Eamon's *glamourie* had nothing to do with it.

"Bryce?"

"Hmmm?"

"I'm sorry."

Bryce shot a startled glance at him before returning his attention to the road. "Don't worry. I don't blame you for the gate anymore."

"That's not what I mean. I mean I'm sorry for being a total douchebag to you and Mal. Neither of you deserved that."

"No shit." But despite the tart rejoinder, a smile quirked Bryce's mouth. Then he sighed. "I appreciate the thought, but it's irrelevant now. This whole thing—" He waved one long-fingered hand. "I mean, I'd feel a hell of a lot better if it *was* your fault."

Gareth straightened in his seat. "You just said— I can't affect anything not within reach of my voice."

"I know. But you can see my point, can't you? If this isn't a localized problem with a localized cause—you—then it's systemic."

"Systemic?"

"All gates everywhere. The whole Faerie ecosystem. This spell is monumental. The druid council has always felt that a spell of that magnitude couldn't be adequately controlled and managed from *inside* the biosphere it was trying to manipulate. When the elder gods created Faerie, they were outside it."

"So you think . . ." Gareth swallowed, a pit opening in his belly.

"I think the whole thing is spinning out of control. Eamon and the Queen, the druid council, they all emphasized the importance of balance—between Seelie and Unseelie, high fae and lesser fae, Faerie and the Outer World. But balance is precarious. If something has thrown the spell off-kilter, if one of their calculations was incorrect, if one of the components of the spell was missing—"

"You mean me, I suppose."

"I don't *know*!" he shouted, pounding the steering wheel. "That's the problem. But if Faerie implodes, it'll throw the Outer World off too. We may not be looking at only the destruction of Faerie, the death of everyone inside—we might be looking at the destruction of everything."

Gareth stared at Bryce, appalled. "It can't be— I mean, simply removing one person from the sphere . . ."

Bryce shot a sidelong glance at him. "Not one. Two."

"You mean you think Niall—"

"What I think is that making decisions based on incomplete information is a recipe for disaster. Someone's hiding the truth. The question is: who's hiding it, and from whom?"

They pulled into Bryce's driveway, and he punched the button to open the garage door.

"So what can we do about it? If there's no way to get in, how do we find out what's happening inside?"

Bryce turned off the car but didn't make a move to open the door. "I don't know. The archdruids are getting together a sort of super circle—seven times seven—to see if they can scry what's happening. But they're hampered because druids are usually barred from Faerie."

"But you got in."

"Only because I had the cooperation of a royal. If you can't get in now, it's not likely I'd be able to get any closer to Faerie than to Reykjavik. Come on. Maybe David's heard something by now." Bryce's voice held a note of desperate hope. "Maybe they're back and we've worried for nothing."

But you don't believe that, do you?

Bryce led the way out of the garage and across a narrow grass verge to the house next door.

Gareth forced himself not to run. He'd finally gotten Niall back—who could blame him for wanting to stay close? Especially now that Niall remembered enough about their relationship to be ready to resume it.

Gareth hit the door before Bryce, his need to see Niall again outweighing manners—*it's not his house anyway; it's Alun and David's*. When he burst into the living room, David was perched on the edge of an armchair. Niall was sitting on the end of the sofa, head bowed, elbows on his knees. The tension in the air was so great that Gareth felt as if he were striding through treacle.

When Niall didn't look up—*Why won't he look at me?*—Gareth's anxiety spiked. "What's wrong? What's happened? Did you hear— Is it Alun? Mal?"

"No, no." David surged out of the chair with a quick glance at Niall. He bit his lip. Goddess, David was total shite at hiding his feelings. *Something* was definitely wrong. "That is, we don't know for sure. Did you find a gate?"

Bryce trod heavily into the room and parked himself next to the fireplace. "No. It was the same as the one in the park."

Niall dropped his head into his hands, fingers threaded through his hair. The sleeve of his borrowed henley rode up over his wrist.

The skin was smooth and unmarred.

"Niall! Goddess bless, you're healed." Gareth rushed to the sofa and dropped down next to him. He drew a tentative finger over the spot that only an hour or two ago was livid with healing tissue and scars. Niall twitched, but didn't pull away. Gareth glanced at Bryce, shamefaced. "I'm sorry I didn't give you enough credit. Thank you."

Bryce frowned, squinting at Niall from behind his glasses, his head tilted to one side. "I don't think it was my doing. There's something—"

Niall leaped up from the sofa and strode across the room. He wasn't holding his shoulders with the same tension as he had earlier, as if the touch of his clothing had been torture against his healing back. He turned to face them, but his expression was closed down.

"Yes. I'm healed. But that doesn't matter." He stared intently at Bryce. "What do you think it means, the inability to access any of the portals?"

Bryce blinked at the change in Niall's demeanor. "I . . . don't know exactly. That's what we're trying to figure out. But in the absence of any other information, we're just stabbing in the dark. Even if the Circle manages to scry into Faerie tonight, they don't have any sort of focus."

"Focus?"

Bryce ran his fingers through his hair, setting it sticking out in all directions. *Such an unlikely match for Mal, who's always so aware of how he looks to others.* "Think of it like trying to spot a specific bee in a clover field while looking through a long, narrow tube . . . when you're not even sure where the field is."

Niall nodded as if that made perfect sense. "If you had something . . . some component of the Convergence spell, would that help?"

"Help? Are you kidding? That would mean everything. But we can't even get into Faerie. How the hell can we get anything related to the spell?"

"Well, as to that . . ." Niall reached into his pocket and withdrew a small velvet bag. "I believe this is what you're looking for."

Bryce took the bag, his eyebrows bunched over the top of his glasses. "What is it?"

"He called it a binding stone. It was supposed to be presented at some point in the ceremony. I'm not even sure what point. He — He was supposed to signal me when it was time."

"'He,' huh?" Bryce opened the bag and upended it. The instant the contents dropped into his palm, his eyes widened. "This is an adder stone. A *Gloine nan Druidh.*" The stone was dead black and perfectly round. "It's been coated with something. Pitch? Something else too, but that begs the question: what the hell is one of these doing in Faerie?"

"Not one," Niall said. "Two. The Queen has the mate to it. I expect the coating was to shield it until it was time for it to be used."

Bryce's eyes narrowed. "If the Queen has the mate, it would make sense for Eamon to have this one. So why doesn't he? Is *this* what cause the spell to mutate?" He lunged for Niall, and Gareth stepped in front of him.

"Stand down, Bryce. He's been through enough."

"Out of the way, Gareth. I'm not going to hurt him." The fire in Bryce's normally mild brown eyes belied that. "But I need to know. If he stole it, if that's why he ran, he could have put Mal and Alun in danger." He clenched his fist around the stone and glared at Niall over Gareth's shoulder. "Are you taking vengeance on Eamon for kidnapping you? For torturing you?"

"Eamon didn't torture me. He saved me."

Gareth turned at the stunned outrage in Niall's voice. He put his hands on Niall's shoulders and gave him a tiny shake. "You may not remember it, Niall, but he's the one who took you. I saw him, that last night in Corwen."

Niall blinked, the anger on his face fading, replaced by . . . shame? Regret? Sorrow? It was hard to know. "You saw me go off with Eamon?"

Gareth nodded. "Yes. Even if you don't remember everything, I do. And I know you wouldn't have left me voluntarily."

Niall's gaze locked with his. "I wouldn't have. Believe that. No matter what, you have to believe that."

Hope burbled in Gareth's chest. "You remember more? You remember that night?"

Niall closed his hands around Gareth's wrists gently. His mouth quirked up in an almost smile, a ghost of his former cheeky grin. "I remember, Gareth. I remember everything."

The dawning joy in Gareth's eyes nearly stole Niall's resolve. *This is the last moment when he'll still love me.* But he fought the urge to stretch out the moment. Taking a breath, he dropped his human mask and bared his true nature.

Bryce gasped and David murmured in distress, but Niall's gaze never left Gareth's as confusion replaced joy.

"No." Gareth shook his head, his hands raising as if to ward off a blow. "You— It can't be. You're—" Hurt followed by revulsion chased across Gareth's face as he backed away until he bumped into Bryce's shoulder. "You're fae. You're *Unseelie*. You're one of *them*." He turned away, face to the wall, shoulders shaking.

Niall's chest felt as if it were packed with ice. He wanted desperately to soothe, to comfort, but he'd lost that privilege. *He might never be mine to comfort again.*

David edged away and tugged on Bryce's sleeve. "Um . . . Bryce? Can you show me that thing about the . . . the thing?"

Bryce was goggling at Niall, his gaze tracing a path in the air. *He's got druid sight. He can see my aura now.* "What?" He shook his head as if he were coming out of a trance and glanced at Gareth's back. "Oh. Right. The thing. Sure." He let David tug him out of the house, although he kept glancing over his shoulder at Niall the whole way.

Niall waited until the door closed behind them. "Not much for subtlety, your brothers-in-law, are they?" When Gareth didn't respond, Niall inched toward him, craving the touch of his hand. A glance. Even the shrug of a shoulder. *Something*. But when he tried to place his hand on Gareth's back, Gareth jerked out of reach.

"Don't touch me."

"Gareth. I'm sorry. Sorrier than you can ever imagine that I —"

He whirled, his curls writhing around his head as if the *ethera* were dancing there. "*You're* sorry? You think I can't imagine regret? Remorse? *Disgust*? Do you know what I've done in your name to my family, my Queen, my realm? All because of my poor kidnapped lover, the human victim? Do you know what I've done to *myself,* thinking I brought it on you by my attention? I know all about those things, and more. And it was all because of a lie."

"It wasn't *all* a lie. I loved you. I love you still—"

"Stop. Was this the plot all along? Just one more attempt to destroy me? First my dog, then my horse, then my groom? Then what? My virginity? My— my heart?"

Niall grimaced, tempted to fob off the question, but the time for lies was past. "In a way, but not how you think."

Gareth snorted, eyes flashing. "How *I* think? You have no idea how I think. I'm not sure I do either, because everything I've done in the past two hundred years, every action, every thought—Goddess, every *song*—has been colored by what happened to you. The memory of my perfect lover. My grief at his death—yes, I thought you'd died, either in Faerie or somewhere lost in the Outer World in some time not of your choosing, a random place and time that I had no hope of finding. *A fork in the stream and we meet. An eddy, a stone, and we part*. What a cosmic fucking joke."

"Gareth, if you'd let me explain—"

"You didn't have amnesia, did you?"

"Well. No. But I'd heard you talking to Alun, how you felt about the Unseelie. I didn't want to risk . . . to risk . . ." *This. I didn't want to risk this.* "I thought if I could just have a little more time to recover, I'd be ready to face you again. To explain—"

"Do you know . . ." Gareth advanced on him, teeth bared, "I was ready to forswear my heritage. Have Bryce sever my connection to the One Tree. Make me mortal. Because I couldn't stand to live without you forever in a kingdom half ruled by the man who'd stolen you from me, who'd brutalized you, who'd . . . who'd k-k-killed you."

Niall reached for him, this wild and vicious stranger who'd possessed his gentle lover. "Please, love, if you'd only let me—"

Gareth backed away. "They were right about you. They were right all along."

"Who was?"

"The Voices. The criminal dead." His lips twisted in a sneer. "My fucking legacy."

"You don't understand. If you'd let me—"

"No more." Gareth shook his head. "I can't— It's too much. I can't talk to you, I can't *see* you, not with two hundred years of deceit to unwind." He gripped his hair with both hands. "Goddess, I've got a concert tonight. I—" He whirled and bolted for the door.

"Gareth! Wait, please."

Gareth didn't stop, and the slam of the door behind him rattled the pictures on the wall.

Chapter Eighteen

Niall's shoulders sagged, and he dropped onto the sofa, belly roiling. "Shite." What was he supposed to do now? He should have found another way. He shouldn't have ever left Faerie in the first place. "I should have taken the crossbow bolt and ended it all there. Better for both of us."

The French doors creaked open and David peeked inside. "We saw Gareth peel out of here like his hair was on fire." He came in, Bryce behind him. "Are you okay?"

Niall slumped back on the sofa and gazed up at the two men. "I don't suppose *achubydd* can heal stupidity, can they? Or time-surf? Because I've bolluxed things up from the first moment I met him, and my decision-making isn't getting any better. It appears that when given the choice between any two options, I've always chosen the wrong one."

Well, that had been his one undeniable skill, hadn't it? To instantly see which path would lead to the maximum amount of chaos. He'd never realized he'd be one of his own victims.

Bryce advanced on him as if he were in a trance. "Eamon's brother. David told me, but I should have realized it from your aura. It's almost identical, except his had red undertones and yours are blue."

"That's because his mother was a Welsh lake maiden and mine was human."

David sat next to him and took his hand. The warmth flowing into Niall threatened to soothe his lacerated feelings. *No. I'm not worth it.* He snatched his hand away. David glared at him. "Let me guess. You don't think you deserve to feel better."

"I don't."

"That is just so . . . so *Alun*."

Bryce dropped down on Niall's other side. "Mal too. I think it's a Kendrick family failing."

David scowled. "Well, the youngest Kendrick hasn't ever suffered from that. He spent most of his life convincing his brothers they were right to feel unworthy."

"Don't." Niall rose, suddenly feeling hemmed in. Danu's tits, he'd spent two hundred years chained in a cave, but it took two men sympathizing with him to make him feel like a prisoner. "He has every right to be angry. It was a betrayal from the first. Maybe it turned into something else later, but it didn't start out as anything more than one of my gods-bedamned wagers."

"Do you mean you *planned* to abandon him?"

"Abandon him? No. I was supposed to kill him."

The two men stared at him, eyes wide and mouths identically agape. Niall nearly laughed, because two less identical bookends would be hard to find.

David recovered first. He shut his mouth, and his throat worked as he swallowed. "K-k-kill him?"

"Oh yes. It was to be my crowning achievement. Proof I wasn't a dilettante worse than any of the sycophantic courtiers, since at least they stroked my father's ego, whereas I did nothing but flaunt his authority at every turn."

"But you— I mean, I know Mal and Alun have . . . you know . . . done that. Killed people. But that was in combat. Or to carry out a sentence."

"Do you think that makes the death any more justified?"

David frowned. "I have to admit, as a nurse and I guess as an *achubydd,* I've never liked the idea. But there's at least one person I would have preferred was erased from the world, preferably before he was ever born." He shared a glance with Bryce, and they both said, "Rodric Luchullain."

"Tiarnach's esteemed colleague. Excellent choice."

"Were you a warrior too?"

"No. That's the irony. Or is irony the word I want? I was the only greater fae in the Unseelie court who'd never killed. I confined my mayhem to murdering reputations. Even during the Oak Wars, I refused to join the combat."

Bryce nodded as if he were on the same pacifist train, but David simply asked, "Why?"

"Because the people who died were never the ones who caused the conflict. They were just fae going about their business, following their instincts and nature, until the politics swept over them like a wave. Do you think the greater fae risked their precious necks in those bloody woodland skirmishes? Not likely. They sent out the cannon fodder. The lesser fae died in droves while the greater fae stood back and waited until they could indulge in their pretty swordplay."

"I thought—that is, Alun has always said that the Daoine Sidhe lived for war, which is why they're such a pain in the butt now that they don't have anything better to do."

"They may have lived for war, but not for battle. They didn't ride in on their precious steeds until the field was already littered with the bodies of the foot soldiers, the lesser fae. I wonder if the elder gods foretold that? That's why lesser fae can reproduce but the greater fae require divine intervention—or an unwilling fertile partner."

Bryce nodded. "Mal told me he wasn't born like we are. But Heilyn had offspring when we met."

"Yes. The lesser fae aren't as long-lived as the greater, but that may be because they've always been abused and sacrificed at the whim of the greater, who always seem to be the ones in power."

Bryce regarded Niall, head tilted to one side. "You know, you sound more like a revolutionary than a murderer."

"Much good it did me. The best I could do was annoy them. I hadn't any real power to effect change."

"But why kill Gareth?"

"It didn't start out that way. It was originally a way to prove that subterfuge could get better results than head bashing. During the wars, because I can pull my mother's human guise over me at any time, I could mask myself from the enemy. Infiltrate. Bring back news." He snorted. "Not that I brought back *all* of it. Just enough to try to keep our own troops from slaughter, never enough to decimate the opposing ranks. Because what choice did any of them have, Seelie or Unseelie? They had their orders to die on command."

"Not exactly a shocker," Bryce said. "War has always been harder on the front lines. That's why it's better to avoid it."

"Try telling Tiarnach that. He doesn't appreciate the subtle distinction between physical force and societal subversion. I made the mistake of challenging him."

That night, Tiarnach had been brooding at the head table in the Great Hall. The usual sycophants had been at his elbow, plying him with mead and flattery, while the rest of the court feasted with one eye on the King—because no one ever knew when he'd take it into his head to make an example of one of them for some imagined slight.

Niall avoided the feasts altogether if he could, since they were nothing but an excuse for the greater fae to lie to one another about their exploits, drink too much, and make work for the Keep staff. They'd become doubly tedious now that Tiarnach was obsessed with his ludicrous vendetta against Gareth Cynwrig. Niall arrived—late as usual, and the instant he'd swaggered into the Great Hall, Tiarnach called him out.

"You! Coward! I know what you did." Tiarnach glared from his perch on his pretentious throne-like chair. Danu's tits, did the idiot need the throne to remind him of his power? Maybe he used it to remind everyone else of his power—just as he always wore his crown. *Bastard probably wears it to bed.*

Niall spread his arms and bowed. "I admit it. I ate the last venison pie. It put up a valiant fight, but—"

"Silence! I speak of the desecration of the war spoils: your unlawful removal of my warriors' trophies."

Trophies. The last had been the head of an elderly bauchan, Gareth Cynwrig's poor groom. The sight had so distressed Peadar and the rest of the staff that Niall had removed it in the night and buried it under a rowan tree.

He forced his expression to remain bland and kept his gait even and unhurried as he trod between the long tables to stand before Tiarnach. "Surely we're not at war any longer. Isn't that what the Unification treaty was about?"

Tiarnach's jaw worked, his eyes flashing red. Niall hoped his own never did that—it was disgusting really. "As long as there are Seelie swine in Faerie, the war will never end."

"Hmmm." Niall tapped his chin. "That's not what you swore to the Seelie Queen that day in the Stone Circle."

"What I said matters not. It's how we were bred, in our bones and blood." The toadies flanking Tiarnach nodded in pompous approval, which naturally encouraged him to natter on. "Seelie and Unseelie will never mix, just as no high fae would sully his honor to pander to the lesser."

"Honor?" Niall laced his tone with astonishment, glancing around at the crowd to gauge its temper and perhaps identify a like-minded rebel or two. *Not promising, but when has that ever stopped me?* "I wasn't aware honor was one of our tenets. Surely that's the purview of the Seelie. You've mocked them often enough for it."

"You owe me fealty as your King, as your . . . father." Tiarnach hunched over his flagon. "Yet you do nothing but sow discord in my court, depriving me of one advisor after another —"

"Ask yourself what value their advice, when they could be seduced by their own avarice and ambition. I did you a favor."

"You think you can do better? You think you can rid the Queen of her bard?"

"I couldn't very well do worse than your bumbling assassins."

The smile that spread over Tiarnach's face caused the bauchan serving him to tremble and spill mead onto the tablecloth, earning it a backhanded slap from Tiarnach's currently favored courtier—what was his name? Gwin? Tionn? Niall never bothered to remember their names. He only paid attention when he wanted to remove one, and that slap had put this one in his sights. He'd ask Peadar later who it was.

Tiarnach stood. "Hear this," he boomed, quelling all other conversation in the room. "Until such time as Niall MacTiarnach rids the Seelie Queen of her bard, he is banished from this court and from Faerie." He stared at Niall, eyebrow raised. "You have your orders."

Niall nearly backed down. To accomplish the task fully in the Outer World would be difficult. Who knew whether the bard ever ventured there? But then his own smile answered his father's.

A challenge. What better way to pass the time, away from court and his father's presence. Although he'd miss his brother, Peadar, and the other staff. Worse, they'd miss him, with no champion to protect them from his father's worst excesses and the casual cruelty of the rest of the court. He'd speak to Eamon before he left, to engage his assistance—

"Leave. Now. This instant. My guards will escort you. You think yourself so clever and resourceful? See how you manage with nothing more than your so-vaunted wits."

A murmur swept through the crowd, and Niall caught the satisfied smirks on the faces of his most vicious critics. How they'd love to see him sweat, see him struggle, see him fall. He refused to give them the satisfaction. He straightened his shoulders and forced a confident grin. "I've never failed yet when I've set my sights on something. You'd best keep that in mind, Father, before you make a threat you might be hard-pressed to keep."

He turned and walked straight out of the hall, well ahead of the guards when he passed through the door.

"Master." At Peadar's whisper, Niall's stride faltered, but he recovered before the guards could notice. "Your cloak. And—" He thrust a leather pouch, heavy with gold, into Niall's hand.

Niall took the cloak, but closed Peadar's hand around the pouch. "Hold on to this."

"But, master, you will need it."

Niall gripped Peadar's shoulder and grinned down at him. "You may need it more. Besides—an adventure! I could ask for nothing better . . . although I appreciate the cloak." He flung it around his shoulders and fastened it with a copper oak leaf brooch. Take care of yourself, my friend. Go to Eamon if you need anything."

Niall clutched the edge of the mantel until his knuckles whitened, the scene still fresh in his memory. "It was ridiculously easy to track Gareth to the eisteddfod." He released his grip and faced the two men again, smiling crookedly. "His reputation was . . . shall we say . . . formidable?" *:Rock star!:*

"So you destroyed Gareth by making him fall in love with you and then leaving him?" David's eyes clouded like a storm over a lake. "Really?"

Niall shrugged. "No. I fear the joke was on me. I'd intended to find his weakness, get him to indulge it until it consumed him, just as I'd done with so many other corruptibles. But with him, I found I didn't want to. Instead, I was the one who fell." He touched a picture on the mantel, Gareth and Mal flanking David and Alun at what must have been their wedding, judging by their clothing. "My weakness, as it turns out, is Gareth."

"But he says he saw you leave with Eamon. If you didn't intend to destroy him, then why not come back?"

"Ah, but you're forgetting the terms of my banishment. I needed Eamon's help to get back into Faerie before I'd fulfilled them. I couldn't return until I'd rid the Seelie Queen of her bard."

Bryce's eyebrows shot up. "You were going to keep the letter of the order, not the spirit?"

"Got it in one, Sir Druid. The way I planned to rid the Queen of her bard was to propose that I be allowed to take him as consort. Then he'd no longer be Seelie. Or at least, not entirely."

"I take it," Bryce said, his tone dry, "that the King didn't see that as a brilliant policy decision."

"No. Not one for subtlety, my dear father. He considered it a betrayal of family, King, and court. He ordered me to kill Gareth outright. Ordered me to bring him to the Stone Circle and slit his throat on the altar." Niall closed his eyes, the horror of that notion twining thorns around his heart. "I refused. He swore I'd follow his orders—that Gareth would die and that mine would be the hand to do it. When I refused, he—well, he sentenced me to serve at the underworld forge as a slave to Govannon until I repented and carried out my task."

"Wait a minute." Bryce leaned forward, the light of a druid in pursuit of knowledge in his eyes. "When Eamon deposed the king, he took him and Rodric to the underworld. You're the one he rescued that night."

"Yes."

David frowned. "But why were your wounds so fresh? Had he . . . beaten you?"

"*He* didn't. He wouldn't sully his royal hands with any weapon less exalted than his sword. But he ordered Govannon to do it. Every year, on the anniversary of my folly, Tiarnach showed up at the forge and asked me if I'd repented. When I said no, he'd have Govannon flog me." Long habit made him curl his shoulders forward, as if anticipating the first blow.

"Later on, he'd have the flogging first and the question afterward. He wanted me to beg, you see. Beg to kill Gareth."

David was solemn. "But you didn't."

Niall glared at him in disgust. "Of course not." He scrubbed his face with both hands. "Two weeks before Eamon released me, Tiarnach told me he'd tired of waiting. After the beating, he said he'd killed Gareth himself."

"Ooohh." David's eyes shone with unshed tears. "You must have . . . wow. I don't even know how you must have felt then."

"I felt like Tiarnach was damn lucky I was still shackled to the rocks," Niall growled, "or I'd have strangled him with my own chains. Since they were forged by a god, they'd have had half a chance of doing the trick, too."

"That must have been one hell of a beating, considering the state of your back when you arrived."

"Oh. That. That was actually the accumulation of all the beatings that I've received since I last escaped into the Outer World. The underworld is a place out of time, out of space, you understand. Anything that happens there—well, it has to happen again when you leave, unless you're escorted by someone with proper authority. It's supposed to discourage prisoners from escaping."

David leaped up. "You have to tell Gareth. The whole story."

Niall retreated behind a wingback chair, in case David decided he needed comforting again. "He doesn't want to hear anything more from me. Besides, how would 'I was sent to kill you but decided to fuck you instead' go over? Doesn't make me sound like an honorable kind of man, does it?" He spread his arms and took a bow. "But I'm Unseelie. I don't know what honor is."

"Stop it. You fae are just . . . augh!" David clutched his hair. "You're so fixated on your stupid tenets, and how everyone has always followed them in the past, that you never think of how open to interpretation they are. I'm surprised your heads haven't all exploded from the contradictions."

"Well, I can't say I haven't tried to skate on the edge of them myself."

"Everybody does. They have to. But it's easier to follow other people's patterns and paths than to make one of your own. That's why fae have such a hard time with change. Personally?" David crossed his arms and stuck his nose in the air. "I think you're all just lazy."

Niall was surprised into a laugh. "You've never seen how hard the lesser fae work to keep up with the capricious orders of the courtiers."

"Not physically lazy. Actually, I think inaction is one of the problems. I mean you're all so freaking *ancient* that you can't think outside your own little box. Don't you see? You sacrificed *everything* for Gareth. Don't you think he'd appreciate that?"

"Not with the way he feels about Unseelie."

"Gah!" David grabbed his hair again. "Why are you fae so freaking *stubborn*? The reason he feels that way about Unseelie is because of *you*. Because he thinks they abducted and brutalized you." David squinted one eye, releasing the death grip on his hair. "And actually, they did. Well, one of them did, but not in the way he thinks. If you *explained* to him—"

Niall folded his arms across his chest. "And make me sound even more pathetic than I am? No, thank you. Besides, I don't want him to come to me out of gratitude or obligation or pity."

"Well, I think he has a right to know."

"No!" Abandoning the chair's dubious protection, Niall dodged around it, palms up in supplication. "Please. Don't tell him." He dropped his arms to his sides. "If we're to find our way through this, we'll have to do it with our eyes facing forward, not back."

"Weeeellll, I still think you should tell him. I mean, look what hiding information from him has gotten you so far. You think keeping this from him will make him happy?"

"I think what would make him *happy*," Niall said, baring his teeth in the mockery of a smile, "is if I disappeared again."

"You are *sooo* wrong. If there's one thing I've learned in my nurse's training—the psychology part—you can't take away someone's cause without giving them something in its place. He's been focused on you and your fate for so long—what's he going to replace that with?"

Niall looked away from the sympathy of David's gaze. "Whatever it is—whoever it is—it'll be better for him than I am. I should go."

But where? He had no home here, no clothing, no money, no acquaintances other than Gareth and his family and friends—who, when given a choice between an Unseelie con artist and the one true bard, would probably make the right choice.

:Trust us!:

Ah well. The *ethera* were on his side. But he rather doubted they could run to a stiff drink, let alone a getaway car.

David apparently reached the same conclusion because his eyebrows shot up. "Go? Where?"

"I don't know. Somewhere . . . else. So it's not awkward when Gareth comes home after the concert."

"Oh, that's not an issue. He usually gates back to LA after—d'oh! He can't. No gates. Hmmm." David screwed his mouth up, thinking. *One more person who has to solve the problem of Niall O'Tierney.*

"You can stay at my place." Bryce had been so silent in the shadows that Niall had forgotten he was there.

"Really?"

"I'd rather have you than Gareth. Besides, I have a feeling there's a hell of a lot more you can tell me about the spell, and our time is running out."

Chapter Nineteen

Gareth should have known better than to try to play while rage was banging around in his head like a fourth-rate drummer. Neither of his guitars would stay in tune during the sound check—and his instruments were *always* in tune. It was one of the perks of being a bard.

Unless the bard was so off the rails that he could barely remember a G7 chord, let alone the intricate finger-picking of most of their songs.

"Shit on a pogo stick, Gareth." Hamish threw his drumsticks on the stage. "Do we have to do this whole thing a cappella? Bad enough your guitar sounds like a panther shifter in heat—"

"Watch it, kangaroo," Tiff growled.

Hamish ignored her, which never happened. "Whatever's eating your ass is bleeding over to the rest of us. Josh's violin. Spence's rig. I mean can an electronic keyboard even *go* out of tune? Even my drums sound sour. If this is what getting laid does for you—"

"Shut the fuck up, Hamish!" Gareth hurled a cable across the stage, where it slid along the deck, causing one of the roadies to jump aside.

"Oho. So you *didn't* get laid. Shite, I thought the way you and Niall were eye-fucking each other during the show last night—"

"I said *shut the fuck up*. Goddess strike me blind, you *never* know when to quit. No wonder Tiff won't give you the time of day."

Hamish surged up off his stool as if he were about to leap over the drum kit. Given the power in his legs, it wasn't beyond possibility. Gareth bared his teeth and bunched his fists, ready for the fight—*craving* the fight. Hells, he'd have welcomed the gods-bedamned Voices if only to have someone to argue with, but they were silent. Probably off gloating in their spectral pub, the arseholes.

Someone touched Gareth's shoulder, and he whirled, fist cocked, only to meet Josh's eyes, wide with shock and hurt. Gareth didn't know whether he'd have thrown the punch at his best friend—he'd like to think he was better than that—because Spence caught his wrist.

"If it weren't for the fact we've got a show in an hour, I'd break your fucking arm," Spence growled, his eyes taking on the reddish glow of a werewolf about to shift.

Gareth met his furious gaze. "Do it." The pain in his body would be a thousand times easier to bear than the pain in his heart. It was building inside him, a vast angry sea of red, threatening to burst through the breakwater and swamp him, drown him.

"Spence." At Josh's gentle tone, Spence's eyes faded from red to brown. "It's okay."

"It's not." But Spence let go of Gareth, only to snake his arm around Josh's waist and pull him halfway across the stage, well out of Gareth's reach. "Nobody threatens you. Especially not some asshole who's supposed to be your friend. Who's supposed to be a friend to all of us. What the fuck, Gareth?"

This was worse than when Niall had left. Then, he had only his own grief for love lost. But now? He'd always imagined himself better than Gwydion, more compassionate, more *moral*. But he'd taken his grief and turned it into a bludgeon to pummel his brothers, his friends. Even his music had been warped by it.

Gareth turned away and hunched over his guitar again, trying to bring it back into tune. "Never mind. Let's just get this done."

"Done?" Hamish smacked his high hat with a clang. "I'd say we're *over*done if we can't even manage a fecking sound check."

Josh pulled away from Spence, who tried to catch him but fell back at the fiercest look Gareth had ever seen on Josh's face. He approached Gareth so warily, Gareth discovered a blue undertow of sorrow in the red sea of his anger. Josh had never been afraid of him before.

He pressed his lips together, holding in the venom, beating back the tears, and allowed Josh to take his guitar from his unresisting hands.

"Gareth, I'm not sure what's going on, but for this show, I think you're on vocals only."

"But Josh—"

Josh cut a glance at Spence, and he subsided into glowering silence. "I'll handle lead guitar. Spence can pick up rhythm with the synthesizer. We've done it before."

Hamish slumped on his stool, arms crossed. "Not for years. Shite, this show is gonna suck."

Tiff, who'd been silent, watching them all with the not-wary gaze of a hunting cat, hung her bass around her neck. "You telling me you can't handle a change in our set list, kangaroo? I thought you had more balls than that."

Hamish glanced between Spence and Gareth, and for once, he didn't goad anyone. When was Hamish ever subdued? "Bring it, kitty cat. I'm game."

"All right then." She signaled to a couple of the roadies. "Repatch the amps and strike Gareth's instruments. He's on mic alone tonight. Josh, draw up a new set list. Songs that don't depend on the violin arrangement."

Gareth let them hustle around him as he fought the urge to scream at the top of his voice. Maybe he'd channel a little early Roger Daltrey tonight. Add in a "Won't Get Fooled Again" scream. Yeah. That was it. His music. He'd use his music to channel his feelings, just as he always did.

"One thing," he said, his voice rough and scratchy. "'Lover's Reel' is off the list."

Josh met his gaze for a long minute. "Of course."

As it turned out, they should have canceled the show anyway. Josh was perfectly competent on guitar—bordering on brilliant, actually, if Gareth wanted to admit it. But he should have known better than to sing when his own emotions were running so hot and dangerous.

He was a fucking bard, for shite's sake. His voice *amplified* emotions in his audience. He prided himself on playing those emotions as precisely as any instrument, but tonight, he hadn't been able to separate his own feelings from the performance. He channeled his rage, his betrayal, his—yes, his hate—into every word, every note.

And the audience picked up on it.

Instead of dancing, fights broke out in pockets throughout the crowd. Even the ones who didn't turn on their neighbors sported angry expressions, fists punching the air when they weren't punching each other.

He'd stormed offstage at the end of the show before any of the rest of the band. They'd all been on edge too, responding to the unbridled passion in his vocals. Even the dampening effect of the electronics couldn't rob his voice of its bardic power.

He rushed down the hallway to his dressing room and slammed the door behind him. Sweat dripped down his face and soaked the back of his T-shirt. He leaned against the door, chest heaving, unable to catch his breath. This wasn't the usual postconcert adrenaline rush. This was something else. He should have felt some kind of catharsis after a release like that, but he didn't. If anything, the red swirled higher until his very gaze was tinged with it.

He stumbled forward to stare at himself in the mirror. He looked exactly as insane as he felt, his hair in sweaty clumps. He laughed mirthlessly. Niall had always loved his hair. That's why he'd never—

Fuck that. Fuck Niall. Fuck everything.

He dug in his case and pulled out a belt knife, then grabbed a hank of his hair and started sawing at it. "Fuck this. All for—" He winced as the blade caught on his hair, pulling at his scalp. "Nothing. All for nothing." He dropped the handful of curls onto the floor and grabbed another handful. "I could have been there for Alun. For his *real* grief." More curls joined the growing pile on the floor. "I could have—"

Hamish burst through the door. "I don't know what the hell that was, Kendrick, but— Jesus fuck, what are you doing?"

Gareth glanced at himself in the mirror. Half his hair was gone, leaving a ragged mess on the top and sides. "Getting a haircut."

"Yeah? Well if you're going for mullet-nouveau, I don't think it'll ever catch on. Gimme that." Hamish grabbed Gareth's arm. They grappled, Hamish *woofing* when Gareth landed an elbow in his belly. But then Hamish dug his fingers into the tendons of Gareth's wrist, and Gareth dropped the knife with a cry.

Gareth backed away as Hamish scooped the knife off the floor. "You're not going to—"

"Stab you? Get real. Although if I were you, I'd steer clear of Spence for the next little bit." He dug in his pack and pulled out a pair of shears. "Good thing for you I never travel without my scissors."

"You what? Why?"

"I'm always shaggy after a shift, so I give myself a trim. Come here."

Gareth choked on a hysterical laugh. "You think I'm going to let *you* cut my hair?"

Hamish raised an eyebrow. "A baboon with a lawn mower would do a better job than you're doing. Give over."

Gareth made himself hold still—or as still as he was able—while Hamish approached and started snipping at his mangled curls. Tremors still racked his body from time to time, and when they did, Hamish would pause.

"You need help, Gareth. Whatever happened, you need to get over it. If this is coming from me—I mean, I'm the first guy to say yes to a little fracas, right? So if I'm saying you're over the top, you know you're really *over the fucking top*. You need to come down." He tossed his scissors in his bag. "There. Not exactly *GQ* worthy, but at least you won't scare any children. Although . . ." He pawed through his bag, pulled out a knitted beanie, and tossed it at Gareth. "Here. Best not to take any chances on that."

Gareth glanced at his reflection. He didn't remember the last time his hair was this short. It was odd. Lighter. As if he'd shorn himself of part of his personality.

Maybe that's a good thing.

But he needed more. He yanked the beanie onto his head, a fuck-ton of rage still swirling in his belly. "Take me to that shifter bar."

Hamish squinted one eye at him. "If you want a drink, mate, I can hook you up with beer or whiskey. No need to go out in public. Besides, it's fight night. Crowd'll be a bit rough."

"I want to go to a bar. *That* bar. If you don't want to come with me, I'll go by myself." He shrugged into his jacket. The roadies had packed his guitar cases with the rest of the band's gear, so he had nothing but his duffel. "See you back in LA." He started for the door.

"Shite," Hamish muttered. "You realize, don't you, that we're all stuck here until you give us a Faerie ride back home?"

Gareth froze. Shite. He'd forgotten. "I—I can't. The gates are all locked for some reason."

"Outstanding. Guess we'll be cadging a ride with the roadies tonight."

"I'm not going back. Not tonight." Gareth strode toward the door, but Hamish blocked his way.

"Going back to your BIL's house?"

"Hells no." Gareth bared his teeth. "I'm going to get drunk."

"You're a bard. You can't get drunk."

"I can damn well try. If that doesn't work, I'll get hammered some other way."

"Shite on a pogo stick." Hamish ran both hands through his hair. *Wonder if mine'll stick up like that now?* "Josh'll kill me if I let anything happen to you. Come on. I'll take you to the bar as long as you give me your keys."

For about ten seconds, Gareth considered resisting. He didn't want to agree to anything tonight. Didn't want to give in. Wanted to fight against everything.

Fight the truth.

But with Hamish looming over him, he gave in. "Fine. But we're not leaving that bar until I throw a punch at *someone*."

Everything hurt. His hands. His ribs. His face.

His heart.

Hamish hadn't quit muttering under his breath since he'd hauled Gareth out of the basement of the shifter bar. How could everything hurt this much when he'd never even made it to the fight pens?

"If you hadn't blocked my punch, I could have taken that guy out."

Hamish signaled to exit the freeway. "If I hadn't blocked your punch, your other hand would be broken, and you'd have more than a black eye. That bloke was a fecking grizzly shifter, you daft twit. Next time you go off the rails, pick a fight with a bunny rabbit or a koala."

The anger that had gotten buried under pain resurfaced. "You think I can't hold my own in a fight?"

"I think you make your living with your hands and voice, and the angel face doesn't hurt. If you put those at risk, how will you pay off the medical bills?"

Gareth slumped lower in his car seat and stared out the window with the eye that wasn't swollen shut. "Don't need that. Fae heal fast, and my brother-in-law is an *achubydd*."

"Yeah? From what I've seen of your BIL, he's not a fan of flat-out stupidity. I'll bet you anything you like he'll let you stew in your own mental juice."

Unfortunately, Hamish had a point. David, while as empathetic as anyone in either the Outer World or Faerie, had little patience with foolhardiness—which he let Gareth know when he tried to sneak into the house. He'd have been more successful if Hamish hadn't been tailing him and banging into the furniture, bringing David charging out of the kitchen.

"Seriously, Gareth? A bar fight?" Fists planted on his hips, David glared at him, and though David was at least six inches shorter and many pounds lighter, Gareth cringed as he had when his playing hadn't met Gwydion's approval. Gareth's only solace was that David was alone in the house—that Niall wouldn't see his state. "Even The Who confined their untold destruction to the stage. And what's with the hat?"

Gareth tugged off the beanie, wincing at David's expression of horror. "That bad?"

"It's . . . um . . . a bit unfortunate, yes."

"What can I say? Hamish sucks as a barber."

"Honestly." David held out his hand imperiously. "Let me see your fingers."

Gareth extended his throbbing right hand. His fingers were already swollen and purpling at the knuckles. *Good thing we don't have another gig tomorrow.* He braced himself, but David's touch was gentle as he examined the damage.

"You've breaks in the neck of these two metacarpal bones, here and here." David touched the knuckles below Gareth's ring and little fingers. "Know what they call that?"

"Really fricking painful?"

"A brawler's fracture."

Hamish chuckled. "Too right."

David glared at Hamish from under his bangs. "I suppose you were right in the thick of it too. Why didn't you stop him?"

"Oi, mate. I tried. If I hadn't hauled him off that grizzly shifter, he'd have a sight more than a busted hand and a black eye."

David squinted at Gareth's chest. "Don't forget the ribs. Three of 'em."

Shite, no wonder it hurt to breathe. "Wasn't Hamish's fault."

"No? Well, I blame everyone. So I suggest you get on to wherever you need to be, Hamish, and let me fix this."

"Think you can fix his hair too?"

David raised one eyebrow. "I doubt anyone could fix that. I'm an *achubydd*, not a miracle stylist. Shoo."

Hamish clapped Gareth on the shoulder once—*ow*—and left.

David shook his head. "Honestly, Gareth. After a couple thousand years of life, I'd expect you to have more *sense*." He nodded toward dining room. "Go sit in one of the chairs, backward, and I'll see what I can do."

Gareth trudged over to a chair and arranged himself as ordered. David banged around in the cabinets for a few minutes before washing his hands and carrying a first aid kit to the table.

Gareth blinked at the kit. "Do you need that? I thought—"

"Obviously you didn't think. So I'm going to help you remember. The ribs and the hand—oh, and your hip. Don't think I missed that limp, Mister Sir. Those I'll take care of the supernatural way. But the black eye? Nope. I'll give you the same treatment I'd give any human idiot who let his temper override his intelligence. You can think about it every time you look in the mirror."

Niall would see. Niall would know.

But so what? You don't care what he thinks anymore, right?

But he'd know how much it *mattered* to Gareth. How devastating the truth was. The only thing he had left was the tattered remains of his pride.

"David, please. I don't mind the pain, but—" He swallowed against a lump in his throat. "Never mind."

David's touch, light and somehow impersonal, nevertheless sent soothing warmth through his chest and abdomen. "I know. I can see that pain too, you know. But you have to deal with it yourself—you and Niall. It's not an injury I can heal. There. Turn around now and let me see your hand."

Gareth complied, breathing a relieved sigh when David's healing touch knit the bones in his injured hand. He really hadn't been thinking, had he? Letting his hurt and anger get the better of him, so much so that he'd lashed out in a way he could never expect to win. He'd had little combat training. But in a way, he'd wanted the punishment. *For my behavior. For my naïveté. To atone for what I've done to my brothers.* So why didn't he feel better now? Maybe keeping the black eye was a good idea.

"I'm sorry."

David glanced up. "For being a dope?"

Gareth smiled wryly. "Not entirely. For making work for you."

"I don't mind that. It's what I do. And I can feel your gratitude, which means you're giving me back everything I'm sharing."

"That's not all, though. I'm sorry for how I acted, how I treated Alun all those years. What I said to Mal about Bryce. My hostility toward Bryce."

"Well, not that I disagree, but why the sudden change?"

"Because it was all for nothing. A lie. An illusion. A trick."

David released Gareth's hand, a frown puckering his forehead as he poked in the first aid kit. "Maybe you should talk to Niall before you jump to that particular conclusion."

"Why? Our whole relationship was a fraud, at least on his part."

"You need to talk to him. Seriously. Close your eye, please."

Gareth crossed his arms as David wiped some cool, astringent-smelling lotion on his face. "There's no point."

"There's *every* point. Honestly, you fae are so blasted *stubborn* sometimes. Things are not black or white, right or wrong, Seelie or Unseelie. There are shades of gray here, and more popping up all the time. I think this whole Convergence is a perfect example of how you need to adjust your world view. Be a little more flexible, for goodness' sake."

"Flexible." Gareth snorted, then winced at the twinge in his bruised flesh. "I'm not certain that word exists in the fae lexicon."

"Then put it there." David shook a couple of blue-green capsules into his palm and handed them to Gareth with a glass of water. "Here. The fae equivalent of ibuprofen."

Gareth swallowed the pills. "Where—" Did he want to know? If Niall was gone, then Gareth didn't have to face him. But where could he have gone in this place and time? Gareth had brought him here and then abandoned him.

Serves him right.

But did it? That's what fae nobles had been doing to humans for time out of mind.

Except he's not human.

Gareth had no desire to discuss their past relationship—or their nonexistent future one, for that matter—but he should at least make sure Niall had the resources to survive in the Outer World. Assuming he didn't want to return to Faerie. Assuming Faerie even existed anymore.

"Where is he?"

"I'll tell you tomorrow. In the meantime, go sleep it off, because I am so over all this freaking fae *drama*!"

CHAPTER TWENTY

As dawn pinked the sky outside, Niall stared bleary-eyed at the pages of notes on the table between him and Bryce. "I'm sorry I can't remember more. Usually my memory is better than this, but I wasn't paying much attention at the time."

"No, you've been amazingly helpful." Bryce threaded his fingers through his hair, looking as weary as Niall felt. "We've been looking at this all wrong. The druid circle's spell looks for *movement*—that's the only way to detect anything. But I forgot. In Faerie, time moves differently. Slower than the Outer World."

Niall shrugged. "Sometimes. It depends."

"On what?"

"Who knows? Faerie has its own rules and moods."

"You make it sound like a person."

"Well, it is, more or less. It's a child of the elder gods as much as the fae are, if you look at it the right way. Especially since we know its heart—the One Tree—is sort of the same as the Seelie Queen."

Bryce leaned forward, his gaze intense behind his glasses for all that his eyes were red-rimmed. "But see, that's where I think you're missing the bigger picture. I saw that the Queen was the One Tree the first time I met her, but she's not *all* of it. The Unseelie King is supposed to be its roots. It's the balance that Cassie is always after me about. Without the trunk, the branches, and the leaves, the roots have no purpose. But without the roots? The trunk will topple, and the leaves will wither for lack of nourishment."

"So—"

"So this mating was inevitable. I think the elder gods may have planned it from the first. The tree metaphor gives you something physical to relate to, and if I've learned one thing about the fae in the last few weeks, it's that they have a tough time with philosophical concepts."

Niall frowned. "Hold on. What about the tenets of both courts? Aren't those concepts?"

"No. Don't you see? They were presented to you as fixed. Concrete. Almost as physical as the One Tree. Have you—has anyone—ever *seen* an actual tree that's the One Tree?"

"I haven't. But if I wanted to, I could find it." He pressed his fist to his chest, below and to the right of his heart. "We can feel its pull, like a compass."

"So why haven't you ever tried to follow it?"

Niall frowned, bewildered. "What would be the point?"

"*That*—" Bryce jabbed a finger toward Niall "—is what I'm talking about. You never even considered asking the question, did you? The primary artifact of Faerie, and none of you has ever bothered to look for it. Because it doesn't exist. Not as a tree. It's even more of a concept than the tenets. It's an . . . an organizing principle. Not a physical thing at all."

"But you said the Queen—"

"She's the embodiment of it. She and the King—like an engine that keeps it running. But think how hard that must be. The tenets were a fail-safe, like sub-points in the grand Faerie outline. But really it's more like a parent-child relationship. I mean an actual parent-child relationship."

"You mean the Queen and King are the parents of all fae? That doesn't quite work, since fae procreation is quirky at best and nonexistent at worst."

"No. Not of the fae. Of Faerie itself."

Niall reared back in his chair. "How can the parents be enclosed in the child? That doesn't make sense."

"That's because you're thinking of it physically or biologically. This is *conceptual.* The parents are responsible for the well-being of the child, but they also have to manage it. Think about it. An infant has no organized thought patterns—it has to learn. It learns from examples and rules until it's able to make decisions on its own."

"You mean . . ." Niall's eyes widened. "The Unification. The Convergence. They're like . . . like . . ."

"Like puberty and adulthood. Faerie is maturing. Changing. Adapting. The parents—the Queen and Eamon—are guiding the maturation process. But the Queen was essentially a single parent for a long, long time. I think Faerie turned into a juvenile delinquent."

Niall could relate, since he'd been the equivalent himself. "She certainly got no help from my bloody father."

"Exactly. So the Convergence is overdue by a couple of centuries at least. The fae are like the neurons of the meta-child's brain, and it takes cooperation from all the neurons to evolve to the next level."

Niall quirked an eyebrow. "I think you're taking this metaphor a little too far."

Bryce waved a hand dismissively. "Whatever. You get my point, though, right? It wasn't until I found out about how the elder gods and the druids created the fae for . . . for convenience that I started thinking about it. Because the fae haven't been *allowed* to think about it—the only ones in Faerie who had a clue were the King and Queen, and they kept it a secret, cloaking it in freaking bogeyman stories."

"Humoring the kids," Niall murmured.

"*Protecting* the kids. Druids couldn't be trusted not to exploit the situation back then—they had to learn to police themselves. It should have been introduced gradually before, but the single mom had enough on her hands dealing with her crazy coparent —"

"Don't I know it."

"Not to mention her equally crazy boyfriend and the equivalent of a hormonal teenager."

:Drama queen!: Niall snorted.

Bryce frowned. "What?"

"Oh nothing. I get these mental text messages from the *ethera*. They just referred to Faerie as a drama queen."

"*Ethera*?"

"Like . . . like spirits, I guess you could say. The embodiment of the Outer World. They like talking to me."

"Is that why you speak in the current vernacular instead of the language of Georgian England?"

"I suppose. It might be my human mother's blood. I evolve with the Outer World as much as with Faerie."

Bryce blinked. "A child of two worlds. Holy crap. And your wounds—you say a god inflicted them?"

"Yes. Why is that making you look as if a giant lightbulb just flashed on in your head?"

Bryce leaped up and grabbed a stack of oversized charts from the breakfast bar. "Remember you said that your father didn't understand the subtlety of depriving the Queen of her bard without actually killing him?"

"Sure."

"Well I think the magician who's driving this spell has trouble with subtle interpretation too." He spread a chart on the table and pointed to some kind of colorful arcane code. "This is what we've been able to determine from the sources available to us—which we're pretty sure are the same ones that the magician is using too, since they came from the same place."

"Where's that?"

"Originally? The library at Alexandria."

Niall blinked. "The one that burned?"

"Yes. But luckily, a circle of druids had seen this first, and since their—*our*—traditions are all oral, they'd committed it to memory and it got passed down, then transcribed by a few heretic monks who were burned for their trouble in the Spanish Inquisition."

"Nobody expected that, I'll bet."

Bryce blinked at him. "Seriously? Monty Python?"

Niall smirked. "What can I say? The *ethera* are fans."

"Anyway, the spell of binding says this: 'There at the altar, at the center of all, the heart of the child of two worlds, god-touched, laid open for the good of all.'"

Niall's veins felt as if they'd been filled with ice. "I was supposed to be a sacrifice? Fionbarr was going to cut out my heart on the altar?" Did Eamon know? He'd begged for Niall's presence, had given him the token to be presented at the crucial moment. Was that so he could be overpowered by Fionbarr and slaughtered for the good of Faerie?

Would Eamon sacrifice him if he thought it was best for the realm?

"Hey hey hey." Bryce grasped his shoulder. "Don't go there, okay? Because you're not the only one who fits that bill. Not the way I see it."

Niall took a deep, shuddering breath. "I'm . . . I'm fine. Is it—Could it be Eamon? He's a child of two worlds too."

Bryce shook his head. "Not entirely, no. His mother was a fae, even if from a different branch. Besides, he hasn't been god-touched. There's only one other fae who meets both criteria."

Bryce met his gaze calmly, obviously waiting for Niall to make the connection himself—and when it happened, the ice in his veins cracked. "Gareth. He's Gwydion's pupil. God-touched. But he's not a child of two worlds."

"Since your disappearance, he has been. His life is rooted in the Outer World by choice, not by curse. We assumed he was the intended sacrifice, since we didn't know about you. If the two of you hadn't bolted, I'm convinced that one or both of you would have been gutted on the altar. And from what we can determine, that would have been entirely the wrong thing to do."

Niall jumped up, sending his chair toppling onto the floor. "'Wrong thing to do'? Is that what you call it? My brother wanting to murder me, murder Gareth, all while pretending to want me to be part of the future of Faerie?" Niall barked a laugh. "Well, I guess if my heart created the new realm, that's one way of ensuring I'd be 'part' of it."

"Niall, that's not what I mean. I don't think Eamon or the Queen had any idea about this. He showed you the plans, didn't he? He asked you to look at the spell and the schematics?"

"Yes. But maybe they weren't the real ones. Or not the complete set."

Bryce's gaze softened. "Niall. Do you really think your brother would sacrifice you? He went to a lot of trouble to rescue you."

"Yeah." Niall swallowed. "But maybe that's why. He needed an . . . ingredient for his bloody spell."

"From what you know of Eamon, would he be likely to read the arcana of the incantation? Would he understand it if he did?"

"He . . . I don't know. He's smart, but he's . . . well, upstanding and straightforward. He never expects deviousness. It's one of the reasons Tiarnach was always able to keep him in line. Eamon always expected the best from him—took him at his word." Shame swamped him, because he'd exploited that quality once himself: his brother had been the first target of Niall's pranks when they were boys. Eamon had fallen for it every time, never holding a grudge, but never learning caution either.

Niall stared at Bryce, shame banished by dawning horror. *Shite. He* still *hasn't learned*. "Someone's lying to him. But why?"

Bryce leaned forward on the table, the chart crinkling under his elbows. "We think it could be one of two reasons: either the magicians made the wrong assumptions about the nature of the spell, but expect it to deliver the desired results; or they deliberately chose the bloodier path because they *know* it will yield a different outcome."

Niall frowned. "A different outcome. What kind of a different outcome?"

"That . . . we're not quite sure of. The only thing we know for certain is that the addition of blood to the equation will not result in a peaceful and uneventful merging of the two spheres."

"What will it do?"

"We're not sure of that either. The Convergence might succeed, but not peacefully—when bloodshed initiates the event, odds are it will generate more bloodshed. The spell might be intended to create a new order of things—cement the privilege of the high fae, for instance. Eliminate certain races either by design or as a by-product of the energy needed to power the spell."

"'Eliminate'?" Niall croaked. *What a sterile fucking word for murder.* And Niall would wager another two hundred years at the forge that the Daoine Sidhe wouldn't be the ones *eliminated.* It would be the lesser fae. Peadar. Heilyn. The entire Keep staff. "Why not call it what it is? Genocide."

Bryce inclined his head. "No argument here. Aside from the humanitarian and ethical considerations of that kind of horror, targeted extinction of that sort never works. It would completely destroy Faerie, which depends on the symbiosis of the races to maintain balance. I mean, the high fae *literally* cannot take care of themselves. Do they imagine that eradicating the species they see as inferior will make their lives better? Are they that shortsighted?"

Niall snorted. "Easy answer: yes. Plus they're precisely that entitled and arrogant. The way they see it, if they want to keep or increase their influence when the spheres merge, then somebody else's influence needs to diminish." *:Zero sum!:* "Even if the ones who lose were never in the game in the first place, like the lesser fae." Niall punched his palm. "As if Eamon would allow that to happen."

Bryce traced a blue line across the paper under his elbow. "That's the other thing, though. The spell may not have been intended to retain any of the former power structures. Including Eamon, the Queen, or even the One Tree."

"You mean—they'd want to put someone else in charge? Who, for fuck's sake?"

"It could be the magicians themselves, setting up a theurocracy. But there's another possibility that came up when Mal and I helped Eamon. Someone gifted Rodric Luchullain with a silver prosthetic hand, and he was convinced he was the second coming of Nuada Airgetlám. If the magicians have found another candidate—"

"They don't need another one." Niall's belly knotted as he remembered the conversation in the throne room, which hadn't sounded like a conversation between guard and prisoner. "They've got Rodric."

Bryce went pale. "Luchullain? They can't. Eamon escorted him to the underworld himself."

"Well, he got out. Fionbarr convinced Eamon that he and Tiarnach had to be present for the Convergence. Shite." Niall let his head fall back against the wall behind him. "He needed him all right—but not for the reason we assumed. Although why they'd see him as a viable King . . ."

"You mean because he's an overly ambitious, narcissistic sociopath who craves power and doesn't care what he has to do to get it?" Bryce's tone dripped disdain. "Trust me, the magicians aren't the first shortsighted idiots to pick that kind of candidate."

"So what do we do? Can the druids cast some kind of counterspell? Use the binding stone somehow?"

"Not from out here. To send the spell into a different path, complete the Convergence without undue bloodshed, we need to *be* there, and there's no way to get in."

Niall swore under his breath. Then froze. Slowly, he straightened in his chair. "What if there were a back door?"

CHAPTER TWENTY-ONE

Gareth was still sitting at the table, staring broodingly at his third cup of coffee, when the French doors were flung open and Bryce strode in, dumping an armful of rolled-up charts and mysterious equipment on the table.

Niall lurked behind him, hovering in the doorway, head down. Gareth averted his gaze, staring at the coffee cup again.

"Nice shiner," Bryce said.

"Thanks. Sorry you weren't the one to give it to me?"

Bryce shrugged. "We're past that now."

Niall gave a low-voiced curse and crowded past Bryce's shoulder. "What happened to you?"

Gareth regarded him, forcing his face to remain impassive. "I ran into a door."

"Gareth—"

"It's none of your business, Niall."

Niall backed off, frowning, to stand in the corner of the dining room, as if he were waiting for the best opportunity to bolt. *He's so good at choosing his entrances and exits. He's the one who should have been a performer.* Oh wait. He was one. The best Gareth had ever seen.

He fooled me completely.

David bustled in from the other room, pulling on a gray blazer over a fresh dress shirt, one of his signature bow ties already in place. "Bryce? Is something the matter?"

Bryce took a giant breath, and Gareth tensed, waiting for the bad news. But although Bryce didn't smile, he didn't look overly grim either. "No. We're not sure, but we think we may know how to get into Faerie."

David's eyes widened. "Truly?" He flung himself at Bryce, hugging him around the waist. Bryce patted David awkwardly on the back. While David was as impulsively affectionate as a kitten, Gareth had noticed that Bryce seemed uncomfortable with physical contact with anyone—other than Mal presumably. *And I don't want to think about the kind of contact* they *get up to.* David stepped back, swiping a hand under his eyes. "I'm so—Wait. You said we *might* have a way? Not for certain?"

"Frankly, it's kind of a long shot." Bryce nodded at Niall. "He'll fill you in while I get the gear together."

"Gear?" David blinked. "We need gear?"

Niall stepped forward. "Gear and a good couple of hours of travel, according to Bryce."

"But . . . but I can't go. I have a session with the vampire council and if I miss it—"

This time, Bryce initiated contact, gripping David's shoulder. "It's okay. You need to stay here anyway. In case—" He swallowed. "In case they come back. Besides . . ." He let go and stepped back. "I'm just the driver. I can't make the trip any more than you could. It's a fae-only thing."

"Oh. Okay. I guess. But—"

"We need to move quickly," Niall said. "I'll tell you what I know while Bryce gets ready."

After sharing an odd glance with Niall, Bryce left.

"So," Gareth drawled. "Leaving again? Seems to be a specialty of yours." *He doesn't need my help after all.* Gareth wasn't sure if he was relieved or disappointed.

"Make up your mind, boyo. You either hate him or you don't. We vote for hate—not like he doesn't deserve it."

For once, the Voices might have a point. Unfortunately, two centuries of emotional commitment wasn't that easy to slough off.

Niall's lips quirked in an apologetic smile. "I'm sorry."

"Sorry?" Gareth had intended to keep his voice modulated, but that came out as a near shout. "If that's all you—"

"I'm *sorry,*" he said, his voice gentle, "because you have to come too."

Gareth sucked in a breath. Go back to Faerie? Face his mistakes? Face his brothers? Let them know how bloody wrong he'd been all this time? Face the Queen?

Worse, spend an unspecified amount of time with Niall? Everything else would be child's play compared to that.

"No."

Niall straightened his shoulders. "This isn't about you and me anymore, Gareth. This is about Faerie. About my brother and yours. About all Celtic fae, greater and lesser. If you're the man I've always believed you to be, you don't have a choice."

The anger shrieked through Gareth like a banshee wind. *What of the man I've always believed* you *to be? Where is* he? Gareth knew the answer: nowhere, because he'd never existed. *But, Goddess, I want him back.*

David tugged at Niall's sleeve. "So where are you going?"

"It's a place near what Bryce says is the Deschutes National Forest."

"Near Bend?" David's eyebrows bunched in confusion. "But I thought we'd determined that all the gateways are shut down."

"It's not a gateway. Precisely."

"But it leads to Faerie, right?"

"More or less."

David squinted at Niall. "More *more* or more *less*?"

Niall shrugged. "We won't know until we get there. But what other choice do we have?"

David sighed and dropped into the chair next to Gareth. "You're right. I just wish things were a little more *concrete*."

Gareth placed his hand over his brother-in-law's. "Concrete? Weren't you the one who was urging more flexibility just now?"

David scowled. "Yes, and I'm not sorry for it. But this . . . What is it exactly, Niall?"

Niall rubbed the back of his neck, not meeting their eyes. "Well . . . It's what you might call a cave. A cavern. An underground . . . thing."

Gareth sat back, arms crossed, trying very hard to keep his vow not to speak to Niall. He needn't have worried, not with David around.

"An underground thing?" David snorted. "Well, *that's* comforting. Could you be a little more specific? And maybe a little more optimistic? Lie to me, for goodness' sake. I need *something* to get me through the next few hours."

Niall sank into the chair across from David. *Still not brave enough to face me.* Which was good. Which was spectacular, because Gareth's emotions were seesawing like a bad soprano. "It's a path. To the underworld."

David goggled. "The underworld? You mean like . . . like *hell*?"

Gareth took David's hand. "The underworld is just that—under the world. It's another realm, like Faerie in a way, but it's more . . . pervasive. And fluid."

"Great. *Now* things are flexible. In *hell*." David blinked. "Wait. Is that why you always swear by 'hells' instead of just 'hell'? Because there's more than one?"

Gareth nodded. "Every culture has their own."

"Which one is true?"

Niall chuckled. "They all are."

David slid down in his chair until his head rested on the top rung of its back. "Great."

"Dafydd *bach*, the underworld—or underworlds, I suppose I should say—aren't necessarily a place of torment or punishment." Gareth caught Niall's startled jerk out of the corner of his eye, but didn't let it distract him. "They're just another place. What happens there, who lives there, what's located there, depends on the culture and mythology."

"So what do you expect to find at the end of your path, Niall?"

Niall met David's gaze somberly. "The Flaming Abyss, and the forge of Govannon. And beyond that, the stairway into the dungeons under the Unseelie Keep."

David's lips parted in a soundless O. "And the entrance to hell is in the Deschutes National Forest? Seriously? How do you know that?"

"I've been there once before, so I have an affinity for it. Bryce was able to cast a spell to pinpoint the precise spot. He'll drive us, but he can't go with us."

"Why not?" David smacked the table with both hands. "I'd think the more people to help, the better. And Bryce is a druid."

"Exactly. The problem is with the Convergence spell, and no non-fae can be inside—especially a druid."

"Why druids especially?"

"Because they helped make Faerie from the outside. They can't be inside when it's remade or they risk—"

"The balance. Yeah yeah yeah. I get it."

"That's not all." Niall shot Gareth a glance—apology? Shame? Sorrow? He couldn't tell, but there was nothing in it of Niall's old confidence. "Bryce believes that the spell hinges on me or Gareth, possibly both. And Gareth may be the only one with the power to fix it without killing us—and everyone else too."

"That does it then." David turned to Gareth and extended his palm. "Give me your hand."

"Uh ... okay." Gareth laid his hand on David's and immediately felt the warmth of *achubydd* healing surrounding his eye, soothing the throbbing flesh until it felt as good as new. Gareth touched his cheek with tentative fingers. "Thank you, *bach,* but you didn't have to do that."

"Yes I did. If you're going to hell so you can rescue my husband, the least I can do is make sure you don't feel worse *before* you go than after you get there."

Gareth stared out the window as Bryce navigated the unpaved roads through the forest, still thinking about what Niall and Bryce had told him on the way. The conclusions they'd drawn about the spell were chilling enough that Gareth had managed to put aside his own personal issues. *At least for now.*

"Are you sure this is the place?" Bryce slowed the LEAF to a stop. "Not much around here."

"I'm sure." Niall pointed out the windshield. "I can feel it, now that we're close enough."

Bryce pulled over to the side of the road and turned off the car. "Are you sure you don't want me to wait here for you?"

"No point." From where Gareth was sitting in the back seat, he could see Niall pat the pockets of the tactical vest he'd borrowed from Bryce. "Assuming we can make it into the central cavern, where the path leads down to the forge, we won't come back this way. With luck, we'll be heading on into Faerie from there."

"You've got the contact stones?"

Niall patted his chest pocket. "Right here."

"Remember, the quartz is for when you make it into the cavern. The agate—"

"If we need a pickup. I've got it."

"All right."

They all climbed out of the car. Bryce opened the hatch and handed them their ridiculous helmets with the flashlights embedded on the front. Gareth didn't want to admit that he was uneasy about the first part of the descent. The underworld—assuming they managed to get that far—wasn't the issue. It couldn't be worse than Caer Ochren after all.

But they'd be going somewhere that had never known sunlight, the weight of the earth pressing down on them. After his years in Caer Ochren, never seeing the sky, he'd developed claustrophobia.

His quarters, carelessly arranged by Arawn, had been more or less comfortable, but the damned place was constructed out of bones—the walls, the floors, the ceilings—and had no windows. No matter how many rugs he'd put down on the floor, how many hangings he'd draped on the walls, he'd still known they were there. And the Voices never let him forget.

The cave couldn't be as bad as that, surely. And at least the Voices were still silent. He halfway wished Bryce were coming with him. Hells, he halfway wished for the Voices—because he still had no desire to speak to Niall.

He followed the two of them as they picked their way across a field dotted with scrub oak. Niall stopped in the middle.

"Here."

Gareth looked around, bewildered. The field was flat, no cave in sight. "I don't see—" Niall pointed down, at a hole in the ground barely wider than his shoulders, and the hair on Gareth's neck rose along with the panic in his belly. "That?"

"It opens up once you get inside."

Gareth swallowed. "Comforting."

Bryce handed them several energy bars and a canteen each. "You have to be careful not to contaminate the ecosystems of these caves. Don't leave anything behind. Don't mar any surfaces. Don't—"

Niall slung the canteen over his shoulder. "Believe me, Bryce, we know how to take care of the environment." He lifted an eyebrow at Gareth. "After all, we're both fae."

CHAPTER TWENTY-TWO

The cave antechamber was smaller than Niall remembered. Or maybe it seemed smaller because he was sharing it with a still pissed-off bard. The anger fairly rolled off Gareth in palpable waves. The *ethera* were disturbed by it, twittering in distress without offering any intelligible remarks.

Fine. If Gareth didn't want to speak, Niall would indulge him. It was the least he could offer in return for his betrayal. If he'd been guilt-ridden over lying to Gareth when they'd met, it was nothing compared to the crushing weight of knowing what a shambles he'd made of Gareth's life by letting the deception go on.

But his vow of silence lasted perhaps ten minutes. He sighed. "We've got a long road ahead of us. Why not just pretend?"

"Pretend?" Gareth's voice was rough.

"Yes. I don't hope for lovers or, gods help me, even friends. But at least pretend that we're . . . companions, seeking a common goal. Pretend you don't hate me. You're a performer. Surely you can manage that."

"Didn't do such a good job last night."

"Is that where the black eye came from?"

"Not exactly. That was afterward. I pretty much trashed our concert. More fights broke out in the audience than in the last battle of the Oak Wars."

"Bit of an overstatement, don't you think? That battle was bloody awful."

"You weren't at the concert."

"No." Niall forced himself to keep his voice level, his gaze fixed straight ahead into the depths of the cave illuminated by his headlamp. "I wasn't." It was probably for the best. If he had been, Gareth's voice would have entranced him again, and he'd have been tempted to do something stupid like fall on his knees and beg for forgiveness.

He might still do that anyway, not that it was likely to do any good.

They reached a rough wall. Gareth stared at it. "Dead end. Now what? If we don't—"

"Shush."

"Shush? Seriously?"

Niall glanced from his study of the wall back at Gareth. "You spend the last however many hours giving me the silent treatment, and now—when I actually need the silence—you decide to pipe up?"

"I—" Gareth snapped his mouth shut and crossed his arms. "Fine."

"Thank you." Niall ran his fingers lightly over the wall, listening for a change in the *ethera*'s distressed chatter. When it came at last, he bent closer. *There*. The mark he'd scratched in the wall when he'd passed through before. He looked up, and there it was—the gap that led to the next cave, nearly hidden in the shadows of the irregular ceiling and trailing roots from plants overhead.

Gareth peered at the mark. "That's an ogham N. Like my tat—" Gareth stopped and cleared his throat. "Your initial. You've been here before."

"How else do you think I knew about it?"

"I don't know. You and Bryce are the ones who plotted this adventure. For all I know it was a druid spell, and you're just as much bound to him as Mal."

Niall shot him a disgusted glance. "For one thing, Bryce would never cheat on your brother, even with another familiar. For a second thing, what makes you think *I* would cheat on you?"

Gareth blinked. "You— When you went with Eamon . . ." He clenched his eyes shut. "He's your brother. You didn't fuck him."

"Too right. I'm not a bloody Welsh elder god. They're the ones who were all about the incest."

"That was nothing but post-Christianity propaganda, and you know it."

Niall shrugged. "Not like it was unheard of in other pantheons too. But I'm not an elder god, and I never cheated."

"You expect me to believe that? Two hundred years in the Unseelie court, and don't think we haven't heard stories about the orgies."

"If that's what you've heard, whoever made up the tale had a better imagination than a bard. The Unseelie court is about as boring as I expect the Seelie court is these days. Intrigue and one-upmanship and power plays, all for nothing. Besides, I wasn't there."

"You weren't . . . Then where were you?"

Niall didn't miss the hurt accusation in Gareth's tone, the question obvious: *If you weren't there, why weren't you with me?*

"Someplace else. Now give me a boost. We need to go up."

Gareth scowled, but braced his back against the wall and laced his fingers together. Niall placed one booted foot in Gareth's hands and pushed off with the other, managing to grasp the rough edges of the opening, thanking Bryce's forethought for the leather half-gloves. One foot in the indentation in the wall that had allowed him to descend all those years ago, and he was up and through, straining to lever himself until he could sit on the edge of the hole.

He sat for a moment, catching his breath, and looked around.

The ceiling of this cave was like a stone wave breaking overhead, the floor cobbled like a sun-baked riverbed. At the far reaches of the light, the ceiling was low enough that they'd have to crawl on hands and knees until they got to the entrance to the central cavern. Then they'd have to slither on their stomachs like a couple of tunnel snakes.

Niall's newly healed back twitched when he remembered the roof of that long stretch, covered with jagged rocks like hag's teeth. It had scraped him even rawer in his last visit. At least this time he was wearing a shirt and one of Bryce's tactical vests —although they'd have to empty the pockets. Crawling along on their bellies would be painful enough without the pressure of their lumpy supplies.

He peered down at Gareth's anxious face. "See that recess? Put your foot there and take my hand. I'll pull you up until you can grab the ledge."

Gareth clenched his jaw and nodded, then took Niall's offered hand in a strong grip. *Musician's hands.* Niall braced himself to take Gareth's weight, but Gareth had no more trouble scrambling up the wall than a mountain goat.

When he was perched on the ledge, Niall raised an eyebrow. "Impressive."

Gareth shrugged. "Hamish likes rock climbing. I go with him sometimes."

"Good to know." Niall stood and brushed off his pants, nodding toward the back of the cave. "This is phase two. We'll follow this to nearly the end, crawl through another low tunnel, then into the central cavern and down."

Niall began unloading batteries and a pocket knife and energy bars from his vest. "While we can still stand upright, better transfer all your gear." He slapped the pockets on the outside of the legs of Bryce's loaner pants. "I don't recommend having anything under your chest when you crawl through here." He glanced down at the pockets on the vest. "In fact, I'd suggest turning this around backward, except the ceiling is likely to catch on the fabric of the zippers and we'd get stuck."

"Stuck? In here?" Gareth's voice rose on the last word.

"Not here. At its lowest point, we can still get by on hands and knees. But in the next bit, it's barely the height of our bodies. The floor is sand, though, so we can dig out a bit." He might need to dig out a lot. The last time he took this route, he wasn't nearly as developed through the chest and shoulders. "I'll go first. You're smaller than I am, so if I can make it, so can you."

Gareth's eyes were wide in the light from Niall's headlamp. He clutched the pocket of his vest, where the spare batteries lay. "I—I'm not sure I can—"

"Hey hey hey." Niall gripped Gareth's shoulders. "It'll be all right. After that bit, the cavern opens up. The path is a bit narrow and the pit it circles is deep, but at least we can stand. You're not bothered by heights, are you?"

"Not heights. No. But this." He gestured to the walls around them, the ceiling so close overhead. "No escape. If our lights were to fail, we'd be in the . . . in the dark."

Gareth trembled, his headlamp wavering, and Niall couldn't help it—he took Gareth in his arms, holding him close. Gareth kept his hands fisted at his sides, not returning the embrace, but at least he didn't pull away.

"Tell me what you need to make this better," he murmured. Gareth's hair, so different with the curls gone, feathered against his cheek. "I'll do anything you want."

Gareth chuckled weakly. "Go back?"

"Well, almost anything." He pulled away so he could meet Gareth's gaze. "We have to keep going. For your brothers. For mine. We have no choice."

"I know. And Goddess knows I'm used to having my path dictated for me. But what if—"

"No what ifs. Once we're through here, we won't be in the dark entirely. We'll be able to see the flames of the Abyss. Will that help?"

Gareth shrugged. "It'll have to. Let's get it over with."

Despite his obvious fear, Gareth kept pace with Niall until they had to drop to their hands and knees and go single file. When they reached the tunnel entrance, Niall stopped and turned sideways.

"This is it."

Gareth's mouth dropped open. "You call that a *tunnel*? I'd call it a fucking mousehole."

"I'll talk to you as I go, all right? You'll know exactly what I'm seeing, what I'm doing, how far I've gone. Will that help?"

Gareth nodded, then dropped his gaze, which meant that suddenly their hands and knees were the only fully illuminated things in the cave. He raised his chin again with a gasp. "Yes." The wild way his eyes darted around the shadowed recesses of the cave belied the word.

"All right then." Niall tried to put as much reassurance in his tone as possible. "No point in hanging about, eh?"

Gareth shook his head. "None. Good . . . good luck."

Niall made himself grin, the same way he'd have done in centuries past before he embarked on one of his usual harebrained schemes. *Like falling in love with a Seelie bard.* "Not needed. I've done this before, remember?"

Niall wiggled headfirst into the tunnel. Danu's tits, had it been this shallow when he'd last passed through? *None of that. Have to reassure Gareth.* "Nothing to worry about. I'll just push the sand aside. Open the way for you to slide through, slick as you please."

He heard Gareth's laugh, echoing weirdly in the outer cave. "Are you talking about the tunnel or sex?"

"Could be both." He used his forearms to shove sand away and to the side. *Please don't let me hit rock. Please don't let me hit rock.* "Preparation. That's the key. Not that the channel won't be tight."

"How tight?"

"Tight enough to hug you." Shite, it better not be *that* tight, because those spikes on the ceiling were worse than Niall remembered, snagging on the fabric of his vest. Gareth wouldn't appreciate that. "But deep." He shoved more sand out of the way, increasing the clearance. There was one spike longer than the others, directly in his path. He remembered that one: it had gouged a bloody slash in his back.

Could he change direction? Detour around it? But if he did, there was no telling whether he'd get them lost for good.

"Niall? Are you all right?" Gareth's expressive voice couldn't disguise his panic.

"Oh yes. Fine. Just catching my breath, you know. Wouldn't want to finish too soon."

He squirmed forward another few inches and scooped sand away from under the overlong stone tooth. He eyed the clearance and scooped some more. And more. And more. It was one thing for his back to be lacerated—he was used to it. But not Gareth. "Just dealing with a . . . protuberance."

He squirmed onward, the stone scoring his back but not too badly. He could smell the distinctive scent of the Abyss now, although it had a fainter, smokier tinge than he remembered. Was it because they were so far away from it? *Think about that later.*

He emerged onto the path, panting, and scrambled around to call back through the tunnel.

"I'm out. The path is clear enough for you. Just beware of—

"The protuberance?" Gareth's voice seemed so far away. Faint. Was that fear? Niall wished they could have gone through side by side, but if wishes were granted, he'd have spent the last two centuries with Gareth.

"Exactly."

He could hear Gareth humming softly, although the melody was jerky. *Sounds like a man crawling through a twelve-inch-high tunnel on his belly.*

"Keep going, Gareth. It's not too far. I'm right here. If you—"

"Niall?"

"Yes?"

"Shut up."

"Right."

Niall stood and studied the cavern. The pit was as wide as he remembered, but the path that circled it down into the earth was narrower. He hoped Gareth was telling the truth about being inured to heights, because Niall couldn't see the bottom of the pit, not even the distant glow of the fires. He sighed. They had long trek ahead of them.

He turned, listening for Gareth's hum, but heard nothing. Terror spiked through him and he dropped to his knees next to the tunnel mouth. "Gareth? Are you all right?" No answer, and the terror spiked higher. "Gareth? Say something? Are you stuck? Can I—"

A hand thrust out of the tunnel mouth, and Niall, giddy with relief, grasped it to pull a panting Gareth free. He toppled onto his back, his head over the edge of the path, Gareth on top of him.

Gareth's eyes popped wide. "Gwydion's bollocks."

"It's all right." Niall wrapped his arms around Gareth, steadying them both, although the rocks in the path were cutting divots into his arse. He stroked Gareth's spine. "Just breathe for a moment and then crawl backward. Slowly."

Gareth clenched his eyes shut for a moment and nodded, his chest expanding in a singer's breath. Was it Niall's imagination, or was he lingering with their bodies pressed together from chest to knees—

And Niall's shoulders with nothing under them but air. *Not the best time to hope for a reconciliation.*

Gareth eased back onto his knees, then onto his arse, his back against the cavern wall. He held out a hand and helped Niall sit up.

"Well. Let's never do that again."

So much for that hope. "Sorry. I just thought you needed a little assistance—"

"I meant the caves, you twit. Now. What's next?" The ground trembled beneath their feet, and they both steadied themselves against the cavern wall. "Uh . . . is that normal?"

"We're in the fucking underworld. I don't think there's any such thing as normal."

Gareth hated being weak enough that he craved Niall's touch. *It's only because of the cave, the descent.* It couldn't be because he still craved *Niall.* Not after the lies. Not when he was a gods-bedamned Unseelie *prince.* Although when Niall had pulled him out of that tunnel, and Gareth had fallen on top of him—

Stop it.

He followed Niall down the path, keeping his eyes firmly on Niall's feet in front of him and *not* on the pit they were circling. Despite his declaration about not fearing heights, even a glimpse of that vast void turned his insides to jelly.

One step after another. That's all it takes. But he needed a distraction. He'd sworn not to talk to Niall, but it wasn't as if he had a lot of other options.

The further down they traveled, the warmer the air grew, until Gareth's hair stuck to his sweaty forehead and his shirt clung clammily to his back.

"So. You made this trip before, did you?"

Niall glanced back at him over his shoulder. "Yes. The other direction though. Trust me, going up was way harder than going down."

"Then why do it?"

Niall turned back, and his shoulders moved in a half-shrug. "Seemed like a good idea at the time."

"That's not an answer."

"It's the only one I've got." He trod closer to the edge of the path and peered over. Gareth wanted to grab him and pull him back. "I don't understand. Why are the fires so low?"

"You want them to be *hotter*?"

"It's not a question of want. It's how things ought to be. And something's wrong."

"Well we knew that."

"Something in Faerie, yes. But the underworld isn't part of the Faerie sphere, nor the Outer World. It exists outside of both. Last month the fires reached—"

"Wait." He grabbed Niall's arm. "You made this trip *last month*?"

An odd expression flitted across Niall's face. Guilt? Regret? "No. But I was in the underworld last month. Granted we're not quite at the bottom yet, but the fires are still too fucking low."

"What should—"

An eerie wail echoed through the cavern, as if some giant were mourning at the bottom of the pit. Even in the reddish light of the cavern, Gareth could see Niall blanch.

"Shite. Come on. We have to hurry."

He broke into a run, rocks skittering under his boots, and Gareth had no choice but to follow. After another three circuits of the cavern, the flames were visible below them, and sweat was running freely down Gareth's chest.

He could do nothing but pound after Niall, praying that neither one of them would slip and tumble over the edge.

Suddenly the ground leveled out, and Gareth nearly ran into Niall, who'd stopped in the middle of a sort an antechamber off the main cavern, its floor worn smooth as if from eons of foot traffic. A huge anvil stood in its center, an equally gigantic bellows lying abandoned on its side, with jumbled heaps of scrap metal lining the walls and piled in every crevice.

It dawned on Gareth where they were: the underworld forge, realm of Govannon. But where—

Niall swore and darted forward.

An enormous figure was crouched in the embers at the back of the cave, flames licking his flesh, blistering and blackening it, yet not consuming it. Why didn't he step out? Then Gareth saw the shackles at his wrists, attached to gigantic rings set in the cavern wall. Someone had bound him there and left him.

Gareth stumbled forward. "Is that—?"

"Govannon. But how . . . Shite. He doesn't deserve this. Nobody deserves this. Where is the . . ." Niall raced to the nearest pile of metal and began sorting through it, casting pieces aside to clash and clang against the stone walls.

"What are you looking for? How can I help?"

"His hammer. It's the only thing that can hope to break those chains."

"But even if we find it, can you wield it? It's bound to be proportional to him, and he's as big as a house."

"I'll find a way."

Gareth glanced around helplessly, his gaze pulled by the sight of the god huddled and groaning in the flames with chains pooled around his feet. *Wait a moment.* Gareth eyed the monstrous links, counting them, estimating their size and number.

"Niall?"

Niall didn't stop heaving metal about. "What?"

"Look at his chains."

"I have done. That's why I'm trying to find the blasted hammer."

"No, I mean *look* at them. There's plenty of play in them. He could walk out of the fire if he wanted to."

Niall tossed a broken sword aside, but instead of joining Gareth by the anvil, he strode right up to the edge of the flames.

"Govannon. Come forth."

The huge smith didn't respond, merely hung his head as flames licked along his flesh, singed his black hair, turned the manacles on his wrists molten red.

"Govannon! Who did this to you? Where are Tiar— the others who should be here?"

Finally Govannon raised his head, focusing on Niall, his eyes mirroring the flames that played sullenly around him. At the despair, the anger, the inhuman fury in those eyes, Gareth wanted to pull Niall away, back into the cavern and up to that thrice-blasted tunnel. But Niall didn't even flinch.

Gareth couldn't breathe, and not only from the sulfurous stench of the flames—and Govannon wasn't even looking at him. How could Niall bear it? And why did Niall act as if conversation with a god was nothing out of the ordinary?

"Why do you return, Niall MacTiarnach? Do you so miss your captivity that you want to resume it after only two score days?"

Two score days? Gareth tottered, steadying himself on the wall with one hand. Had Niall been here so recently? And why? He edged forward and caught Niall's arm. "Captivity? What's he talking about?"

"Nothing." Niall shook off his hand and moved closer to the flames. Goddess, even standing as far from them as possible, Gareth still felt as if he were being parboiled, but Niall hadn't broken a sweat.

"Govannon. I see the fault lines in your soul, cracking wider by the moment. You must lay down your burden of guilt over your nephew's death. Otherwise, you will shatter."

Govannon raised his head and glared at Niall, his eyes redder than the flames that surrounded him. "Mine is the hand that forged the spear, mine is the hand that threw it. My spears throw ever true, so mine is the blame."

"It was an accident."

"Does that make him any less dead, or me any less his murderer?"

"And will punishing yourself in this way bring him back?" Niall's gentle tone didn't seem to console Govannon, who turned away, hunkering down amid the flames.

"Plague me no more, Niall MacTiarnach. Leave me to face the End of Days thusly, atoning for my crime."

Niall's shoulders tensed. "End of Days? What do you mean?"

"You know. You must feel it. The trembling of the spheres as they're poised on the brink of collapse."

Niall glanced back at Gareth, but Gareth could swear his widened eyes contained guilt as well as panic. "I thought those were just ordinary tremors. Earthquakes."

"You knew they were not. If Faerie falls, the underworld will crumble. Without either, the Outer World cannot long stand." His blazing eyes seemed to sear right into Gareth's soul. "Make your own peace, before it is too late."

"Bugger that." Niall moved as if to step into the flames, but Gareth caught him.

"Are you mad? He might be able to handle the fire, but he's a god."

"He's also the one with the answers. And I don't care if he's a god, a demon, or my fucking madman of a father, he doesn't deserve this." Niall turned back to the giant figure in the flames. "Govannon, I ask you again. Come forth."

"And I tell you again, Niall MacTiarnach—no." He regarded Niall, his head canted to one side. "Any road, why would you show pity on me, after I tormented you for two hundred years?"

Two hundred years?

The words twanged in Gareth's head like a dissonant chord. He wrapped his fingers around Niall's biceps. "That's the second time he's referred to you as if you'd spent— Goddess, Niall, is *this* where you've been since you left me? Is *he* why you couldn't come back?"

"No." Niall's tone was sharp, his arm like stone under Gareth's hand. "But even if he were, would you leave him to suffer? If so, you're not the man I took you for."

CHAPTER TWENTY-THREE

Gareth's eyes went wide in the flickering amber light of the flames. "That's not what I— Please, Niall. Tell me why you stayed."

Now he wanted to hear Niall's side of the story? For a musician, Gareth's timing sucked. "We can hash it all out later, all right? For now, help me get him out." Niall scrabbled at the coil of chains with the broken sword, wishing for something with a longer handle—but Govannon had never, in all the years Niall had spent as his minion, forged a single spear. The heat traveled up the metal far too quickly, warming the hilt until Niall was forced to drop the sword with a clang against the stony cave floor. "Shite."

Gareth's forehead wrinkled in a frown. "You'll never get him out that way, not if he doesn't want to come."

Niall whirled on Gareth, the sense of urgency, of time slipping by, underlined by the now continual tremors in the stone under his feet. "Do you have a better idea?"

Gareth's mouth quirked. "Happen I do," he said, letting his accent broaden, the same way he'd done in the past when he and Niall had masqueraded as Yorkshiremen for some lark or other. He moved back until he was standing next to the anvil, motioning Niall to join him.

Niall glanced at Govannon, who was still crouched sullenly in the flames. *What do I have to lose?* He joined Gareth, who'd begun to drum a soft cadence on the anvil—nothing too loud or heavy, since the anvil wasn't the ideal drum—but a definite counterpoint to the rumbling in the ground.

Then he began to sing. Welsh words, ancient words, words that stroked Niall's spine with a longing that he found hard to resist—the desire to approach Gareth, the solace he promised, the peace at the end of the day.

Niall edged toward him, swaying to the rhythm of Gareth's fingers on the iron, to the timbre of his voice, the ache of the melody. Mesmerized, he barely registered a clink and drag of metal, the stentorian breath of the god behind him. Then Gareth's voice died away, and Niall's heart cried out at the loss.

"There," Gareth whispered.

Coming out of the music coma, Niall realized that Govannon's breath wasn't emanating from the fire anymore, but from right beside him, above him, next to Gareth, as if he too had felt the siren pull of that voice.

Of course he did. Gareth was singing to him. *I was simply caught in the fortunate undertow.*

"You." The manacles on Govannon's wrists fell away and clattered to the ground. "The only one who has ever sung that song was my brother, Gwydion."

"Not the only one. He taught it to me, because I too have brothers that I love."

Govannon laid a huge hand on Gareth's shoulder, dwarfing him. "Thank you. I had not thought to hear it again, with him vanished to the stars and me banished to the depths."

"You're welcome."

Niall watched as Govannon's flesh healed under his eyes. *Guess godly flesh is an advantage. I'll have to tell David—*

No. Regardless of whether he and Gareth were able to repair the damage to the spell, Niall had no illusions that he'd ever be welcome again in the Kendrick family. If he was lucky enough to survive the mangled Convergence—if any of them were—he'd stick to the Keep, out of Gareth's sight, out of his life. *I protected him from my father for two hundred years. I can protect him from myself for the rest of time.*

But first, he needed information. "Govannon, who chained you? I didn't think anyone had the power."

"A spell from the before-time. The magician had it, although he has no notion of what it is he does."

"The magician. You mean Fionbarr? I thought— Isn't he the architect of the Convergence spell?"

"He thinks he is. However, the working was laid before ever the Tuatha Dé set foot on the land. But he seeks to subvert it. To move backward, not forward as was intended."

"You mean Bryce was right? This is the evolution the elder gods expected? Are the lesser fae to be elevated too?"

"Elevated?" Govannon studied Niall as if he were speaking an unknown tongue. "What mean you by that? Their size is one of their advantages—they can live in burrows and bowers that larger fae cannot."

"Right. But I mean granted equal rights. Not relegated to second-class citizenship."

Govannon's bushy eyebrows drew together. "Class is a political notion, not a natural order. All fae were created to serve the gods and assist the druids in preserving balance. Greater fae are larger. Lesser fae are smaller. That is the only difference."

Niall blinked. "Wait a minute. You mean 'lesser' and 'greater' refer to *size,* not rank?"

Govannon peered down at him as if Niall were a complete idiot. "Yes. And in longevity. The smaller bodies burn energy faster and so must be replenished and replicated."

Gareth shared a wide-eyed stare with Niall. "I think the whole class hierarchy of Faerie just imploded."

"I knew it." Niall punched his palm. "I *knew* the lesser fae were more than servants and chattel. But why doesn't anyone know this?"

"The truth can be lost over the ages, or hidden, when there is advantage to be gained." Govannon sighed, stirring eddies in the dust. "Time is long, Niall MacTiarnach. When the elder gods retreated, abandoning their creation to spin on its way alone, they left the door open for change, and for corruption."

"You know . . ." Gareth took a step closer to Niall, "I've often wondered what concessions the Queen had to make to forge the Unification treaty. She was certainly willing to sacrifice *you* for its sake. I wonder if she sacrificed the fate of the lesser fae as well."

Niall thought of Tiarnach, retreating further into power-madness and paranoia over the years. Suppressing the truth was certainly to his advantage. He remembered the revolutionary murals painted by lesser fae in their Keep hallways. Maybe that was how they kept the memory alive from generation to generation, as their freedoms had slowly been eroded.

"If yon magician," Govannon said, "continues on his path, if he is able to complete his abomination of a spell, he will do more harm than he knows, subvert the true order, the true balance. To accomplish what he wants, he must power the spell with magic not his own." He eyed both of them with something like sympathy. "His first intent was to use you."

Niall's shoulders slumped. "So Bryce was right. The spell requires a god-touched fae."

"Not only god-touched, but one who had shown loyalty and steadfastness. You were his first choice." Govannon's gaze slid sideways to Gareth. "But not his only one."

Fear skated across Niall's skin. "No. If the only way we can fix this is with my sacrif—"

"You don't understand. His spell is not intended to converge the spheres and heal Faerie—it's intended to break it apart. He is a fanatic. A follower of the old ways."

"If that's so, why did he chain you in the fire? You're one of the old pantheon. For that matter, why did you *stay* in the fire when you could have walked out at any time."

"A spell. I had to be called out by one of my own." He inclined his head at Gareth. "Which the bard did, by singing my brother's words. I doubt the magician expected such a thing. As I am of Dôn, not Danu, to him, I am a false god, one to be cast aside if he is to return the Tuatha Dé to power above the ground."

"In the Outer World?" Gareth asked. "That makes no sense. Ireland isn't the same as it was back then. How does he expect to overcome modern weaponry, governments, technology."

"How else? Magic, and the ascendance of the supernatural."

Gareth frowned. "That would never work. The population of the Outer World is vast, more than he could ever hope to control."

Govannon merely looked at them with something like pity, and the other shoe dropped. "The spells last summer. The ones Bryce tried to stop, the ones that threatened the Outer World water supply. He plans to reduce the population. Return it to the levels of the ancient times."

Niall paced across the cavern and back. "But that would be a slow process. If he's intending this coup to take place now, tonight—"

"The destruction of Faerie will cause devastation across the Outer World," Govannon rumbled. "More than you can imagine. He thinks to strike two hares with one arrow—eliminate the inconvenient folk while bringing his own chosen sovereign to power."

Gareth looked up. "How do you know all this?"

Govannon narrowed his eyes, and for the first time, Niall realized what it must have been like to face him in battle. "First, the two who took your place here did not bother to hold their tongues in front of me. Second, the mage could not resist gloating, after his trick trapped me in the flames."

Niall stopped mid-pace. "There's no possible way he could have done that, I don't care how powerful a mage he is. No way —"

"Unless you allowed it," Gareth said gently. "Niall spoke of your guilt. Believe me, I know how it feels to betray a relative."

Niall cringed, remembering Gareth's words about how he'd treated his brothers, all because he'd believed Niall human and kidnapped. "I think this may be irrelevant in any case. It sounds like we can't simply waltz in and allow him to power the spell with my heart—"

"No!" Gareth's shout stopped Niall in his tracks, and for a moment, Niall believed that Gareth might still harbor some feelings for him that hadn't been tainted by his deception. "I mean, it would be counterproductive anyway."

Of course. It has nothing to do with me. "As far as we know. But what other choice do we have? Bryce said the calculations for that spell were incredibly complex. We can't just invent one on the path between here and the Stone Circle."

"You don't need a spell," Govannon said. "You have a bard. A bard trained by my brother, with all the old songs only my brother knew. And those songs can only be truly accompanied —"

"By his own harp," Gareth said, a defeated slump to his shoulders. "But I don't have the harp anymore."

Niall met Gareth's gaze. "Where is it? You had it in the Keep before the feast."

"How do you know?"

"I saw you there. I had . . ." Niall swallowed, acutely aware of Govannon's dark gaze on him. "I had only that morning found out you weren't—that Tiarnach hadn't murdered you. I wanted to talk to you, but . . ." He shrugged. "I didn't think it would go well."

Gareth's laugh was tinged with hysteria. "No. I don't imagine it would have, given the later events."

Niall forced himself to walk over and face Gareth. "I should have done it anyway. I'm sorry I didn't then. I'm sorry I didn't tell you the truth from the beginning. But—"

"But you paid for that too, Niall MacTiarnach," Govannon rumbled. "Every year, for two hundred years, you refused the King's demand that you kill the bard. Every year, you chose the lash over that betrayal. Surely if I've atoned for my sin, you have as well."

"Wait a minute." Gareth grabbed Niall's arms in a steely grip. "Do you mean to tell me your brother brought you here to—"

"No." Niall sought Gareth's eyes, willing him to understand. "You mustn't blame Eamon. He was only doing as I'd asked. When you and I were together, I had been exiled from Faerie until I completed a task. I had a brilliant notion of how to fulfill that task without . . . without—"

"Without killing me?" Gareth said gently.

Niall nodded. "But I couldn't get back into Faerie on my own. I needed Eamon's escort. He tried to intercede, as I understand, but—"

Gareth clenched his eyes shut. "Goddess, I'm an idiot." He raised shaking hands to his face. "The first time I met Eamon, he was a monster. Someone told me—was it Alun?—that he'd been cursed for disloyalty to the King."

"He tried to convince Tiarnach to listen to me. Apparently Tiarnach wasn't in the mood for conversation that day—or any day for the last two centuries. But the first thing Eamon did after deposing the King was to come here and release me. So please, don't hate him. He saved me."

"And you saved me." Gareth stepped closer. "Why didn't you tell me?"

"I'm not interested in your gratitude, Gareth. And I'm not interested in having this conversation now." Gareth jerked at the harshness of Niall's tone, but didn't push for more, thank the Goddess. "You had the harp at the feast. Where is it?"

"I hid it in the ceilidh glade in the Seelie realm. I had intended . . . I planned to sever my connection to the One Tree, to live in the Outer World as a mortal. Because I couldn't—"

Govannon stood; at his full height his head nearly brushed the jagged teeth of the rocks on the roof of the cave, although Niall knew for a fact he didn't always appear that tall. He must want to make a point. "Niall MacTiarnach is correct. This conversation must wait. For now, you must hurry before the mage adjusts his spell to drain all the lesser fae."

Niall gritted his teeth. "Right. Let's go."

"Hold on a moment." Gareth glared up at Govannon. "I have no idea what I'm supposed to do here. Can you give me a few more instructions?"

"No."

Gareth threw up his hands. "Wonderful. I could end up doing just as much damage as this rogue magician."

"You are a bard. With the harp in your hands, you will know what to do."

"And what is that, exactly?"

Govannon peered down at him, a perplexed scowl on his face. "Heal, of course."

Niall grasped Gareth's arm, but released it at his startled glance. "Sorry. I . . . ah . . . if it makes a difference, I have full confidence that you'll manage it. You've never given a performance yet that didn't reach the audience in exactly the way you intended."

"You didn't see last night's concert," Gareth muttered.

"But that proves my point; you were angry and you didn't want to be angry alone. Gareth, I may not believe in much—I've always been the fellow who's tried to prove the opposite point just out of obstinacy—but I believe in you."

Gareth glanced down, his throat working, but he nodded.

Niall nodded too. "Good. In the meantime, I intend to make sure that Tiarnach and Fionbarr and Fionbarr's candidate for the new dictatorship don't have a chance to repeat this little experiment." He strode over to the pile of scrap metal in the corner and began sorting through it. He'd seen a better attempt at a sword in here somewhere when he'd been searching for something to free Govannon with. Now where—

"Those will not do." Govannon picked up the bellows and handed them to Niall. "I will forge you another weapon. One that will strike true. One to save Faerie, not destroy it."

Niall took the bellows. "Do we have time for this?"

"Do you wish to hurry off to your own execution? With no weapon, you'll have nothing to hold off the mage while the bard weaves his spell. Would you leave him vulnerable, all for want of a little patience?"

Niall glanced at Gareth, who looked away. Was it the fires in the forge, leaping higher now that Govannon was back at his post, that washed Gareth's cheeks with red? "Of course not."

Niall took his old post and worked the bellows, falling back into the trancelike state that had allowed him to toil all day, every day, for so very long. As Govannon worked, the weapon taking shape in his hand, Niall faltered for one moment.

A spear.

The one thing the god had never forged since the day he'd killed his nephew. Perhaps he'd come to his own healing after all.

The hiss as Govannon plunged the spear point into the barrel of water next to the anvil startled Niall from his work-trance.

"That was . . . fast," Gareth said, his eyes wide.

"Was it?" Niall glanced down at the bellows in his hands, at the spear point cooling from molten gold to red to black. "I didn't notice."

"Well, it's the fastest I've ever seen, and I used to hang about in the armory and smithy in Annwn whenever I got the chance."

Govannon handed the spear to Niall. "This will find its target always. So be very certain before you cast it that you know at whom you aim."

Niall accepted it, testing its perfect balance. "Don't worry. I know who needs to die." Tiarnach, first and foremost.

Govannon closed his hand over Niall's on the spear's shaft. "I should tell you, Niall MacTiarnach. This spear will never kill one of your own blood, so if you have that thought in your head, dismiss it."

"But—"

"You should think twice and thrice about whether you wish to shed any blood yourself at all. By right, you are neither judge nor executioner. Perhaps you should leave sentence and punishment to those entitled to such duties."

Niall glared up at the god. "I'll do whatever I need to do to save my brother, the Queen, Peadar, and the rest. If the spear won't rid the worlds of Tiarnach, I'll do it with my bare hands, but I won't let him threaten Gar— anyone again."

"You cannot save the worlds with the blood of kin on your hands. It cannot be you who strikes the blow."

Govannon reached up into the dark recesses of the cave and retrieved a curved horn, strapped with gold-studded leather. Niall blinked. That hadn't been there before, nor in the years he'd spent in this very cavern—and he'd had plenty of time to study every single cranny.

Niall accepted it reverently. "This . . . this is Herne's horn." *With this, I could summon the Wild Hunt. And once on the trail, Herne and his hounds never fail to bring down their prey.*

"Yes. If you would rid the worlds of those who mean them harm, leave the punishment to him."

"I'll— Thank you." Niall wasn't sure whether he'd be able to resist ending the men who'd planned this kind of destruction, but the more options the better.

"Go now." Govannon turned his back on them, staring into the flames.

"If we go—" Niall approached him, but didn't touch him. One didn't touch a god without permission. "You won't go back into the fire, will you?"

He glanced down, his lips easing. Not quite a smile . . . rather the retreat of solemnity. "No. Besides, if you fail, I shall be destroyed quite sufficiently without any further effort on my part."

Lovely. Nothing like the rock-solid confidence of a god to send them merrily on their way.

CHAPTER TWENTY-FOUR

Gareth followed Niall to a narrow opening in the cave wall that was mostly hidden in the shadows. He glanced behind him once. Govannon wasn't much like his brother Gwydion. For one thing, he was corporeal, whereas Gwydion wasn't—or at least wasn't most of the time. He also lacked Gwydion's hubris. Never once in all the time that Gareth had been Gwydion's unwilling pupil had he ever shown the least remorse for his actions. Govannon, on the other hand, was still mourning and guilt-ridden over an accident.

Brothers. Relationship doesn't equal similarity.

Niall pointed up a narrow path, the floor cut into irregular steps. "This way. It leads to the Keep dungeons."

"How do you know? You remember it from when you were imprisoned?"

Niall glanced back at Gareth and grinned crookedly. "Was hoping we wouldn't have to go through that. But I used to sneak down here as a boy, too. Spy on Govannon through that very crack."

"You— you were a boy once?" Gareth could have kicked himself at displaying astonishment. He still wasn't sure he'd forgiven Niall for his past behavior. But two hundred years' worth of slavery—for Gareth's sake? It was difficult not to cut the man some slack for that.

"Yes. My mother was human, so I was born in the usual way. Not like you Seelie blighters, springing magically into being."

"Just because we didn't have to endure puberty doesn't mean we didn't have to learn."

"Well, puberty. Didn't miss much there. Turns out pubescent half-breed fae are as wild as a phooka on a mead spree. I don't recommend being one, or being *near* one."

Gareth chuckled, and for a while was content to follow Niall up the rough staircase in silence. But when Niall slowed down, his breath changing from even to halting, Gareth caught up with him. "What is it?"

Niall nodded, jerking his chin up ahead of them. "Look." The stairs were blocked by the body of a trow, its neck turned at an impossible angle, even for one of its kind. "Now we know why Tiarnach's guards didn't seem too concerned with actually guarding him. They weren't his guards at all."

Niall edged past the body, and Gareth followed. "Do you think the plot is more pervasive than we thought?"

"I don't know. But Eamon told me there were factions that weren't happy with the restrictions the Convergence would place on them."

"Alun said the same about the Seelie court."

"I don't know what the problem is. They can hardly run rampant in the Outer World like the old days anyway, so it's not like they're losing much."

Gareth glanced back at the body of the guard before a twist in the stairs hid it from view. "Maybe that's the point though. Maybe there are fae on both sides who actually like the idea of breaking Faerie open like an egg, regardless of any havoc it might wreak, so the Outer World can be their playground again."

"A total regime change." Niall frowned, playing his flashlight on the steps as the light of the Abyss faded and the stairs wound into darkness. "With the return of Nuada Silverhand, gods save the bloody fools."

They climbed in silence for another few minutes. "Niall?"

"Hmmm?"

"Why did you agree to leave with me? That day in the Stone Circle. You weren't going to come, were you? Already denying any memory of me. What made you change your mind?"

"Oh you know me. Game for a lark. Always was."

But even in the relative darkness, able only to see the light playing on the stone stairs and the tension in Niall's wide shoulders, Gareth could detect the lie. "That's not the real reason. Won't you tell me?"

The flashlight beam wobbled as Niall took a huge breath. "I saw Tiarnach in the woods with two guards. One of them was aiming a crossbow at your back. It was either scarper, or take the bolt myself, and I didn't fancy that. My back had enough problems."

"So you saved me. Again."

Niall's shoulders lifted in a shrug. "I'm not keeping score, Gareth, if that's what you think. You don't owe me anything."

I'm not sure that's right. I think I might owe you everything. But Gareth wasn't sure he was ready to admit that yet—at least not to Niall. He had to convince himself first—and find his own way to atone. Although he hoped it wouldn't be quite as extreme as Govannon's method.

Ahead of them, the darkness began to fade to dimness, then a shaft of torchlight pierced the gloom as they rounded the last turn in the stairs. They emerged into a narrow corridor, lined on one side with barred cells, all of them thankfully empty.

"This way." Niall led Gareth up another winding stair, and at the top, they discovered the bodies of two more trows. "Shite. Eamon won't have any subjects left at this rate." He loped forward, through an archway and into the throne room. It was empty, thank the Goddess, of either the living or dead. Niall stopped and faced him, planting the butt of the spear on the flagstones, Herne's horn bumping on his back. "I need to get to the Stone Circle as soon as possible, so I think we split up now, yes? You need to go get the harp."

A pang of worry pierced Gareth's chest. *I don't want to be parted from him. If Fionbarr is still planning to sacrifice him . . .* "I think we ought to stick together."

Niall grinned crookedly. *Don't fall for the charm. Just don't.* "As grand as that would be, love, we don't have the time." He winced. "Sorry. That slipped out."

Gareth didn't want to admit that the endearment warmed him more than the flames of the Abyss. "It's all right. But we don't know what we'll be facing. Don't you think it would be a good idea to have each other's backs?"

"Perhaps. But at the moment, I'm more concerned that nobody has Eamon's back—or your brothers' backs when it comes to it. We'll do a lot more good if we stick to the plan. The main thing here is to repair the spell—accomplish the true Convergence—and you're the only one who can do that."

Gareth nodded, still uncertain how exactly he was supposed to manage that. Govannon's confidence that he'd know what to do was hardly reassuring considering the fatalistic way he seemed to be preparing for his own destruction.

"That's the barber." Niall turned and took two steps before he stopped. "Ah, bugger it." He whirled and strode back to Gareth. "I know you may never forgive me for the past, for the deception, for being the thing that you hate—"

"You're not."

His lips quirked. "That's something, I reckon. But Gareth, you have to know—if this is the last time we're to see one another, if it all goes wrong—I never regretted the cost to myself. My time in the forge, my father's anger, I'd take it all again. It was worth it. *You* were worth it. You were the best thing in my life." He reached out and stroked Gareth's hair with a tentative finger. "I miss the curls, but you're still the most beautiful man in all the worlds to me."

Gareth closed his eyes against the want. How much of his hatred was born before he'd met Niall, and how much was the result of misunderstanding his departure?

Niall's hand fell away, and Gareth opened his eyes as Niall stepped back.

"Here." Niall unhooked the strap of Herne's horn from his shoulder and held it out. "I think you should take this. It will be much safer with you in the glade than it will with me in the Circle."

"But what if you need to blow it, to summon Herne?"

"I doubt he'd come for me." A smile glimmered in Niall's eyes. "You realize this whole conversation is a load of double entendres."

Gareth barked a laugh. "Only you would think of that now."

"Eh, what can I say? The edge of danger was always my favorite spot." He leaned forward and pressed a soft kiss high on Gareth's cheek. "Stay safe. You can do this, I have absolutely no doubt."

This time, he turned and strode across the room toward a half-height door in the corner, his borrowed sneakers squeaking against the stones. Gareth sighed. *Time to do my part, I guess.*

Gareth made his way to the Keep entry, shame scalding him when he remembered his scene with Alun the last time he was here. *So many misconceptions. So much misplaced anger.* Against Eamon, against the Queen, against his brothers. Should he have directed his anger at Niall all that time? Did he regret his time with Niall?

No. Never that. Niall had brought him to life in a way that he'd never experienced before.

Gareth pushed open the Keep door, narrowly dodging a stone that fell from the lintel. The massive gate stood ajar, hanging askew on a single hinge. Not a week since, the gate had stood tall, the door sturdy and guarded. In Faerie, those few days in the Outer World could be measured in hours, in minutes, yet this much destruction had already occurred.

Govannon had the right of it. Faerie was disintegrating around them.

He quickened his pace, a sense of urgency driving him into a near run. He was tempted to run flat out, but the road which had been smooth before was now pitted with potholes.

He hummed a marching tune to himself, then stumbled to a halt when he realized where he'd learned that particular melody. From Gwydion—he'd used it to rally the troops from Gwynedd on their march south to Dyved. *So what?* The use the music was put to wasn't the fault of the melody.

Besides, for the first time in his life, he was glad that his tutor had been an arrogant, bloodthirsty, warmongering bastard, because he needed to channel some of that single-minded conviction today.

When he burst into the empty ceilidh glade, he was more appalled than he had been by the pitted roads and deteriorating Unseelie Keep. Whereas in the past, the moss that carpeted the glade could withstand the entire host of Seelie fae dancing the night away at a quarter day feast, now his footprints crushed the browning moss, marking his trail.

When he reached the oak where he'd secreted the harp, he was half-afraid to pick it up, considering he'd all but forsworn it when he'd left it here. But when he lifted it from its case, the strings sang briefly, a soft chime of welcome, as the instrument fitted into his hands as if he'd been born to play it. *As perhaps I was.*

He and his brothers had never asked why Arawn had chosen to have them spawned. Perhaps this was part of the tapestry woven by the elder gods all those years ago.

He stood, cradling the harp in one arm. *Now comes the hard part.* Maybe in the few minutes it would take him to reach the Stone Circle, the elder gods would get off their collective duffs and give him a fucking clue about what to do.

CHAPTER TWENTY-FIVE

Moving through the underbrush silently was not an easy task. Luckily, Niall's ability to move stealthily—a requirement in his days as a free trader—hadn't deserted him. He crept through the trees until he was directly behind the northernmost menhir, with a clear view of the altar. Fionbarr was standing atop it, as if he hadn't moved in all the time Niall and Gareth had been gone—and perhaps he hadn't. Time moved differently here, so their few days in the Outer World might have been mere minutes to the throng on the plateau.

Keeping low, Niall slipped out of the trees and threaded his way through a knot of lesser fae.

"Highness." The feeble croak stopped him. He looked down. Peadar was huddled on the ground amid a cluster of the other Keep staff. Heilyn lay unconscious next to him along with three of the bauchan's young. Shite, were they still breathing?

Niall dropped to his knees. "Peadar. What's going on?"

"Bad things, Highness. Very bad."

"Where's Eamon? The Queen?"

Peadar pointed one shaking finger. "Yonder. The mage, he did something. Looked for you, he did, but you weren't there. Turned to us, asking no leave."

Niall scanned the lesser fae. Nearly every third one was crumpled unconscious. *The bloody bastard's draining them. "Magic not his own" my arse. Not on my watch.* "Hold on, my friend. I'll fix this."

"You can't, Highness."

Niall forced himself to grin in his old insouciant manner—although considering how the blood was pounding in his temples with the rage surging through him, he wasn't sure how reassuring it was. He gently disengaging Peadar's hold. "Would you like to place a little wager on that?"

Niall motioned to a nearby duergar. It wasn't one that he'd drunk with, but that didn't matter—a debt owed by one was a debt owed by all. "You know who I am?" he murmured.

"Aye. The iron-bellied prince."

"I'm calling in my favor. You and your lot protect Peadar and the others there, and I'll call us square."

The duergar nodded and gestured to his mates as Niall picked his way through the huddled crowd until he reached the barrier. Here, he could see what the altar had hidden from him before: Eamon, sitting with his back against one of the inner ring of bluestones, with the Queen sprawled across his lap, her eyes closed and her face as pale as new snow.

The Kendrick brothers stood guard in front of them. *Thank the Goddess Eamon has the support of men of integrity.* But what could the two of them do against the rest of the host assembled inside the Circle? Seelie and Unseelie both shifted with unease, as if they were trying to decide which side to take, which path would gain them the most advantage.

One of the binding stones lay on the altar next to Fionbarr's feet. Its outer coating was gone and it pulsed with malevolent life. Fionbarr glared at Eamon. "I tell you again, Eamon MacTiarnach. Give me the stone."

Eamon cradled the Queen closer to his chest, and Niall could see that her fingers were no longer as white as her face, but brown and mottled, like the bark of a tree. "No."

"Then you give me no choice." He gestured to Rodric. "Take it."

Rodric Luchullain swaggered to the front of the altar, flexing his silver hand, and though it didn't seem to be very mobile, it sparked like captive lightning. "With pleasure."

Niall strode forward, breaching the barrier. "Hold up. I believe you were looking for me."

"Niall, no!" Eamon cried, "Run!"

"I've tried that, and it didn't turn out so well. But it looks like this party isn't turning out as you'd planned either. For instance, I don't recall Tiarnach being invited, nor Rodric Luchullain either." Niall took a stance next to Mal Kendrick, adding another body between Fionbarr and Eamon. "As I recall, they were supposed to be confined to the dungeons. How is it that they managed to escape, Fionbarr?"

The magician looked down his nose. "I don't answer to you."

"Who do you answer to then? This blighter," Niall pointed to Rodric, "who's failed to usurp two other thrones? You really think he's up to the task of taking on another? How many times does he need to prove he's not able to—"

"Jack himself off in a sack," Mal muttered.

Niall grinned at him. "I think I like you."

"Can't say the feeling's mutual, *Niall*," Mal growled out of the corner of his mouth. "Because seriously, why aren't you dead? For that matter, why aren't you *human*?"

"Long story."

"When we've gotten rid of this blighter, I may take care of the death matter myself, to pay you back for breaking my brother's heart."

"You'll have to get in line for that," Alun said. Although he didn't take his attention off the group by the altar, his voice held more menace than a troop of redcaps.

"Let's table that discussion, shall we?" Despite the Kendricks' hostility, Niall still felt safer at their sides than with anyone else in the inner Circle. "Fionbarr, we need to talk."

"I have no desire to match wits with you, Niall MacTiarnach."

Mal gaped at him. "Niall *MacTiarnach*? You're a bloody Unseelie *prince*?"

"Not really the most pressing issue now, is it?"

"I'm going to kill you twice, you bloody liar."

"I'll put it on my dance card, which is getting quite full of people who want to do other things with me than dance. Take Fionbarr, here. Why don't you tell our lovely friends what you intended for me, eh? Not much point in hiding it anymore, this being past the eleventh hour and all."

Fionbarr's lips twisted in an evil smile. "You sound as if you don't need the information."

"I don't. But Eamon does. So do the other fae who'll be affected by your little world-building plans. The humans might have a stake in it too, but I note none of them have been invited to share their opinion."

"Their opinion doesn't matter. It's the dawn of a new age—the return to the golden age of the Tuatha Dé."

"Fuck me backward," Mal muttered. "Not this again."

"What—" Eamon glanced between Niall and Mal. "Niall?"

"I'm afraid your pet mage doesn't have your best interests at heart." Niall replied. He glared at the nobles. Some of them looked as bewildered as Eamon, but others clearly knew Fionbarr's plan. "He's not offering you the freedom you imagine, you know. Didn't you hear him? He wants the pure-blood Tuatha Dé to rule. How many of you can count yourselves among that number?"

"I do," Rodric shouted. "All the Daoine Sidhe do."

"So you'll be the overlords, then?"

Rodric glared at Niall. "I'm not some paltry *overlord*. I am the rightful king, as this proves." He thrust his silver hand in the air.

"All that proves," Mal said, "is that you're a traitorous wanker who's just as likely to electrocute his own dick as piss into the wind."

Alun didn't take his eyes off the group by the altar. "Mal—"

"Aw, don't make me stand down, Alun."

"No. You should be precise, however. Rodric Luchullain is an irredeemable, narcissistic sociopath and mass murderer. He's racist, classist, and motivated entirely by his own self-aggrandizement. Those who imagine anything different are only fooling themselves."

Despite the gravity of the situation, Niall grinned. "Well, damn, Lord Cynwrig. Tell us how you really feel."

Alun's sword point dipped toward Fionbarr. "That includes you, Fionbarr. He's not Nuada Airgetlám, so don't expect him to behave in any way honorably."

Tiarnach scuttled forward and clutched the hem of Fionbarr's robe in one clawlike hand. "You promised to return my crown."

Fionbarr glanced down. "No. I promised to crown the true king, not an incompetent half-Fomorian tyrant." He raised his hands palms out, and a collective moan rose from the lesser fae.

"Enough!" Niall called. He caught a movement in the trees outside the ring of menhirs, a flash of a pale face under honey-gold hair. *Gareth.* He edged toward where Eamon was sitting. As he'd hoped, Fionbarr's adjusted his stance to face him, away from where Gareth lurked. "I propose a bargain, Fionbarr."

"A bargain?" Fionbarr scoffed. "With you? I'm not such a fool. Besides, I need not parley with you. I hold all the cards in this hand."

Niall pulled the velvet bag out of his pocket. "But you don't have the other binding stone."

"Niall, no!" Eamon cried.

Fionbarr's eyes blazed. "Luchullain! Seize it!"

Rodric barreled toward him, but Niall upended the bag, showing that it was empty. "Ah ah ah. Call off your goon or you'll never have it—and besides, that's not how you want me to end, now, is it?"

"Stand down," Fionbarr ordered. "Where's the stone?"

"Oh no. I'm not stupid enough to turn it over without a few guarantees." Niall hoped Gareth was ready, because he was about to play his last card. "I'll give you the stone, but only if you let them all go. The lesser fae. Eamon and the Queen. All of them."

Fionbarr sneered. "If you know so much, you know why I'll not do any such thing."

"You only needed them because you didn't have me. Well, I'm here now. If it takes my heart's blood to save Faerie—" He ripped his shirt open from collar to hem. "—then take it."

CHAPTER TWENTY-SIX

Goddess, Niall, what are you doing? Gareth crouched in the trees, frozen, as Rodric Luchullain grabbed Niall's arm and towed him toward the altar where Fionbarr was gloating, brandishing his fucking enormous knife. The crowd outside the Circle, all lesser fae or nonhumanoid Unseelie, muttered and keened in distress.

Think, think. He needed a diversion, something to disrupt the ceremony, distract Fionbarr, until he could figure out what he was *really* supposed to do.

He was a bard, damn it, not a soldier or a mage. He knew nothing about strategy or tactics or monumental magic.

But I know how to sway an audience.

The throng of fae gathered for the ceremony wasn't any bigger than the crowd at a Hunter's Moon concert. But they weren't properly contained in a circle, damn it, so he couldn't make them dance.

If I can't make them dance, could I get them all to sing? Their combined voices would make one hell of a distraction. A song, a simple song, one that they all knew. An old song, too, one that called to the heart of Faerie.

The first song. An ode to change, to growth, to rebirth. To the joy of song itself.

He began to sing the Middle English version, since for many, that had been the last time they'd visited the Outer World.

Svmer is icumen in
Lhude sing cuccu
Groweþ sed
and bloweþ med
and springþ þe wde nu
Sing cuccu

The song spread in a ripple through the fae on the outside of the Circle: trows and duergar picked it up, a bass line and rhythm as solid as anything Tiff or Hamish could lay down. The brownies and bauchan followed Gareth's lead on the round, with dryads, bwci, wights, and redcaps joining in. He caught the echo of it from the lake at the foot of the tor, the river that wound through the woods: glaistig, nuckalavee, kelpies.

Inside the Circle, Rodric gestured wildly at Fionbarr, his face contorted in rage and his mouth moving, although his words were drowned by the wall of sound rising from the throats of nearly all the fae present. Fionbarr raised his hands, but he could do nothing against a true bard and the combined fae chorus.

Then Niall took up the song in his strong baritone, despite being restrained by Rodric. *I'd recognize his voice anywhere.* That booming bass must be Eamon. *Niall's brother. Not my enemy.*

The power rose around them, *from* them, an almost palpable presence on the plateau. Gareth knew, beyond any doubt, that with Gwydion's harp, he could harness that power and do anything with it—including stopping Rodric's heart and sending Fionbarr to the flames of the Abyss where he'd chained Govannon. *Anything at all.*

"Go on, boyo. Do it. Just like Gwydion did. Take what you want."

This isn't about what I want. Gareth had to concentrate to sing while arguing with the Voices.

"Then what Niall wants. What your brothers want. An end to Rodric Luchullain and no questions asked. An end to all of them—the Unseelie."

This is not about me. There's no longer a 'them,' no matter what you want me to believe. The only 'them' I want to end is you.

So Gareth did it—he harnessed the merest tendril of the combined power and nipped the connection at the root.

He couldn't be sure, but for a single instant, as they dispersed into nothing, he thought he detected relief from the Voices who'd done nothing but torment him for most of his life. *They were trapped too—without Annwn, without Caer Ochren and their bones, they had no anchor but me.* He peered up through the rustling leaves. *Be free. Be at peace. But be gone.*

He glanced down at the harp. *This isn't* my *battle. It's* ours. Remaking Faerie didn't depend on the power and desires of any one person, fae or human. Remaking Faerie needed them all, working together as one.

So he set down the harp. And altered the lyrics:

Seelie and Unseelie all
I sing with you
With all speed
In word and deed
We'll Faerie make anew
As our home too

Not his finest poetry, but this wasn't the time for cleverness and plays on words. Simple and direct, accessible and singable by all, it fit the tune and fit the spell. The fae nearest to him picked it up, and it spread more quickly than the original round. Miraculously, despite the sheer numbers, the variations in physiology and musicality, no one sang out of tune, their counterpoint precise.

And Faerie answered.

The ground trembled, the stones spoke as the spheres aligned, moving under his feet. Around him, the trees reached up, branches no longer drooping, leaves uncurling.

And inside himself, Gareth felt his aspects becoming one—the self who hated how he'd been trained with the self who loved music so much he couldn't count the cost; the self who demanded strict adherence to the rules with the self who could compromise and forgive.

Inside the Circle, a deafening *crack* reverberated through the air. When Gareth finally shook off the residual euphoria of the song enough to be aware of his surroundings, Mal was holding Fionbarr at swordpoint, and Rodric lay on the ground at the foot of the shattered altar, Alun looming over him. Gareth frantically searched for Niall. *There.* He had Tiarnach backed against one of the trilithons, Govannon's spear at his throat.

"Niall! Don't!" Gareth shouted, but his voice was lost in the deafening cheer from a pack of trows.

The spear might not kill Tiarnach, but if Niall spilled his kin's blood in the Circle, with the spear that Govannon himself had warned him not to use for that purpose—

Gareth sprinted for the Circle, all the fae, Seelie and Unseelie, making way for him with obeisance he didn't deserve. *You did it—all of you did this yourselves.* As Gareth sped by, he noticed Eamon urging the Queen to her feet.

"Niall, stop," he panted as he fetched up next to the remains of the altar. "You can't do this!"

Niall's gaze never wavered from his father's terrified face. "Why not? If it weren't for him—"

Gareth placed his hand over Niall's on the spear shaft. "If it weren't for him, we might never have met."

"For that, I could almost forgive him. But he told me you were—" Niall's throat closed up with remembered grief. "He told me you were dead."

Gareth chuckled, a sound so incongruous in this setting that Niall tore his gaze away from Tiarnach's wild-eyed face. "He's not the only one inside this circle who's bent the truth for his own purposes."

Niall's belly plummeted to his feet. After all this, if Gareth wasn't ready to forgive him ... "I thought ... in the throne room, when we—" He stepped away from Tiarnach, letting the spear point fall. "Never mind. It's all right." No it wasn't. It would never be all right, not if Gareth wouldn't forgive him. "I'm sure Eamon can find enough to keep me busy in the Keep for another couple of centuries so I won't bother you—"

"Hey." Gareth closed his fingers on the back of Niall's neck. "I'm counting on you bothering me frequently, from now until the End of Days."

"You mean . . ." Niall faced Gareth, not caring when Tiarnach scuttled away. "You forgive me?"

Gareth nodded, his fingers trailing from Niall's neck, across his jaw, to brush his lips. "Yes."

"You might," Mal growled from his spot in front of the altar's remains, "but I'm not sure I can, nor Alun either. You suffered through *all* the bloody hells after he—"

"Enough, Mal." Gareth cast one quelling look over his shoulder. "It's time for you and Alun to let me fight my own battles."

"Gareth—"

"I agree that brothers should stand together, and if I need your help, I'll ask for it. But for this . . ." He held Niall's gaze, and Niall's breath stalled. "I'm good."

"Niall." Eamon's panicked voice cut through Niall's preoccupation with Gareth's eyes. "Something's wrong. Caitrìona—she's not recovering."

Niall grabbed Gareth's hand—he wasn't about to let him go now—and hurried to where Eamon was still kneeling on the ground, the unconscious Queen cradled against his chest. Her fingers had transformed completely into leafing twigs, and only her neck and face were still pale-skinned, although the bark-like mottling was creeping up her throat as they watched.

Niall dropped down next to Eamon, Gareth at his side. "But the Convergence is complete. Everyone in Faerie must be able to feel it." The surge and sparkle of renewed energy was intoxicating—witness the chain of trow snaking around the outskirts of the plateau, pulling random fae of all races into their earth-shaking line dance, the words of Gareth's song still on their lips.

Gareth's song. His grip tightened on Gareth's fingers, and he brought their joined hands to his chest. "You can do it. You can restore her if you sing."

Gareth shook his head. "If the combined will of the fae couldn't—"

"I don't mean the Convergence song." He kissed Gareth's knuckles. "I mean the songs you sang to heal me in the Outer World."

"I—" Wide-eyed, Gareth's gaze bounced from Niall to his brothers, then to Eamon, who nodded. "All right." He choked on a half-laugh. "Maybe I was too hasty setting aside the harp."

"You don't need the harp." Niall kissed Gareth's lips softly. "Only your voice—and your heart."

Gareth closed his eyes for a moment, then released Niall's hand to take the Queen's. He started to hum, and Niall recognized the same song about talking to the trees that Gareth had sung on their first abortive attempt to reenter Faerie. But then he changed to a minor key and began to sing in Welsh.

Goddess bless, the *power* in that voice. It swirled in the air around them until Niall could swear it was corporeal, something he could reach out and twine around his fingers. It invaded his chest, filling him with a wild golden joy, lifting his heart until he was convinced he could do anything. But while every fae inside the Circle swayed in time, and even the raucous line dance outside the Circle changed its rhythm, bark crept another inch up Caitrìona's throat.

Gareth broke off. "I can't—"

"Bollocks," Mal said. "You can do anything. I watched you heal your own hand when— Ah, *shite*."

Gareth blinked at Mal, the muscles in his jaw bunching. "You saw that? *You* told Arawn I was a bard?"

Mal nodded miserably. "I'm sorry. I only wanted to keep you safe."

"When will you and Alun realize I can take care of—" Gareth carded his fingers through his hair. "Never mind. It's all right. From what I've learned lately, it was all part of the elder gods' plan. How else could I have led the chorus today? But . . ." He glanced at the Queen. "I can't reach her. There's something canceling out my voice—like a harmonic that's wrapped her in some kind of shell."

"Not a harmonic. A pulse." Niall leaped to his feet and strode over to where Mal was looming over Fionbarr. "It's the binding stone, isn't it? This is your doing."

Fionbarr bared his teeth, seeming unconcerned about Mal's sword at his jugular. "Yours too. If you'd taken responsibility for once in your life, sacrificed for the good of all—"

"Good of all?" Niall grabbed the front of Fionbarr's pretentious robes. "Don't you mean the good of *you*? And it looks like I wasn't the only sacrifice you'd planned. Stop the spell."

Fionbarr glared at Niall. "Why should I? Magic has its own momentum, and since you and your histrionics blocked the second half of the binding, you'll need to live with the consequences." He glanced toward the Queen, a sly smile on his face. "Although you might want to move her to a more convenient location. Once she takes root, there's no going back."

Niall let go of Fionbarr and spun to face the Kendricks. "We have to find the stone and neutralize it."

Mal eyed the pile of rubble that used to be the altar. "How do you propose we do that?"

Niall dropped to his knees. "We dig." Gareth started to rise, but Niall motioned him to stay put. "Not you, love. Keep singing. Leave the stone to us." Niall began to sort through the debris.

Fionbarr cackled. "What do you imagine you can do, even if you find it? It's beyond any fae intervention now, even mine."

"We'll see about that," Niall muttered. But Danu's tits, the altar had been huge. It would take hours, maybe days, to unearth the tiny stone. He'd need an army of—

"Master?" Peadar touched Niall's elbow. "If you will permit?"

Niall's eyes widened at the flock of lesser fae at Peadar's back. "You're all right? All of you?"

"Yes, Highness. And willing to serve our true Queen and King."

"Then let's do this."

Peadar beckoned to his fellows, and the lesser fae moved forward in orderly rows, each carefully taking a single piece of the shattered altar, then moving aside for the next rank. Even though their burdens were small, there were so many of them that the pile diminished amazingly fast.

They'd cleared only a quarter of it before a brownie cried out, backing away and pointing to the sullen glow of the binding stone. Niall reached out to take it.

"Don't touch that!" Mal barked. "It's a bloody Druid's Glass. If it can turn the Queen into a tree, who knows what it'll do to you?"

Niall rounded on him. "How are we supposed to neutralize it if we can't even touch it?"

"*You* can't touch it. But a druid can."

"In case you hadn't noticed, we don't have a druid in attendance, so unless you've got one in your pocket—"

"It happens I do." Mal sheathed his sword. "Bryce."

"Bryce isn't here."

"No." Mal pressed his fist to his chest, over his fae center. "But he's here. And that'll do." He caught the attention of a nearby Daoine Sidhe and pointed to Fionbarr. "Watch this blighter, would you?" He joined Niall, staring down at the stone. "Being a druid's familiar isn't a one-way street, boyo. I get as much out of it as I give."

Niall cast a harried glance at Gareth, who was still crooning over the Queen. The bark had grown halfway up her throat. Alun had joined Eamon, his muscles bunching as he held the Queen's legs away from the ground. *Oak and bloody thorn.* Her feet were throwing out shoots, attempting to root—*through Alun's thighs.* "Then you'd better *get* as much as you can—right bloody now."

Mal's eyes popped wide. "Shite. Alun—"

"Don't worry about me," Alun said between clenched teeth. "I can handle pain. But hurry. If the bark covers her mouth and nose—"

"Right." Mal flexed his hands. "We need to geld this bloody thing somehow. If I had the least fecking clue—"

"Pitch," Niall said, earning a what-the-blazes-do-you-know-about-it glare from Mal. "Bryce said the other stone was coated in it."

"Grand. You happen to have a bit of that in *your* pocket?"

"No, wise arse, but a forest-dwelling fae could fetch it instantly. A dryad or a—"

"Master?" Heilyn popped up at Mal's elbow, their children clinging to their shoulders.

"Bauchan." Niall saluted Heilyn, who bobbed their head in response.

They held out a palm, offering Mal a ball of black goo that smelled strongly of tar and pine. "Will this answer?"

Mal shook his head with a low chuckle. "Always on the spot with the necessities, you are. Brilliant, mate. Thanks."

Score one point in his favor—he's not an arsehole to the lesser fae.

Stooping, Mal used the sticky pitch to pick up the binding stone, then shoved the stone into the center of the ball with a twig. As soon as the stone was completely encased, he accepted a maple leaf from Heilyn, wrapped it up, and stowed it in his belt pouch. Niall shivered—he wouldn't want the miserable thing that close to his own bollocks, not after it had been activated. Apparently Mal was made of sterner stuff.

Behind them, Eamon cried out and Alun uttered a muffled curse. *Ah, shite. Were they too late*? Niall turned, fully expecting to see his brother bowed in grief, but instead, Eamon's smile was as bright as a new day—echoed as it was by the Queen's. She was conscious again, and though she was still decidedly tree-ish, the bark was receding, her fingers once more pale and graceful, her feet no longer attempting to burrow into the earth through Alun Kendrick's flesh.

Gareth continued to sing, his voice rising in strength and volume, and the Queen's recovery accelerated until she was fully fae again.

Eamon clutched her to his chest and buried his face in her hair. She raised a barely trembling hand to his cheek, and it was as if every fae on the plateau held their breaths as Gareth's final note died away.

"Damn," Mal murmured. "I still can't get over it. Her Majesty in love. You'd never have caught her petting Rodric Luchullain that way. She—*shite*." He tensed, scanning the fae who were clustered around Eamon and the Queen. "Rodric. He's scarpered. Alun, how could you—"

Alun stood, wincing, blood staining his breeches. *Good thing his husband is an* achubydd. "I had a choice to make, Mal, as did you. Besides, I note that Fionbarr is missing too."

"He is? But I told that bloke to—" Mal ran a hand through his hair. "Shite. Handed him right over to one of his minions, didn't I?"

Niall moved past Mal to stand next to Eamon. "Tiarnach's gone as well. I suppose we all made our choices tonight." He smiled tiredly at Gareth. "I can't say I'm sorry, although I don't trust those bastards not to make trouble again."

"You've all done more than I could hope, so please, no self-recrimination." Eamon helped the Queen to her feet.

She tottered a moment before Peadar handed her a staff to lean on. No, not a staff: Govannon's spear. She blinked at it once before planting it firmly in the earth. "The traitors may have escaped, but that is of little consequence. We all live. *Faerie* lives. As we are united, we can await another day for justice."

Gareth cleared his throat. "As to that . . ." He unslung Herne's horn from his shoulder and held it in his palm for a moment, head bowed. He slanted a glance at Niall with a wry smile, then held the horn out—to Eamon. "We have another option, Your . . . Your Majesty."

Niall caught his breath. If Gareth was willing to accept Eamon as King, as someone worthy of fealty, as someone to trust with *Herne's fucking horn*, then he must truly have forsaken his Unseelie prejudices. *And truly forgiven me.*

Eamon took the horn. "Is this—"

"Herne's horn." The Queen ran a finger down its burnished length. "If we sound this, we call up the Wild Hunt. Those we mark as its prey will not escape. Your father, Eamon—"

"I know." Eamon caught Niall's gaze and raised an eyebrow. *Asking permission.* Niall nodded. "But I've given him chances enough. Let Herne deal with him, with all of them. Traitors and conspirators are his rightful prey." He raised the horn to his lips and blew a long, echoing note.

Before it died away completely, a disturbance arose in the woods. All the fae who'd been dancing scuttled away, creating a clear path to where Eamon stood with the Queen. In the shadows under the trees, Niall could make out a tall figure, taller than Eamon and made taller yet by the antlers on his head. His eyes glowed gold, and behind him, the underbrush was lit with dozens of pinpricks of red light—his hounds, the *Cwn Annwn*, awaiting his command.

"You summoned me." Herne's voice, impossibly deep, reverberated in the Circle. "Such things are not done lightly."

The Queen stepped forward, Govannon's spear still in her hand. "We call you forth in full knowledge of what we ask."

Herne tilted his head back as if scenting the air. "Treachery in the air. It calls to me, more than the horn. But . . ." He leveled his amber gaze at them. "A former king? My powers do not extend so far."

Niall stepped forward to stand next to the Queen. "Her Majesty holds the answer to that. A spear, forged by Govannon himself, to strike true against any adversary."

The hounds growled until Herne raised a hand. "Govannon hasn't forged a spear since the death of Dylan of the Waves."

"He did this time."

The Queen flipped the spear with practiced skill. "Will you accept our charge?"

When Herne nodded, she flung the spear toward him. He caught it easily. "You'll see me again when the deed is done." He turned and vanished into the trees, followed by the hounds. A moment later, the pack bayed, the sign they'd caught scent of their prey.

Niall gripped Eamon's shoulder. "I'm sorry. I know you loved him in your way—"

"You mistake. At one time, I felt I had a duty to him, but that ended the day he condemned you." Eamon glanced at the Queen. "My love and devotion is granted only to those who deserve it. For now, we have a new world to celebrate, and it begins with a handfasting. My lady, if you would?" He held out his hand, and she took it. The two of them paced in a stately procession down the path opened by Herne's arrival, the assembled fae falling in behind them.

As Alun limped after them, Mal took his arm. "Looks like you could use a little of David's attention. Shall I fetch him for you?"

"I'd like to say I can handle this, but if you wouldn't mind." Alun glanced at Gareth. "Perhaps you could request Hunter's Moon to join us too? That is, if Gareth is willing to perform at the ceilidh?"

Gareth wrapped his arm around Niall's waist. "I'd be honored. But now that the gates are realigned, I'll fetch them myself. You two go on."

Niall leaned into Gareth's embrace—an embrace offered with no lies between them—until they were alone in the Circle. Eamon had found his partner, Gareth his full confidence. Both of them had claimed their true place in a united Faerie. *Someday, maybe I'll figure out what* my *true place is.*

"Will you help me?" Gareth's breath ghosted against Niall's neck. "To collect the band?"

"I'll come if you like, but they're your mates."

"Yes, but the last time I saw them, I was a dick. It didn't end well. I could use a little backup."

Niall smiled and brushed Gareth's cheek with his knuckles. *Maybe Faerie is irrelevant. We've forged our own true place—with each other.* "I'll always have your back, love. Now let's go bag ourselves a band."

Chapter Twenty-Seven

Gareth laid down his guitar, and signaled to the rest of Hunter's Moon that they could take a break. "You've earned your mead buzz, Hamish."

"Too right. Next time you book us a fae wedding gig, give us more than two moments' notice, eh, mate?" He rose from behind a row of toms. "I'm fair parched. What kind of tucker do you suppose they lay out for a royal splicing, eh?"

As the band packed away their instruments, the spectral music that filled the glade at the Queen's command swelled to fill the silence. It was more than a fanfare this time—almost like an entire orchestra. And it seemed to be coming from . . . Gareth burst into laughter.

"What?" Tiff asked. "Now that you're finally at the point of enjoying jokes, you could at least share them with us."

"Ever wonder where the music came from when we weren't playing?" He pointed at the trees surrounding the glade. Peering through the leaves were a host of small, nearly transparent fae, all of them holding tiny instruments. "They've always been invisible before." Thanks to Niall's insistence, they weren't any longer.

"Figured it was just fae elevator music." Hamish tilted his head as he grinned up at the little musicians. "Not bad, are they? They could use an update in their set list though. Maybe I'll have a word."

He wandered off toward a nearby linden tree and peered up, apparently catching the attention of a rather surly looking lavender fae playing a sackbut. Whatever he said deepened its frown, and it *blatted* a discordant note directly in Hamish's face, which caused his ears to shift immediately to kangaroo form. Hamish gaped for a moment, then burst out laughing, twitching his ears once before shifting them back to human.

It was tough to smirk with a sackbut at your lips, but the lavender fae managed it before dismissing Hamish completely to return to its tune. The tempo, however, picked up significantly.

Gareth hopped down from the dais. The glade had expanded exponentially to hold everyone at the handfasting ceilidh, which appeared to be all the land-based fae, Seelie and Unseelie both. The result was a bit . . . startling. Gareth had never seen a trow dance before. He wasn't entirely sure he wanted to see it again, but he had to give them credit for enthusiasm, if not for grace.

In a way, they reminded him of David, who couldn't dance to save his life. *Although he did that once—and started the chain of events that saved us all. Alun's redemption. My reconciliation with Alun. Mal's journey with Bryce, which led me back to Niall at last.* As far as Gareth was concerned, David was the finest dancer in any world.

Now, David was swaying in the center of the glade, locked safely in Alun's arms so he couldn't damage himself or others with his flailing. The look on Alun's face . . . Goddess, Gareth couldn't remember when he'd ever seen his staid, dutiful eldest brother so at peace.

He searched the crowd for Niall, and spotted him at the far side of the glade, standing next to Mal, laughing with a brownie in a leather apron. Mal had bauchan young on either shoulder and one perched on top of his head, clinging to his hair. Only days ago, Gareth's first instinct at that sight would have been to charge, dislodging and scattering the Unseelie. *But we no longer have Unseelie—or Seelie either. We're all simply fae.*

Bryce was standing next to them, in earnest conversation with a trio of dryads, who were regarding him, big-eyed, with something between terror, respect, and outright adoration. They'd probably never seen a druid this close before. As another repercussion of the Convergence and the odd alliances it bred, a druid—this particular druid—was welcome in Faerie, and the fae had begun a cautious exploration of what that meant.

Regardless of the rocky beginning of his relationship with Bryce, Gareth trusted him to have the best interests of Faerie at heart. He was a good man—deserving of Mal.

Gareth skirted the trees, dodged the enthusiastic revelers until he reached Niall and Mal. "Hey."

Niall grinned at him and pulled him in for a kiss. "Hey yourself. Have you met Peadar?" He put a hand on the brownie's shoulder. "He's one of my best friends."

Peadar ducked his head. "Give over, Highness, do. I did no more than my duty."

"Bugger that. You went far beyond, and I don't forget."

Gareth extended a hand. "Thank you. For watching out for him." Peadar blinked up at Gareth with the same expression the dryads were still training on Bryce, taking Gareth's hand gingerly. But when he would have bent forward to kiss it, Gareth altered his grip and shook instead. "You owe me nothing more than friendship, Peadar. But I'd be grateful if you granted me that."

Peadar bobbed his head. "With pleasure, Bard. You saved our lives."

"No. We saved ourselves—and each other. Exactly as it should be."

Peadar bowed and scurried away. Mal chuckled, causing the young bauchan using him as a perch to squeal. "I think you intimidate him, brother."

Gareth sighed. "I suppose it's inevitable. But I hope it won't last."

Mal surveyed the crowd. Although many species of fae were dancing simultaneously in the circle, not many of them could be said to be dancing *together*. "I expect we'll return to some form of our old contentious ways before long. We're fae, after all." He glanced at Bryce, who was apparently reading the palm of one of the dryads. "Well, most of us are."

"I never told you what Bryce did while you were trapped in here."

"Caused a stir, I reckon. He's not one to sit idly by, my bloke."

"He never stopped trying to find a way to get to you. To rescue you and Alun and Faerie." Gareth glanced sidelong at Mal. "To make me see beyond my own nose."

Mal snorted. "Aye, well, you, me, and Alun—can't say our noses are so small. Sometimes we all need help to see past them."

"He . . . he has a bigger heart and a bigger vision than I do."

"Nah. It's just his job. He's a druid."

"Don't discount it. He loves you."

Mal grinned. "I know. Believe me, I know." He sauntered over and dropped a kiss on Bryce's neck. Bryce glanced up, and the look that passed between them made Gareth's breath catch.

"Remarkable, eh?" Niall wrapped his arm around Gareth's waist. "All the devotion on display tonight. Eamon and Caitrìona—"

"Don't you mean the King and Queen?"

Niall's lips quirked in that familiar sly smile. "Nah. I think we've earned the right to call them by name—at least in private." He nodded at where the two of them were sitting together near the dais, apparently with eyes only for each other. "I think they need a bit of privacy themselves, and speaking of that . . ." Niall let go of Gareth's waist and held out his hand instead. "Come for a walk with me?"

"Of course." Gareth let Niall lead him into the trees behind the dais. In the old days, this would have been Niall's ploy to get Gareth alone for a bit of lovemaking, but his expression was entirely too somber for that.

They arrived at a small clearing next to a chiming brook. Peadar was there, holding something wrapped in a linen cloth. He handed it to Niall and sped off into the underbrush.

Niall studied the bundle for a moment, then heaved a sigh. "Herne brought this to Eamon while you and the band were playing." He unfolded the cloth to display the horn, its leather strap coiled neatly around the base.

"Herne. He was here?"

Niall nodded. "He said—he said that it's done."

"The three of them are gone then. Rodric, Fionbarr, and—

"My father."

Gareth gripped Niall's arms. "I know you didn't see eye to eye with him. I know he's done terrible things, but he was still your father. You must feel—"

Niall huffed out a laugh. "Will you think I'm mad if I say that no matter how much I hated him for what he did to Eamon, to you, to me, that I still craved his affection?"

"Not at all. I never had a father to speak of—although I heard that the fae who spawned us at Arawn's orders was a fellow who'd been cuckolded. I've always wondered if that's why the three of us have never been interested in female companionship. When he created us, he made bloody damned sure we'd never be a threat to him."

As Gareth had hoped, Niall laughed. "I expect Tiarnach wished he'd had as much control over his own sons. He certainly never acted as if he was pleased with us, and Eamon did his best to please."

"You didn't?"

Again that self-deprecating smile. "I did my best to piss him well off. It was the only attention I ever got from him. Although considering events, perhaps I should have been content with being neglected instead."

Niall tucked the linen around the horn again and laid it in a stony recess next to the brook. The half-dozen symbols carved above the opening marked it as a mini-portal, Faerie's version of express delivery. Sure enough, a moment later, the horn vanished. "There's something I need to tell you." He stared at the empty spot for a moment, then sighed again. "I . . . I have to leave."

"Are you—" Gareth's voice cracked. "You're not breaking up with me, are you?"

Niall cupped Gareth's jaw. "No. Never. But I can't be nothing more than your . . ." Niall's gaze lost focus for an instant, in a way Gareth was coming to recognize. ". . . your groupie."

"Did the *ethera* feed you that word?"

He chuckled. "Yes."

"It's *your* doing that they're able to return to Faerie. Just like you demanded recognition—literally—for the musicians. You've done good things."

"Ah well. The *ethera* have done their bit for me. Seemed fitting I'd give something back." He smiled wryly. "And I've always had a soft spot for musicians."

"You could do more of the same. Your brother is the king. Surely he'd grant you a position at court."

"An offer born of obligation rather than suitability? What a disaster that would be." He stroked down Gareth's arms and laced their fingers together, his gaze on their linked hands. "I can't be your true partner if I don't have my own purpose. That's why the fae have dwindled so over the years—we have no context, no place, in the Outer World anymore."

Gareth's fingers tightened around Niall's. "After all this time, I don't want to be without you again."

"Nor I without you. But think about it, love. You have the band, a career, a life that you've built. As for me, during the past two hundred years, I've done nothing but haul scrap metal around the underworld and work giant bellows in between getting flogged to within an inch of my life. What can I offer you?"

"You don't need to offer me anything but yourself. We don't need the money—"

"It's not that. I'm not good with idleness. Call it my Unseelie nature, but when I get bored, I cause trouble."

Gareth nudged Niall's jaw with his knuckles in an attempt to lighten the mood, although he still couldn't quite catch his breath. "You're a Bad Boy. Tiff called it the minute she met you."

"Aye, well, I can't deny it. But I'm trying to be better. I've been talking to Eamon about an idea I've had. Remember how you wanted to pull me out of Faerie because of Fionbarr's rules about all fae and only fae being present during the Convergence?"

"Hard to forget, considering."

"Seems Fionbarr was full of shite. He only wanted all fae inside for the Convergence so he could draw on their energy in an emergency—oh, and because his spell would blow out the walls between the worlds and he placed more value on fae lives than he did on humans. But just because a fae wasn't inside Faerie when the spheres converged doesn't mean they died."

"So that means—"

Niall nodded. "They could still be out there. The Disappeared—Cornish, Manx, Bretons. All the other Celtic fae who've vanished over the years."

Gareth's breath steadied, his grin growing despite Niall's solemn expression. "You want to bring them home."

"At least let them know they'd be welcome should they return." Niall frowned. "Wait—how do you know about that? And what's so damned funny?"

Gareth snaked his arms around Niall's neck, and thank the Goddess, Niall didn't pull away. "You're not the only one who's been planning a quest."

Niall snorted. "It's not a quest. I'm not one of Arthur's bloody knights."

"Of course you're not. They were a bunch of bloodthirsty arseholes, except for the ones who were insufferable prigs. You're much better. But it's still a quest."

"Fine. It's a quest. But that still doesn't tell me why you know about it."

"Because Alun and Bryce broached the same subject. Their Majesties have approved a campaign to locate the Disappeared, find out why they left, and if they're willing, bring them home."

Niall's face took on the yearning look he sometimes wore when Gareth nattered on about the band or music. *He's never had a rewarding occupation, something to make him feel worthwhile.* "It's a go then? I can do it?"

"Yes. With any means necessary, you're to remove the impediments to their repatriation. Make sure they know they have a choice now, a real choice."

"'Any means,' eh? That's a dangerous mandate, considering my track record."

Gareth pressed a kiss on Niall's smiling mouth. "They count on me to keep you in check, I think. You can't get too wild and reckless if you know that should something happen to you again . . ." Gareth locked gazes with Niall, willing him to understand. "Well, I'm not sure I'd survive it."

"Ah shite, Gareth. Way to put pressure on a bloke."

"I don't mean to. Or not much. But we've wasted so much time, Niall. Isn't it our turn now? To be happy? To stage our own convergence?"

"You more than anyone know that the worlds aren't always fair, but I'd say we've both paid a fair chunk of dues." Niall stroked Gareth's cheek with a fingertip. "We've earned our happiness. We'll make our home in the Outer World. You'll have the band, and I'll take on this bloody 'quest' so I won't be underfoot."

"Don't lie. You don't think it's a 'bloody' quest at all. You love the idea."

"I do. But not nearly as much as I love you." Niall threaded his fingers through Gareth's hair and dove in for a kiss that rivaled the heat of the Abyss. When Gareth pulled back, they were both panting, grinding against one another, Gareth with a double handful of Niall's ass.

"I should tell you," Gareth said, voice hoarse with desire.

"The only thing you need to tell me is where we can be alone."

"I can do that."

"Thank the Goddess. Now—"

"But the quest. There's a catch."

Niall rolled his eyes, then ducked down to press his mouth to Gareth's throat. "Of course there is. What?"

"You're not the only one who needs a new job. I'm afraid you'll have a co-quester: my brother, Mal."

Niall laughed, his lips vibrating against Gareth's skin. "Their Majesties are going to trust the two of us on the loose with royal command to do whatever it takes?"

"I'll warn you—there's serious book being made on whether the two of you can accomplish anything without running afoul of the laws, here and in the Outer World both. Or for that matter, killing each other and leaving both Bryce and me to waste away in mourning."

"Is that so, love?" Niall kissed his way up Gareth's neck until he could gaze at Gareth, grinning wickedly. "Care to place a little wager on that?"

Gareth returned the grin, snugging Niall's groin more firmly against his own. "I would never bet against a Bad Boy. Not one with your reputation."

"Wise man." Niall's grin faded into a tender smile. "But if you want a sure thing, here's a tip: the smart money's on happily ever after. For both of us."

The Mythmatched adventures continue
with

SUPERNATURAL SELECTION!

SINGLE WHITE INCUBUS

BOOK ONE

Does a bear shift in the woods?

Well, partially. That was what got grizzly shifter Ted Farnsworth into trouble. He wasn't *trying* to break the Secrecy Pact, but he's the only extroverted bear shifter on the planet and he craves companionship. Signing up for Supernatural Selection, a mate-matching that guarantees marriage to a perfect partner, is the perfect solution. Not only will Ted never be lonely again, but once his new beaver shifter husband arrives, they'll build Ted's dream wilderness retreat together. *Win-win.*

Quentin Bertrand-Harrington, scion of an incubus dynasty, has abstained from sex since nearly killing his last lover. When his family declares it's time for him to marry, Quentin decides the only way not to murder his partner is to pick someone who's already dead. Supernatural Selection finds him the ideal vampire, and Quentin signs the marriage agreement sight unseen.

But a mix-up at Supernatural Selection contracts Quentin with Ted. What's Ted supposed to do with an art historian who knows more about salad forks than screwdrivers? And how can

Quentin resist Ted's mouthwatering life force? Yet as they work together to untangle their inconvenient union, they begin to wonder if their unexpected match could be perfect after all.

Sneak Peek of

SINGLE WHITE INCUBUS

Quentin sighed, eyeing his suitcase. Should he dig out a warmer coat? Not yet. First he wanted to find out if he was quite as alone as he thought. He descended the stairs and fought his way through the weeds to circle the building. It had an impressive footprint—like some kind of inn, judging from the number of floors and windows. Although when Quentin peered through some of them—the ones that weren't boarded up—the inside was a forest of bare studs and plywood floors.

The rear of the place had the skeleton of a deck that, if it were complete, would have a stunning view of the lake and the surrounding hills. He stood looking at it, the chill from the damp ground seeping through the thin leather of his Italian oxfords. Some kind of large bird burst from the trees, startling him, and skimmed across the lake with a cry.

The lake lapped quietly at the shore, but he could hear cascading water and . . . was that someone singing? The sounds were coming from the side of the house closest to the trees. Quentin crept forward until he could peek around the corner.

Holy mother of fire.

There was a man. An enormous man. An enormous *naked* man. An enormous naked man, sluicing himself off in an outdoor shower. Quentin should have shivered just from the notion of what cold water in the colder air would do—not that it seemed to have any effect on Enormous Naked Man's . . . er . . . appendage.

Despite the suppressant still floating around in his system, despite his determination to avoid anyone who wasn't his husband, despite the cold air that ought to have cooled him down to almost zero, heat rose in Quentin's core—and so did his cock.

Oh no. Absolutely not. Even if he weren't contractually bound to someone—who could not possibly be this man, since it was broad daylight and his husband would disintegrate under this much sun exposure—Quentin had sworn never again to let his incubus libido endanger another living person.

And then Enormous Naked Man opened his eyes and stared straight at Quentin.

And smiled.

Devil take it. I am so so so *fucked.*

For a second, Ted thought the guy peeking around the corner was Matt—or maybe Larry, the mechanic from Dewton who doubled as the delivery guy for the lumberyard. Then he wiped the water out of his eyes and realized the guy was way too small and frail to be either one. Matt was taller and Larry was stockier—and neither one of them had black hair and a goatee and looked like the least breeze would blow them off the mountain.

A stranger. And I'm naked. Whoops. Good thing he wasn't here ten minutes ago when I shifted. Because shifting in front of a human? Yeah, that was a sure way to bring the council down on his ass, especially after what Dr. Kendrick had told him this morning.

Ordinarily, Ted would have shifted back to his bear form and shaken the water off to get dry—he'd only stopped out here to shower because he'd run afoul of an illegal dump site when he was lumbering back up the mountain after Matt had dropped him off in town. So he didn't have a towel. Or clothes.

Awkward.

Well, it was his place, damn it. Wasn't he entitle to privacy here? He wasn't expecting anyone until Rusty arrived next week, so he should have been able to parade around as naked as a mole rat if he wanted, with no one the wiser.

And even though shifter blood ran hotter than human, and he'd already started to put on the padding around his middle in the run-up to winter hibernation season, it was still damn cold in the wind off the lake.

"Sorry. I—" he gestured to his body "—wasn't expecting company." If he could just get the guy to go around to the front of the lodge, Ted could shift and dry off. Wouldn't help the no-clothes situation, but he had a stash in the lodge, and a cache inside the tree line for emergencies—or when he was running the Bigfoot scam. He sighed. *Can't do that anymore either.*

But the guy just kept staring at Ted, his eyes behind those rectangular hipster glasses getting bigger and bigger. Which had the unfortunate effect of—what did Dr. Kendrick call it? Sympathetic reaction? Because Ted's dick started to keep pace.

I'm a married man now. I need to keep it in my pants. When I have *pants.* He turned his back. "Could you, you know, go back to your car until I get dressed?"

"I don't have a car." The guy's voice sounded like he was trying to get the words out past someone's fist.

"You too? Yeah, my truck's in the shop, so—" Ted slapped himself on the forehead. *Not relevant.* "If you'd just go around to the porch, I'll be there in a minute and you can let me know what you need."

The guy let out a noise that sounded like "*Awp*!" But since that wasn't a word, it couldn't have been what he'd said. Ted took it for a yes because when he checked over his shoulder, the guy was gone.

A MESSAGE FROM E.J.

Dear Reader,

Thank you so much for reading *Bad Boy's Bard*, the third book in the trilogy that launched my Mythmatched story world. I'm so happy you've taken this journey with me! I'd be immensely grateful if you'd take a moment to leave a review at the retailer and any other site you use for reviews. Believe me, reviews make an *enormous* difference to the health and well-being of books (and not incidentally, to their associated authors!).

Pop on over to my website, https://ejrussell.com, for all the deets on my books—the rest of my Mythmatched tales, my other paranormal rom-coms and mysteries, my contemporary romances, and my one lone historical. If you're an audio fan, you can find the audio scoop there too. The Fae Out of Water trilogy, for instance, is narrated by the wonderful Joel Leslie. (The QR code on the next page will get you there with your smartphone camera or other code reader.)

My newsletter is the place to get the latest dish on new releases, sales, and more. I promise I only send one out when I've got…well…news. You can subscribe here: https://ejrussell.com/newsletter.

All my best,
—E

Also by
E.J. Russell

Paranormal Romance
Mythmatched Universe
Fae Out of Water Trilogy
Cutie and the Beast
The Druid Next Door
Bad Boy's Bard

Supernatural Selection Trilogy
Single White Incubus
Vampire With Benefits
Demon on the Down-Low

Other Mythmatched Romances
Howling on Hold
Possession in Session
Witch Under Wraps
Cursed is the Worst
The Skinny on Djinni
Assassin by Accident (part of Carnival of Mysteries)

Mythmatched Companion Stories
Rusty's Really Bad Day (free to newsletter subscribers)
Second First Date (free to newsletter subscribers)
First Flight (free to newsletter subscribers)

Quest Investigations Mysteries
Five Dead Herrings

The Hound of the Burgervilles
The Lady Under the Lake
Death on Denial

Art Medium Series
The Artist's Touch
Tested in Fire
Art Medium: The Complete Collection (omnibus edition)

Legend Tripping Series
Stumptown Spirits
Wolf's Clothing

Enchanted Occasions Series
Best Beast
Nudging Fate
Devouring Flame

Royal Powers Series (shared world)
Duking It Out
Duke the Hall
King's Ex

Magic Emporium Series (shared world)
Purgatory Playhouse

Monster Till Midnight

Historical Romance
Silent Sin

Contemporary Romance
Camera Shy
The Thomas Flair
Mystic Man

For a Good Time, Call… (A Bluewater Bay novel, with Anne Tenino)

Holiday Shorts (separately)
The Probability of Mistletoe
An Everyday Hero
A Swants Soiree
or all three together in
Christmas Kisses

Geeklandia Series
The Boyfriend Algorithm (M/F)
Clickbait

Writing as Nelle Heran
(traditional cozy mystery)

Crafty Sleuth Series (with C.K. Eastland)
Die Cut
Mixed Media
Found Objects (*coming soon)*

About the Author

E.J. Russell (she/her), author of the award-winning Mythmatched paranormal romance series, writes LGBTQ+ romance and mystery in a rainbow of flavors. Count on high snark, low angst, and happy endings.

Reality? Eh, not so much.

She's married to Curmudgeonly Husband, a man who cares even less about sports than she does. Luckily, C.H. also loves to cook, or all three of their children (Lovely Daughter and Darling Sons A and B) would have survived on nothing but Cheerios, beef jerky, and Satsuma mandarins (the extent of E.J.'s culinary skill set).

E.J. also writes traditional cozy mystery as Nelle Heran. She lives in rural Oregon, enjoys visits from her wonderful adult children, and indulges in good books, red wine, and the occasional hyperbole.

News & Social Media:
Website: https://ejrussell.com
Newsletter: https://ejrussell.com/newsletter

ACKNOWLEDGMENTS

So many things have changed since the launch of the first edition of *Bad Boy's Bard*, but my gratitude remains.

To Rachel, Amelia, L.C. Chase, and the Riptide team for believing in me and the Kendrick brothers' stories, and for giving this book a home for six years.

To Natasha Snow for the lovely new covers.

To NOLAKim and Meg DesCamp for cheering me on.

To my family—Jim, Hana, Nick, Ross, and Billy—for being there for me (even when I'm barricaded in my writing cave).

And last, but certainly not least, to you, my readers, who've loved Mal and Bryce and their adventures from the very beginning—you're the best. Without you, I couldn't keep doing what I love.